The Eight-Team Chronicles

Book 3
The Super Six

ROBIN CHAMBERS

Table of Contents

ROBIN CHAMBERS

For Amy, and for Linda and all those
Who would make good of bad and friends of foes

SOUND ADVICE
Love Learning
Respect Difference
Protect Your Planet

Foreword

During the second decade of our twenty first century (as we now reckon time), I wrote and published my first version of this story. It appeared in seven books under the generic title of *Myrddin's Heir*, and came liberally supplied with chapter references to copious notes at the end of each volume detailing the derivations of uncommon words, literary, historical and geographical references and suggestions for further reading and investigation. It is a series I would have loved to have had at my disposal when teaching high-school English, which I finally stopped doing in 2007.

It is still available for that purpose, as well as for the amusement of any other reader who finds such additional material interesting and informative. Such a format, however, is rare if not unique in fantasy fiction, and a number of people whose opinions I value suggested that I should go on to publish a 'non-didactic' version of what is, they hasten to assure me, a strong, well-written tale!

So this I have now done, and in so doing have included 25 chapters describing formative events in Gordon Bennett's early years that did not appear in the 2017 version. The text has been thoroughly revised, and is, I hope accessible to keen young adult readers as well as to bright children everywhere between the ages of 12 and 112. I have to confess, however, that in the first instance I wrote it for me. Its cadences and its relevance still move me at the age of 82.

Robin Chambers

Chapter 1

X Marks The Spot

Nick hurried along the impressive, wood-panelled corridor. The heels of his boots clicked against the highly-polished floor.

It seemed ironic that his country's first *Space Academy* had been set up in such an old building. Maybe the future is always rooted in the past. Charles Xavier's School for Mutants had been similarly housed.

Nick's flying experience with *Velociraptor* in his early years now stood him in good stead at the Academy. He'd got through the flight simulation part of the course without a single crash, and was heading for high honours in the starship pilot exams.

The extensive playing fields of this former boarding school provided the open space for the academy's more "futuristic" facilities. Biggest of all was that huge launch-rocket hangar with its 400-foot-high door. Nick was headed in that direction now, looking for Gordon.

Gordon was on the fast track for spaceship command. Nicknamed "Flash" by his fellow cadets, he was a born leader, and ace at dealing with aggressive and anti-social behaviour. Qualities like that came in handy when dealing with truculent species like the Klingons and the Borg.

More than one of his fellow command cadets had reason to regret early attempts to check out just how good Cadet Bennett was at dealing with aggression.

As luck would have it, Gordon came around the corner at that very moment, with Science Officer Zack. "Hiya Nick," he called out cheerfully. "You looking for me?"

Maybe it wasn't luck. How did he do that? He always knew when Nick needed him. Nick had no idea how he knew, but he was glad he did.

"Yeah," Nick replied, "I was just coming to find you. There's something I want to show you in the library." Science Officer Zack raised one eyebrow in that disconcerting way he had. Nick hadn't spent much time around Vulcans. Those pointy ears were a distraction.

Gordon put a friendly arm around Nick's shoulders as they changed direction and headed for the library. "What have you found?" he asked. He knew Nick spent a lot of time in the old school library. When he wasn't boning up on the latest space-flight data and course specification manuals, he indulged his interest in yesteryear's great adventurers.

"Well," Nick said, struggling to control his excitement, "did you know that this school was originally set up in the early seventeenth century by Sir Edward Kitchin, a former Sheriff of Chester? He endowed it with funds from the fortune he made in merchant shipping."

"I *did* know that," Gordon said to him affectionately, "because you told me, not so long ago."

"Did I?" said Nick. "Oh yeah, so I did. Well what you probably don't know - because I only just found out - was that Sir Edward Kitchin was Drake's cabin boy on *The Golden Hinde!* She went through the Strait of Magellan in 1578 and captured the *Cacafuego* on March 1st 1579."

"*Nuestra Señora de la Concepción*," said Mr Zack, "known to its crew as the *Cacafuego*. She was sailing towards Panama with six tons of silver and gold on board. It was Drake's most celebrated prize, and made every member of his crew rich, including Ned, his cabin boy."

Nick gazed at him admiringly. "You're very well informed, Mr Zack," he said.

The Vulcan simply raised an eyebrow and continued his narrative. "Ned Kitchin set up this school to encourage a pioneering spirit of adventure in the sons of nobles and commoners alike."

He gazed impassively at the impressive linenfold panelling lining the corridor, his hands clasped characteristically behind his back. "That made it a fitting location for this country's first space academy."

They had reached the old library. Nick led the way to the restricted section, where the librarian jealously guarded the oldest and most precious books. Not that they needed much guarding: most cadets avoided the library. Given the choice, they opted instead to play three-dimensional, first-person shooter games on their Zboxes. Two generations beyond the original Xbox, the Zbox offered a vastly superior range of virtual-reality scenarios.

The library, however, had a good many adventure stories of the more old-fashioned kind. "Here it is," Nick whispered. He reached into a narrow gap between a first edition of King James' *Daemonologie* (1597) and an early seventeenth century copy of the *Malleus Maleficarum*. It was possible that neither book had been moved in the last 400 years. That would explain why the slim volume wedged between them might have remained hidden for that length of time.

Nick had spotted the narrow gap between the two tomes and wondered what was making it. He held it out for Gordon and Zack to see. It was entitled *My Voyages with Sir Francis Drake* by his erstwhile cabin boy Edward Kitchin.

"Are you *still* into pirates, Nick?" Gordon asked. He cradled the volume carefully and turned the first few flimsy pages.

"You're never too old for pirates," Nick said defensively. Two years ago in Year 7 he'd written a story about Sir Francis Drake and his cabin boy Ned. He'd been seriously into the *Pirates of the Caribbean* films at the time, and his tastes hadn't altered much since. "That isn't why I'm showing it to you. Look at the last two pages. They'd never been separated."

Intrigued, Gordon turned to the back of the book. Nick had cut a slit across the top of the two blank end pages, which had been bound as a sealed pocket. He produced his little pair of assistant librarian's tweezers, inserted them into the slot, and partially drew out a thin single sheet of yellowing paper, on which had been drawn a tiny map in now faded ink.

"Whoah!" Gordon said.

Nick carefully slid the map back into its envelope and replaced the book where Sir Edward himself may have put it more than four centuries ago. He reached into his pocket and pulled out a significantly larger, computer-enhanced photocopy. He laid it on the nearest flat surface so that they could all see it clearly. Zack confirmed what Gordon had been thinking and Nick already knew.

"It's a map of the school's hidden passageways, secret doors and underground ways in and out of the building," he said. "Sir Edward had it sealed into the back pages of that book for a purpose."

"I know what that purpose was," Nick breathed excitedly. "The librarian's been here almost as long as the books and he's steeped in the lore of the place. The story goes that Ned Kitchin hid a treasure chest somewhere in the school. It was filled with gold and silver looted from a Spanish treasure ship. His family motto was 'Uti possidetis' which loosely translated means "Finders Keepers".

Nick was almost beside himself. "According to the legend, any boy who found the chest could keep its contents. He was to use them to make his fortune, the way the founder had. But nobody ever found anything, and the legend died out."

Gordon put his finger on the map. "There appears to be a mysterious room here, marked with an X," he said.

"I know," Nick whispered. "It's stranger than fiction, isn't it?!"

Chapter 2

How Deep Is The Ocean?

The smart little trap rolled smoothly along the impressive driveway, the pony's hooves clicking against the tarmac. Miranda caught sight of a herd of deer grazing peacefully among the trees to her right. To her left, the ground sloped gently down to a stream and a pond full of reeds.

She was sitting next to a boy about fifteen years of age. He'd met her at the gate and told her that his name was Duncan. He was taking her in the trap "up tae the big hoos" where her Aunt Matilda lived. Aunt Matilda had married the Earl of Glamis and Cawdor (or somewhere that sounded like that) some years ago.

Duncan clicked his tongue at the shiny black pony and it picked up its heels. His eyes were on the road and his hands firmly involved with the reins. Miranda shot a secret glance sideways at him. She lifted her head to let the air blow through her hair, and wondered what it would feel like to hold his hand. She hadn't been ready to hold Nick's hand in year 7, but now she was in year 9 ...

They rounded the bend and there was "the big hoos". It stood solidly on the high ground ahead of them, surrounded by lawns, and enjoying magnificent views of the surrounding countryside.

Carrickmoor. Her dad had been right: it did look just like that house in *Monarch of the Glen*.

Duncan pulled up outside. Miranda had time to notice the family motto - 'Memor Tua Rei' - carved in the stone arching over the impressive front door. Her aunt bustled out to welcome her. She'd only met her aunt once, at a wedding when she was five. The rest of the family thought Matilda odd. Miranda liked her.

"There you are," she said, "you look just like your mother."

Duncan leapt down and pulled her case from the back of the trap. Miranda climbed down and gave her aunt a grateful hug. She was glad she looked just like her mother. Her mother had died when she was eight.

"I haven't seen you since before your father married again," Matilda said crisply over her shoulder. She led the way into the impressive entrance hall. Miranda felt the temperature drop several degrees. "What's this wife of his call herself again? 'IsaDORa' - ridiculous name."

Miranda smiled to herself. She and her aunt were going to get on.

"I was very fond of your mother," her aunt told her, "and I thought this would be my chance to get to know my interesting niece, now that she's safely into her teens."

They climbed a wide wooden staircase to the first floor. "I believe you like horses," her aunt went on. "Not surprised, very fond of them myself. We have half a dozen stabled nearby."

Miranda felt a quiver of excitement.

"Duncan can take you there tomorrow and you can have your pick. Fergus breeds them in his spare time. Not that he has much." Miranda guessed correctly that "Fergus" was the elusive Earl. "There's a promising stallion that takes a bit of handling, and some rather fine brood mares."

"I've never met Uncle Fergus," Miranda said. She followed her aunt along a corridor to her right. It was flanked by solemn portraits of family members through the ages.

"Few people have, my Dear," Aunt Matilda told her. "He's a busy man, and he doesn't suffer fools gladly. The world is somewhat over-populated with fools, in case you hadn't noticed yet, and too many of them wield considerable power."

She stopped at the foot of a narrower staircase on the left. It went steeply up to a single door at the top. "That door leads to your uncle's private workshop and observatory," she said. "You can have as much fun as you like exploring the house while you're here, but never go up this flight of stairs."

She lowered her voice. "He's just come back from the Western Pacific, where the water is remarkably deep. He's being mysterious but I gather he made a significant discovery out there. He's writing a paper that he thinks will shake the world to its very foundations."

They carried on along the corridor, past several more identical doors and towards a large window that flooded the end of the corridor with welcome light. The last door on the left had a photo pinned to it. It was of Miranda eight years ago, when she was five. She was wearing a tee-shirt that said "Here comes TROUBLE" in big letters.

"This is your room," Aunt Matilda said. "I thought the picture would help you find it again. There are 97 doors in this house, and they all look the same. Your bathroom is through here." She opened the door opposite to reveal the large, wooden seated, porcelain and enamelled, iron conveniences that had been state-of-the-art in 1875.

Duncan had followed them with Miranda's case. He put it down outside the room and retreated a few steps. "I'll be awa' tae help ma faither," he suggested.

"Right you are," her Ladyship said crisply, "after you've put the rig away and taken care of Polly."

"Aye," he agreed, "That an a'."

"Thank you very much, Duncan," Miranda said.

"Ye're very welcome, Miss," he said. He gave her another brief glimpse of those strong white teeth, before striding away.

"What tartan is that?" she asked her aunt as the boy and his kilt disappeared around the corner.

"Duncan is a Campbell," her aunt replied. "They're a proud clan. His family has been on this estate for generations." She opened the door to Miranda's room and marched in. Miranda picked up her suitcase and followed.

"Oh, WOW!" she exclaimed.

The room was south-facing and vast, with a beautiful bay window. Warm afternoon sunlight was flooding in. Against one of the wood-panelled walls was a four-poster bed, with rich velvet hangings tied back to the ornately carved posts. "Think of all the people who must have slept in that bed!"

"I'm afraid so," her aunt agreed. "Not to worry: we've changed the sheets." She pointed at a splendid, bow-fronted wardrobe with massive drawers underneath. "There's enough room in there for your things. I hope you remembered your fancy dress costume."

"Yes I did," Miranda said. She set her case on the bed and unzipped it.

"The fancy dress extravaganza is on Saturday in our ballroom. We're helping to raise funds for a football field and a play-park just outside our local village." She smiled. "It will be a chance for you to meet some of the local youngsters."

Aunt Matilda headed for the door. "I thought we could have tea in the library in about half an hour. I'll let you unpack and settle in, and see you down there when you're ready. The library is to the left at the foot of the main stairs."

"Thank you very much," Miranda said.

"Oh no," her Aunt Matilda said, beaming at her. "Thank *you* for coming and brightening up my summer here. I don't see too much of your uncle when he's deep in a project. And believe me, projects don't get much deeper than your uncle's. It simply isn't possible." She closed the door behind her.

Miranda walked over to the window and looked out. The formal gardens stretched some way down the slope before giving way to parkland. It was an impressive place all right. She turned back to this bedroom fit for a queen. "I wonder if Mary Queen of Scots ever slept in that bed?" she thought, and decided that she had. It made the bed more interesting.

She began getting things out of her case. She couldn't possibly be feeling lonely, could she? She'd only been here ten minutes! What had her aunt meant when she said it simply wasn't possible for anyone else's projects to be deeper than her uncle's? What was there in the Western Pacific that was so deep?"

She tried not to think about her dad, 250 miles away in Isadora's tender clutches. She'd promised her mum she would look after him, and she'd done her best, but that had been Isadora's job for a while now. Miranda had her own work cut out being a teenager. Deciding when she should let a boy hold her hand was probably the least of her worries.

Carefully, she lifted a witch's hat out of her case. She remembered making one for Halloween with Grace in a year 7 Art lesson. It had been good fun, and this one was the same design but big enough to fit her now. She was going to miss her best friend this holiday. She supposed she might see her in her dreams sometimes.

That brought back the memory of a dream she'd once had. She still shuddered at it; it had been so real. She'd gone into the woods to take some bread to someone who was sick in bed. She'd known her Gran was already dead, and hadn't known what lay ahead. Grace appeared in the nick of time and rescued her from a very sticky situation. She'd had a friend with her called Zoë.

Funny, the way things happen in dreams.

There was a scraping noise behind one of the wooden panels close to her bed. Miranda froze and listened. Could it be a mouse or a rat scrabbling around inside the wall?

There it was again! This time it sounded like a rusty old bolt being drawn back ...

A whole section of the panelling beside the bed swung open and Grace stepped out, dressed in her latest Halloween vampirette costume. She was followed by the girl she recognised as Zoë from her dream two years ago. Zoë looked equally weird in tattered black rags. Their hair was wild, and they'd stuck wispy, straggly beards to their chins! With those very pale faces, hollow eyes and black lipstick, they looked like a couple of Goths on steroids.

"Grace, Zoë! What are you two doing here?!" Miranda asked them in amazement.

Grace put a choppy finger against her skinny lips. "Ssh!" she said. "We're on a secret mission; there's not a moment to lose!"

"Secret mission?" Miranda said incredulously. "How did you get here before me? How did you get into the house? What are you doing inside the wall?"

"Get your Halloween costume on!" Grace hissed. "There's something the three of us have to do, NOW!"

Miranda dutifully scrambled into the dress her dad had made for her this year. It was their family tradition, though she had to admit she was getting a bit old for it now. She jammed the witch's hat upon her head. "What is it we have to do?" she asked, a little breathlessly.

Grace was deadly serious and very determined. "We have to stop the world from being shaken to its very foundations."

Chapter 3

Finders Keepers

Mr Zack picked up Nick's enlarged copy of Ned Kitchin's treasure map and moved confidently to a remote corner of the library. It was as though he'd been here before and was already privy to the library's innermost secrets.

He removed a bulky copy of William Tyndale's 1526 English translation of the New Testament from the middle shelf of an ancient bookcase. Reaching into the gap, he pressed a section of the panelling behind it. With a shudder, the bookcase swung through 90°, revealing a dark passage.

"In his way, William Tyndale was as great an adventurer as Francis Drake," Zack remarked, stepping into the darkness. "He was martyred for his adventures with the wording of the scriptures, ten years after that book was published." Gordon and Nick followed him through the gap and closed the bookcase behind them.

They found themselves in a very confined space. Their standard issue pencil torches sent brilliant beams of light through the blackness. The narrow secret corridor stretched to right and left, disappearing round a corner in either direction.

Zack consulted the map as if refreshing his memory, turned it through 180° and set off with total confidence. "It's this way," he said over his shoulder.

"I don't know how you know!" Nick protested, bringing up the rear.

"I *do* know how he knows," Gordon told him. "Trust me, it's this way."

They came to the top of a stone staircase and descended. Nick felt the temperature drop several degrees. It was so narrow that their shoulders brushed against the walls on either side. At the bottom was another choice of direction; Zack turned left without hesitation. "Nearly there," he said.

"Nearly where?" Nick asked, just to make sure.

"X marks the spot," Gordon said cheerfully. "You of all people should know that."

Around the next bend they came to what looked like a dead end. Zack shone his torch on the ceiling. There was a skull and crossbones painted on a square panel just above their heads. He flicked the beam to the adjacent walls. There was another on a panel to his left, and a third to his right.

"OK," said Gordon, "all for one and one for all." They each placed a hand on one of the painted panels and pressed. There were three sharp clicks. Zack put his free hand against the end wall and pushed. It swung creakily to one side ...

Beyond it was a small room, no more than nine or ten feet square. It was empty, apart from a wooden table in the middle. Sitting on the table was a dust-covered, brass-bound, wooden chest with stout brass handles at either end of it. Nick felt tears of joy suddenly welling. It was a dream come true!

Gordon's bleeper chose that moment to go off and bring them back to their own century. He unclipped it from his belt and gazed briefly at its illuminated screen. "Emergency mission!" he announced. "Get us out, Mr Zack, shortest route possible."

"Aye aye, Captain," Zack replied crisply, consulting the map. "There's an exit around the next bend."

"Once we're out, we're heading for that disused ancillary transporter facility," Gordon said. "Three to beam up."

Zack nodded: it was as he had thought. The message hadn't come from Starfleet Command. *Velociraptor* would shortly be boldly going goodness knows where, maybe somewhere in the middle of nowhere.

"Grab the box, Nick," Gordon said. "We'll take it with us. You found the treasure map. 'Uti possidetis.'"

Nick tried grabbing the box, and found it was too heavy to lift. Gordon took one of the handles and it became much easier to carry. They followed Zack towards the nearest secret way out of the building.

The three girls crept along the narrow passageway between the walls. Miranda was glad her dad had insisted on her packing that big, heavy torch. He'd been certain it could get pretty dark at night in the middle of nowhere, though she hadn't expected to need it quite that quickly!

She'd given it to Zoë, who seemed to know where she was going. Miranda was more than happy to bring up the rear. What she was doing there in the first place she had no idea. She supposed stranger things had happened in her dreams.

In less than a minute they'd reached a narrow staircase leading up to the next floor. Could her Uncle Fergus's workshop and observatory be at the top? Her aunt had specifically told her she must never go there, though *actually*, she had told her never to go up that other staircase, so technically, she wasn't being disobedient.

These stairs led to an apparent dead end. Clearly they were a secret way to and from whatever lay on the other side of that wooden panel. Miranda had a sinking feeling she knew what it was. Wouldn't it be just like her Uncle Fergus to have a secret way in and out of his den?

Zoë pressed a well-oiled catch on the panel, and it swung open without a sound. They stepped out into a large, bright space. Instead of a ceiling, the room was surmounted by a huge glass dome. There was an impressively large telescope fixed to a swivel mount on a purpose-built platform beneath it.

A man was standing with his back to them, at a table in the middle of the room. It was covered with maps, charts, photos and drawings, and he was writing in a large notebook with what looked like a fountain pen. They stood in a line for a moment, watching him. Miranda's heart was in her mouth.

Zoë pushed the panel shut behind her and it closed with a sharp click. Startled, Lord Fergus Ogilvie, 14th Earl of Gairloch and Cadder, swung around and stared at the three young witches standing in his private sanctum. This was his holiest of holy places where he was never to be disturbed.

He was a handsome, middle-aged man with a well-trimmed moustache and eagle eyes. Miranda thought him very like Lord Carnarvon, a photograph of whom she'd seen recently in a television programme about the real Downton Abbey.

"All hail, my Lord! Hail to thee, Thane of Glamis!" Grace declared dramatically. She nudged Miranda.

"All hail, my Lord! Hail to thee, Thane of Cawdor!" Miranda heard herself stuttering. She and Grace had learned this scene for Drama last October.

"All hail, my Lord, that shalt find kings hereafter!" Zoë announced. That was a curious alteration to the text as Miranda remembered it.

Her uncle grinned suddenly. He probably thought he'd mixed up the dates and it was time for the Fancy Dress Ball. He fell into rôle straight away, which was pretty sporting of him in the circumstances.

"What are these, so withered and so wild in their attire, that look not like the inhabitants of the Earth, and yet are on't?" he asked theatrically.

He pointed at Zoë and Grace. "You should be women," he said with a cultured Scottish accent that was perfect for the part. "Yet your beards forbid me to interpret that you are so." He took a step towards them. "Stay, you imperfect speakers, tell me more."

Grace grabbed Miranda's hand and skipped nimbly around him. Zoë moved quickly to his other side and grabbed Miranda's other hand, then she and Grace joined hands. The Earl was now standing in the centre of their circle.

"Show his eyes, amaze his heart," Zoë hissed. "Come like shadows, so depart."

Miranda felt a power surging through her. A spangling glow surrounded the others, and she realised it was also wrapped around her. She just had time to catch the look of absolute astonishment on the Earl's face. "This is like being beamed aboard a spaceship," she thought, before the room she was in faded away ...

For several seconds, Miranda experienced a curious sense of emptiness, and then the world around her gradually reassembled. She was still holding hands with Grace and Zoë, and her Uncle was still standing, utterly bemused, in the centre of their circle; but they were no longer in his workshop. Instead, they appeared to be standing on the observation platform of an enormous spaceship.

"Pinpoint accuracy, as usual, Mr Nicholas," Captain Bennett said approvingly. "Welcome aboard, Ladies." He stood up and moved towards the Earl with his arm outstretched. "It's an honour to have you with us, my Lord."

The girls dropped their arms, and the Earl took Gordon's outstretched hand. "Where on Earth are we?" he asked wonderingly. He looked around the futuristic flight deck, unaware of its resemblance to the *Enterprise* because he never watched television, and there weren't any cinemas in the tiny local town with the name that sounded like Auchtermuchtyecclefechan.

"Nowhere on Earth, Sir," Gordon told him, and gestured towards the eye level screens. They were docked at a space station approximately 220 miles from the surface of their awesome, rotating planet. The clarity up there was breathtaking.

"I'm Miranda, Uncle Fergus," Miranda said. She came forward, unsure whether to shake his hand or curtsy. She indicated the two girls behind her. "These are my friends Grace and Zoë, and this is - er ..." She looked at Gordon and hesitated.

"Captain Gordon E. Bennett of the Starship *Velociraptor*," Gordon said crisply. Allow me to introduce our flight control officer, Mr Nicholas, and our Science Officer, Mr Zack."

"Fascinating," the Earl murmured, shaking each of the proffered hands and staring pointedly at Zack's ears. "This is a dream of course, but I've never had one so real before. Are we going somewhere?"

"Indeed we are," Gordon told him. "Mr Nicholas, set a course for the far side of the moon."

Miranda admired the dexterity with which Nick pressed some of the many buttons he had to choose from. He adjusted a dial, punched in a set of coordinates and slapped the 'Enter' key on his keyboard with a well-practised flourish.

"Course locked in, Captain," he announced. There was a dusty, brass-bound box sitting on a flat surface next to his pilot's console. That was odd ...

Gordon extended his right forefinger in time-honoured fashion. If you didn't do that in the final examination, you lost points for style. "Engage thrusters!"

The starship's stabilisers were state of the art: there was scarcely any sense of movement as the ship got smoothly underway. 0-60mph in the first second, 60-600mph in the 2nd, 600-6,000mph in the 3rd ... By the 5th second they were travelling at 600,000mph and the moon was getting bigger by the second. In minutes, it was very large indeed, and the ship used its reverse thrusters to decelerate. "Short, but sweet," Gordon commented on the journey they had just taken.

The moon is only one eighth the size of the Earth, but it looks huge when you're only 200 miles from its surface. They had mere seconds to marvel at its craters and enormous canyons before the ship swung into geostationary orbit on the far side. The journey had taken less than twenty minutes.

It's a popular misconception that the far side of the moon is dark. In fact, it gets as much light as the near side. The "far side", however, is always the far side as far as our planet is concerned because it is never seen from Earth.

Captain Bennett flicked the switch on his intercom. "Bridge party to transporter room: seven to beam down, Ms Welsh."

"Right you are, Captain," came the voice of the ship's chief engineer. Her accent was straight out of the Rhondda Valleys.

"Seven to beam down?!" Miranda's Uncle Fergus exclaimed. "There's no atmosphere down there!"

"Down where, exactly, my Lord?" Gordon asked innocently. He led the way through double doors that swished open at his approach.

Chapter 4

Moonbase Omega

When their surroundings came back into focus, they were standing on an enormous, glazed, observation platform at the top of a tower perhaps a hundred storeys high. It looked out over the most impressive space colony any of them had ever seen.

A city stretched for kilometres in all directions.

It was a hive of activity. Interconnecting mid-air monorails carried linked, transparent pods at high speeds between towers about half a kilometre apart. The station towers too were glazed. Lifts conveyed travellers to and from ground level. It was like an overground version of the London Underground.

The city had no roads. The ground was covered entirely by buildings, where its citizens lived and worked. They could see them hurrying to and fro like ants far below. There was about their movements a more unified pattern of direction and purpose than there would have been in any human city.

Far above the building they were in was an overarching structure made of interlocking triangles. The triangles must have been huge. They were covered in some sort of lightweight polymer. Gordon guessed that the species that had built this city had chosen a very deep impact crater and roofed it over to make it invisible from above.

He was reminded of the time when the gorillas' tracking beams pulled *Velociraptor* towards that huge pyramid on the Planet of the Apes. There had been an illusion of solidity there too, but inside it had been full of space.

From where they were standing, the "roof" was so high it looked like an oddly spun spider's web. Clearly the polymer allowed light in: the sun blazed through with singular intensity. The material must have filtered out the more harmful rays at the ultra-violet end of the spectrum. It was also keeping in the artificial atmosphere and pleasant warmth. Presumably, it was the atmosphere that was holding the roof up there, like the inner skin of a gigantic hot-air balloon.

For a species as advanced as this, it would have been child's play to replicate the pattern of small craters and ridges on the space-side of the roof, making this space station indistinguishable from the rest of the moon's surface.

It was an ideal hiding place.

"Welcome to Moonbase Omega," said a calm, pleasant voice behind them. A young man was approaching them, smiling in welcome. His face and body might have been modelled on an ancient statue of Apollo. He had dark, curly hair and deep, blue eyes, and was wearing a loose white tunic belted at the waist and ending at the knee. His open-toed sandals were tied to his bare feet with gilded leather thongs.

"Fascinating," murmured Zack. Two questions had immediately occurred to him. Did he and Zoë owe their existence to beings like the one who now welcomed them? And why had they now been brought to what must be a very closely-guarded, secret location?

"Those are two important questions," said the young man, smiling at both Zack and Zoë. That totally mystified Nick, Miranda and her Uncle Fergus, who had not heard any questions being asked. "They will be answered in due course."

The young man turned to Grace. With Zoë and Miranda, she now looked even more incongruous in her witchy get-up. He held his hands out to her, palm upwards, in invitation.

"Grace Forrester," he said. There was suddenly real tenderness in his voice. Wondering, Grace took his hands. "You have your mother's eyes," he told her: "flakes of radiant blue among the green."

She fought to keep the tremble out of her voice. "Are you my father?" she asked him.

He squeezed her hands gently. "That too is an important question," he replied. There was sadness and a longing in his voice, as though he had caught, and was mirroring, her mood. "The answer is so much more complicated than you can possibly know." He stroked her cheek. "I have something for you."

He didn't say what it was. Instead, he turned to Gordon. "Gordon Bennett," he said with no less affection, "Ring-Bearer, Torque-Wearer, Myrddin's chosen heir, the Archwizard of Dreams."

"Hi," said Gordon, sticking his hand out a little awkwardly. He was at a bit of a loss, which didn't happen often.

The young man took the proffered hand and shook it warmly. "We have waited many of your Earth years for you," he said. "Your sixteen-greats grandmother was a remarkable woman." The blue eyes twinkled as he glanced at Grace. "It seems that witching still runs in the family."

"Your name is Mabon," Gordon said. "And in some way more complicated than I can possibly know, you are my father too." He held his left hand up. "This is your ring."

The young man sighed. "Yes, and no." He turned to Nick and Miranda. "Tomorrow, you will not remember that you have ever been here; but we acknowledge your importance in our scheme of things. Soon, we will send you each a token of our gratitude."

He turned to the silent, waiting Earl. "And last but not least, we come to you: Lord Fergus Ogilvie, 14th Earl of Gairloch and Cadder and the principal reason that we find ourselves in this space and at this time."

The Earl smiled grimly. "I thought as much. You alter your appearance, of course, in order not to alarm the humans you interact with. Obvious choice of image, I suppose - the Greek Gods - at least for us in the west."

He looked enquiringly at the figure in front of him. "I expect you bear a striking resemblance to Confucius in the East, and to appropriate icons in all the other regions of the world."

The young man regarded him evenly. "You know, of course, why you are here." There was a moment's silence. Miranda looked at her uncle in wonder.

"It has to do with a certain project," Grace told her, "that would shake the world to its very foundations, were it to go ahead."

The Earl's eyes narrowed. "And how," he asked her, "could you possibly know that?"

"Your uncle," the young Greek-God-lookalike informed Miranda, "is one of that rare breed of men and women: a great adventurer. He has been exploring the Mariana Trench in the Western Pacific. It is the deepest ocean on earth, in places more than ten kilometres deep."

"10.91at the Challenger Deep," the Earl confirmed.

"He is about to engage a team of steelworkers and shipbuilders on the Clyde to build a two-man submarine capable of withstanding the enormous pressure at the bottom of such a sea. During his preliminary explorations, he stumbled on evidence that led him to believe there is an alien earth-station down there - of similar size and purpose to the station in which you now stand."

"I'm right, aren't I?" the Earl said, triumphantly. "I *knew* it!"

"Yes, you knew it," the young man agreed, "but very shortly you will no longer know it. It is important for our purposes that no human shall know of it for the foreseeable future."

The observation platform had 360° windows. Access to and from the platform was by a lift, housed in a substantial, round, central column rising through the floor. Double doors in this column now opened noiselessly, and six other identical young Greek Gods emerged.

Gently smiling, they moved with unthreatening precision and purpose to stand beside each of the children. Gordon felt that familiar slipping-into-a-deeper-sleep feeling that normally signalled time-up on a dream.

"Tomorrow," their alien host promised, "you will wake up in your own beds, having had the best night's sleep of your lives to date. You will have no memories of your travels tonight. Lord Fergus will have developed the passion for Egyptology once held by a distant cousin several times removed."

In the time one has when counting down from 10, Miranda heard her Uncle Fergus say rather dreamily: "There is much of value still to be uncovered in The Valley of the Kings."

Chapter 5

Be Careful What You Wish For

The last weekend in March was fast approaching, and Vivian was planning her annual pilgrimage to the dell. She always went back on the same day each year - the last Sunday in March - to sit in the same spot, and clutch the stone. It was the closest she could get to the memory of that first time. She supposed that even now, she retained a hope that maybe, just maybe ... One never knew ...

Elaine would go with her, of course. They had been partners since Grace was born, and their visit there with the Bennett family two years ago had been momentous. The odds on something interesting happening in that dell had shortened considerably after that.

They'd planted acorns from a special oak, the one apparently used in Arden to renew the youth and vigour of a Fairy King and Queen. She wondered how those two young oak trees were getting on. Their rate of growth was staggering.

For Edith and Victor too it had been a 'Road to Damascus' moment; so this time when Vivian asked if they would like to go again and make a picnic of it, Edith was delighted. She promised that Victor would do his best to to have that Sunday off. She mentioned it over dinner that night.

"I'll check the rotas," Victor promised. "It shouldn't be a problem." He glanced over at Gordon. "Is it likely to be as eventful as last time, do you think?"

"I've no idea," Gordon confessed. "I've only been there once, the same as you. It certainly felt special last time. Myrddin said it was one of his portals into our world. I wonder how many others he's got, and where they are."

Victor dipped his fattest chip into the generous dollop of tomato sauce he had plopped on to the side of his plate. "You can ask him," he suggested, "the next time you see him." He took a bite. "Ooh, ah, that's hot!"

Gordon nodded slowly. His current list of questions for Myrddin, as always, was a long one. What Myrddin said to him on his first trip to Avalon had certainly proved true: he still had much to learn in both their worlds.

Victor went through the pain barrier and swallowed his chip. "The trial of that red-haired killer Zack and Zoë identified is finally over," he told them. He sounded grimly satisfied. "The evidence was overwhelming and he confessed. The jury was unanimous: guilty on all counts. The judge sent him down for life; he'll die in prison."

Swansea had come up with the address. He was the registered owner of the dark blue Renault *and* the white van, which he used for business. There was DNA evidence all over both vehicles. They found his stash of grisly relics in a box at the back of his wardrobe.

"That poor girl," Edith murmured, remembering the photo that Victor brought home that afternoon, after Grace and Gordon had helped identify the boys who had vandalised a local playpark.

Victor waved his next chip in the air to cool it. "Those poor girls," he said. "He confessed to the murder of two more: six months to a year apart, each in a different town." He examined the chip closely, as if it might provide a clue to help him understand. "He says another person lives in his head and tells him who to kill."

❧

Later that evening Grace got in touch with Gordon. *"We're all going to the dell again."*

"Yes, I'm looking forward to it," Gordon told her.

"Miranda just rang me. She's over the moon! It's her fourteenth birthday a week on Sunday, and she's just found out her aunt in Scotland is sending her a pony!"

"Whoah," Gordon said. *"That's some present."* He made a mental note to get Miranda a birthday card. Zack shivered slightly, as if someone had walked over his grave.

"Yes," Grace agreed. *"She couldn't stop talking about it. Her aunt's married to some Scottish Lord she met at University. They live in the Highlands somewhere, in a big house. They breed horses and thought Miranda would like a pony. It's jet black apparently, and called Polly."*

"That must have been where she got her location from for that chapter she wrote back in Year 7 English," Gordon suggested. He remembered it because he remembered everything, plus he was still quite proud of the 'Ideas For At Least A Billion Stories' booklet that they'd worked on at the time.

"Yeah. She said she's only ever met her aunt once - when she was five - and she's never met her Uncle Fergus. He's away a lot on expeditions, apparently. His latest one is in the Valley of the Kings in Egypt: looking for a lost Pharaoh."

Gordon frowned slightly: he'd just had one of those "déjà vu" moments. The feeling went away.

"Anyway," Grace went on, *"I've invited Miranda to come with us to the dell and I was wondering if you'd like to invite Nick."*

Gordon glanced at Zack, who nodded assent. *"OK,"* he agreed. They all enjoyed each other's company. It could be fun.

Chapter 6

Somewhere, Over The Rainbow

The four children ran on ahead, while the adults made their way a little more apprehensively along the path towards the dell.

"What are the chances of another manifestation, do you think?" Victor asked Vivian.

She shrugged. "Less, I suppose, with Nick and Miranda here. It's nice to see how well they all get on together, isn't it?"

Edith nodded. "I'm so pleased with the way Gordon is growing up. I was worried for him when he was younger: how other children would take to him."

"He's a very personable young man," Elaine said. "You can be really proud of him."

"We can be proud of them both," Victor said, "and grateful. Those special powers of theirs are already solving crimes and saving lives."

Gordon and Nick came trotting back along the path. They were followed at a more sedate pace by Grace and Miranda. "We think you're going to be surprised," Gordon told them.

"Oh oh ..," Victor said.

"It's a nice surprise," Grace reassured him.

Minutes later, the four adults were standing speechless in the middle of the dell, gazing at two thriving young oak trees in blossom. Their trunks were a full twelve inches in diameter. They towered around forty feet into the canopy.

"They look as though they've been here twenty years," Elaine said. "That's astonishing."

"Why?" Nick whispered to Gordon. They looked like perfectly ordinary trees to him.

"It's just that they've grown a lot since we were last here," Grace explained, truthfully. "We didn't expect them to be blossoming already."

"I think that means there'll be acorns in the autumn," Miranda said. She gazed around the dell, breathing in the heavy scent of the violets. Her feet and ankles were swamped in bluebells. "This is a really magical place."

"Let's make rings around the oaks," Gordon suggested. "The four adults around that one and the four of us around this one. Hold hands, close your eyes, and on my signal make a wish."

"I'm game," said Nick, who had spotted his chance straight away. "It should be boy girl boy girl."

"Of course it should," Miranda agreed, laughing. She'd decided she was game as well.

Victor looked a bit doubtful. "Are you sure, Son?" he asked. It seemed to him a bit like tempting fate. After what happened last time, who knew? The sky might fall in.

"Quite sure," Gordon said. He winked at his dad. "Nothing ventured, nothing gained."

"That's very true," his dad admitted. "Are we up for this?" he asked the three ladies. Edith smiled and took his hand. "I feel like a child again."

"Nobody is to tell anyone what it is that they're wishing for," Grace reminded them. "Your wish won't come true if you tell."

They all took up position around the oaks. Nick took Miranda's hand and Grace's and closed his eyes. He thought this was one of the best moments in his life to date.

"Everyone ready?" Gordon called out. "Right: WISH!"

Seconds passed.

"Can we open our eyes now?" Miranda asked. Nick was holding on for as long as he reasonably could. They opened their eyes ...

The dell looked exactly the same as it had before they had closed them. Victor didn't know if he was relieved or disappointed. Rather self-consciously they let go of each other and stepped away from the trees.

Nick felt a tingle in his hands. Did he just imagine it, or had one of his wishes come true already? It was just possible that Miranda had given his hand a little squeeze before she let go.

"How is everybody?" Elaine asked. "Still in one piece?"

"I'm in ... just the one piece," Zoë said, a little awkwardly.

"So am I," Zack added slowly.

Miranda and Nick looked at them, grinning. "That thing's happened to your voices again," Miranda told them. Nick was confirmed in his view that there was more to this holding hands business than he had previously imagined.

Edith dashed over and grabbed Gordon's shoulders. "Look into my eyes," she demanded. He gave her a quick, impulsive hug, then stepped back, pretending to laugh it off.

"I'm fine, honestly." His voice had dropped a couple of tones. Edith looked meaningfully at her husband, and then at Vivian, who was very quick on the uptake.

"Elaine and I need a hug too," she said. Zoë rushed over and wrapped her arms around them both. Their heads were together for several seconds, whispering, apparently exchanging reassurances.

Nick and Miranda watched this going on, a little bemused. They saw Gordon go over to his father and actually shake his hand! Isn't it strange how they do things differently in different families?

They looked at each other, not wanting to be left out. Their nearest and dearest weren't there to be hugged and shaken hands with. Impulsively, Miranda threw her arms around Nick and gave him a good hug. It seemed the right thing to do. She was so happy about her pony. Her wish had already been granted. Nick patted her on the shoulder. All his Christmases and birthdays had come at once.

"Whoohh!" Gordon's dad said, wiping what looked suspiciously like tears from his eyes. "Did anyone wish for rain?" With surprising suddenness, the sky above the dell had gone grey. The temperature had dropped several degrees, and a breeze was blowing up out of nowhere.

"It looks like we're in for a short, sharp shower," Edith said. There was a little quiver in her voice. She zipped up her jacket. "Let's get under these trees. It will probably only last five minutes."

The adults went back under their oak. The children clustered under theirs. "Sorry about this," Zack said to Nick. "There wasn't any rain forecast."

"What are you sorry about?" Nick asked him cheerfully. "I'm having a great time."

"So am I," said Miranda. She linked in with Zoë and gave her arm an affectionate squeeze. "Thank you for bringing me here: it's a really special place."

Across the dell, the adults were talking quite urgently in low voices. They glanced over at the children from time to time. "Nothing's the matter, is it?" Nick asked. He suddenly felt a little anxious.

"No," Zoë told him, in that sexy low voice that she'd had for a couple of hours two years or so ago in school. "Everything's going to be fine." And, as if what she had just said was a prophecy, the sun reappeared and the rain stopped. Edith had been right: it had only been a short, sharp shower.

"Oh WOW," Nick said suddenly. "Look!"

There was a time when rainbows filled people with awe. They didn't know what made them, and suddenly seeing those colours arching across the sky seemed mystical. They thought it was something supernatural, a sign from God. That was probably when that fairy story was invented - the one about there being a pot of gold at the end of the rainbow.

This rainbow came down right in the centre of the dell. They could clearly see all the colours arching up - red, orange, yellow, green, blue, indigo, violet. Where the bluebells sat in their banded colour they glowed as if the light came from inside them.

The end of the rainbow was right in front of them.

"Gordon and Grace are somewhere over that rainbow," Edith whispered. She gripped Victor's hand. Elaine slipped an arm around Vivian. "They're together," she murmured. "Myrddin will keep them safe." Vivian nodded, staring at the rainbow's end. Her eyes glistened. Her hand wrapped itself tightly around the dreamstone.

Nick rushed out from under their tree. He stood right in the middle of that amazing conglomeration of colour. "It's HERE!" he exclaimed. "The end of the rainbow is right HERE! We have to dig!"

The colours were fading ... As the sun warmed the air, the moisture droplets evaporated. Nick was rooted to the spot, his eyes shining with excitement.

Vivian walked over to him, smiling. She reached into her bag and pulled out a small trowel. "The last time we were all here," she told him, "we did some planting. I brought the trowel again, just in case." She handed it to him. He accepted it eagerly and began to dig ...

Almost immediately, he hit something solid. Wondering, everyone gathered around while he cleared the few inches of topsoil off whatever it was. From the sound the trowel made when it knocked against it, it seemed to be wood. Victor had just decided it must be a root, when he caught the dull gleam of brass.

Minutes later Nick was uncovering a brass-bound wooden box. It looked very old, but the wood was still hard and strong. He was digging like a boy possessed. This couldn't be happening: both of his wishes coming true so soon? It could *not* be happening.

There was a stout brass handle at either end of the box. Nick grabbed one of them and tugged but the box stayed stuck in the earth. Victor stood with his feet planted on either side of it, grasped the handle in both hands and heaved upwards.

"Mind your back, Dear," Edith advised him.

Fortunately, it was the earth around the box that gave, and it came grudgingly out of the ground. He put it down at the side of the hole and stepped back, panting. It is **heavy**," he told them.

Nick stared at it, his heart pounding. Did it look familiar? A feeling that he had seen it before came and went away again. He knelt down and examined it. "It's locked," he said, pointing to a prominent brass-bound keyhole just below the lid.

Zoë put Grace's hand in her pocket. "I woke up a few days ago after a really interesting dream, only I couldn't remember a thing about it."

"That's weird," said Miranda. "So did I."

"Me too," Zack told them.

"And me," Nick added. How strange was that?

"For a moment I heard a man's voice telling me he had something for me," Zoë said, "but I must have dreamt it. The memory went away, but then I found these in my pocket." She pulled out an old bunch of keys.

Nick took them eagerly and began to try them. The third key turned; they all heard the click. He slowly lifted the lid, just as the sun came out above the oak and slanted sunlight down into the dell. Nick's face was bathed in a golden glow as he gazed into the box.

"What can you see?" Zack asked him. Nick threw the lid right back.

"Wonderful things," he replied.

Chapter 7

A Matter Of Life And Death

They were somewhere dark and cold and underground, surrounded by disintegrating death. The air was dank and stank of mould; it caught in the throat and pinched the nostrils. This was a place for hearts that had been stilled, not for hearts still beating.

"Where are we?" Grace whispered. Gordon felt her squeeze his hand. A moment ago, they'd been standing with Nick and Miranda in a hand-held circle round that astounding oak, making a wish. The warm spring air had been heavy with the scent of lilacs. Bluebells were emblazoning the ground.

"I don't know," Gordon admitted. His eyes had been closed while he was making his wish and he hadn't felt his torque take him by the throat. "I can only think we're somewhere in Avalon."

Avalon, Tír na nÓg, the Land of the Forever Young, that region of departed souls. He and Grace were surely once more quick among the dead. What were they here to learn this time? What had they been wishing for?

"I wanted to help all those who die too young," Grace told him. She shivered, remembering the trip she'd taken with Zack to see the Brontë sisters when they were children. It was two years ago now, but the memory of it was as fresh as if it had been yesterday. "Why is there so much misery in the world? Why can't we recycle happiness instead?"

Coincidentally, Gordon had remembered the trip he'd taken with Zoë at the same time that Grace had headed off with Zack. They'd witnessed a riot and a murder. "I wanted to stop those hoodies killing that poor old man. So I was wishing the same as you in a way."

"If this is Avalon," Grace muttered, "then Myrddin knows we're here."

The beam from Gordon's ring grew brighter. It lit the space around their still-clasped hands. He let go of Grace and raised his left arm. The glow drove the darkness back, turning it into more discerning shadows.

They were in a vast, and vaulted, columned tomb. All around were grey sarcophagi, sitting in timeless silence on stone plinths. Their carved, slabbed lids sealed the bodies in: ashes to ashes, dust to dust. It occurred to Gordon that this encrypted space might be below the great hall where Myrddin had introduced him to King Arthur and the Army of the Slain.

Grace tugged on his arm and pointed at one of the stone coffins near where they were standing. Unlike all the others, this one was still open. Its lid leaned ponderously against a nearby wall, waiting. "There's someone still alive in that," she whispered. "She's dreaming in a darkness of her own."

Hardly daring to breathe, they moved across the cold, grey flags and peered into the coffin. Gordon stretched out his ring hand and its light gleamed on the figure of a girl. She was lying on a bed of cushioned silk, her hands folded neatly on her chest. Her eyes were closed, as if in final peace. No breath or pulse betrayed her beating heart, though colour lingered in her cheeks, and her lips were parted in a faint smile.

She was dressed much as Gordon imagined his sixteen greats grandmother would have been dressed when she was fourteen years old, or thereabouts. In height and weight she seemed rather smaller than Grace, though her face was more striking than beautiful in a twenty-first-century sense. She looked quirky and strong-willed.

Above them, off to one side, they heard the sound of metal being forced between a lock and a protesting chain. It was followed by the splintering of wood. Fastenings gave way and a door swung open, bringing dismal light to dust-strewn steps. A long shadow preceded the figure making its grieving way into this last resting place. It was still clutching the crowbar it had used to force an entry.

Grace and Gordon melted a safe distance into the darkness behind one of the marble plinths. The light from Gordon's ring winked out. They heard the unrelenting bar rebound on the stone flags as it was tossed aside. A burning torch waved shadows round the tomb. It was carried by a young man drowning in despair.

Chapter 8

What Are The Chances?

The adults gathered round the excited children to stare at the contents of the brass-bound box. How spooky was it that a rainbow had come down right in the middle of the den, and that Zoë had been able to unlock the box Nick had unearthed with a key on a bunch that had recently turned up in one of Grace's pockets? Could it have anything to do with that dream they'd all had that none of them could remember?

The box was filled with finely engraved gold plate and hundreds of shiny silver coins. They looked new, but had that irregular roundness that signalled early coinage. Victor lifted one out and scrutinised it carefully. It bore the number eight. The name of the king proclaimed on one side was Rex.Philip.V.D.G. Hispan. ET Ind.

"This is an 8 reales coin, dated 1564." He took out a handful. "So is this, and this. They look like a fresh batch."

"PIECES OF EIGHT!" Zack screeched, startling everybody with his passable imitation of Long John Silver's parrot. "Those coins were minted in the same year Will Shakespeare was born."

"I don't believe it," Nick said. "I just wished that one day I might find buried treasure, like a pirate in the Caribbean! What are the chances?!" He was in a state of shock. His almost wildest dream had just come true.

Edith looked meaningfully at Vivian. This was a magical place all right. Here, oak trees grew at twenty times their normal rate. Here, Grace had been immaculately conceived (like treasure planted in a fertile womb). Here, Myrddin, Grace and Gordon passed between at least two worlds, and a child's wish could be granted in the twinkling of an eye.

"Remember your year 7 story," Miranda said to Nick, "about Sir Francis Drake and *The Golden Hinde*? This could be some of the treasure from that Spanish ship. It was shared with the crew when they got back to England."

"They didn't have bank vaults in those days," Zack reminded everybody. "If you wanted to keep something safe you had to hide it. Maybe one of the crew brought his share back to his home near here and hid it in these woods."

"A lot of people died from the plague around that time," Zoë chipped in. "Or maybe someone killed him trying to find it. Either way, this place became its grave."

"The law on treasure changed in 1997," Victor told them. "Now a find like this has to be reported within 14 days to the coroner of the district where it's found. It's then vested to the Crown and transferred to the National Museum of the relevant country." He replaced the handful of coins and closed the lid. "The Secretary of State decides whether or not a reward should be paid to its finder. With a hoard of this quality, the reward could be substantial."

"I don't care about the reward," Nick said. "It's just so fantastic to have found it. I feel like I found it for everyone."

Zoë turned the key and locked the box. "We'd better stick it in the car straight away," Victor suggested. "Once we get back to Nick's house, we can ask Angela if she'd like any help photographing and describing the contents."

"Can we agree on one thing, though?" Vivian asked: "that we don't show anyone where we found it?" She looked anxiously round the group. "Everyone is going to want to know. There'd be thousands of people descending on this dell with metal detectors and spades. It'd be like a plague of locusts. They'd tear the heart out of the place."

Elaine put a comforting arm round Vivian. "We're not going to let that happen. Let's drive to some other spot of common land. We've got plenty of that in Wales. We can choose a nice spot for our picnic and say we found it there."

"I'll dig another hole," Nick declared stoutly. "Gordon will help me."

Zack nodded in agreement. "Might even find more treasure," he joked.

Edith looked stricken. "Before I set one foot out of this place," she declared. "I need to be sure of one thing!"

"Nick, will you and Miranda be OK for a couple of minutes?" Zack asked swiftly. It wasn't really a question.

Nick nodded, looking mystified.

"Families conference," Zoë told Miranda. "We won't be long."

"Fine," Miranda assured her. She and Nick watched Gordon and Grace get into a huddle with their parents on the far side of the den. The adults all looked very worried. Gordon and Grace seemed to be trying to reassure them.

There was something the wrong way round about that.

Chapter 9

Do The Best You Can

The young man placed the torch in an iron ring fixed to the wall near where the coffin lay. He leaned into the open casket. The light played havoc with his tear-stained face.

"O my Love! my Wife!" he sobbed, staring down at the figure lying on its bed of silk, silent in that final resting place. "Death, that hath suck'd the honey of thy breath, hath had no power yet upon thy beauty."

He placed a gentle hand upon her face, clearly amazed at how alive she seemed. "Thou art not conquer'd. Beauty's ensign yet is crimson in thy lips and in thy cheeks, and death's pale flag is not advancéd there. Why art thou yet so fair?"

It was a question that deserved more thought, but the balance of his mind had been disturbed.

"Shall I believe that unsubstantial death is amorous, and that the lean, abhorréd monster keeps thee here in dark to be his paramour?"

That was hardly the most likely explanation, but sorrow sucks all reason from the soul. He shuddered. "For fear of that," he assured her, "I still will stay with thee, and never from this palace of dim night depart again."

He leaned into the casket and caught her in his arms. "Eyes, look your last! Arms, take your last embrace!"

Weeping, he laid the body of his love back on her bed of silk. He reached into his pocket and pulled out a small phial of colourless liquid. He removed the stopper. "Here's to my love!" he declared, and put it to his lips.

"NO!" Grace yelled, on behalf of several million schoolgirls. She sprinted from her hiding place and dashed the poisoned drink from Romeo's lips. "She's not dead! She's not dead! You only had to wait another minute! Look!" Reaching into the coffin, she grasped one of Juliet's hands. "She lives, you glorious, lovesick fool. She LIVES!"

Gordon came out of the shadows into the fading light of the dying torch. He stuck his hand out a little awkwardly. "Romeo Montague, I presume. I'm Gordon Bennett. You won't have heard of me. This is Grace. She speaks the truth, and she has healing hands."

The young man had reeled backwards from the shock of being accosted by a frantic female intent on keeping him alive. Now he was faced with an earnest boy, who spoke his language with a lilting tongue, and dressed in a manner that was passing strange.

"Angels and ministers of grace defend us!" he declared, making a sign of the cross. "Bringst thou airs from heaven or blasts from hell?"

Gordon looked puzzled. "But this *is* Heaven," he pointed out, "nor are we out of it."

Grace had a more pressing matter to attend to. "See where your lady stirs and finds her breath," she declared, "parting the veil of outward-seeming death in search of her most dear and longed-for lord." She stepped to one side. "And yours should be the face she looks upon to comfort her on her return to life."

Romeo stared at Gordon, and then at Grace. "Such welcome and unwelcome things at once, 'tis hard to reconcile," he muttered.

His Juliet's voice, still drowsy from her sleep, drove the last doubt from his still-troubled mind. "O comfortable heaven! Where is my lord? I do remember well where I should be, and there I am. Where is my Romeo?"

Her hands appeared on either side of the casket. She struggled to sit up. He gathered her in his arms. "I'm here my Love, and here I will remain, and never more be parted from your side."

He held her face and looked into her eyes, his tears not now from sorrow but from joy. "For you were lost to me and I to you, had not these two appeared as if from heaven, and dashed the poison from my grieving lips."

And suddenly, the chamber was ablaze with blinding light. It was as if the doorway pointed east and day had dawned, flooding their lives with hope and welcome warmth. Myrddin was making his way down the steps, his ancient, careworn face creased in a smile.

Gordon and Grace ran over to greet him like a favourite grandparent whom they had not seen for quite some time. He stretched his arms out and wrapped them in his cloak, accepting their hugs with a good-natured chuckle.

"Friar Lawrence had the best of intentions, of course," he commented. "But on Earth, if free will is to mean anything at all, the best laid plans do often gang agley." He smiled down at them. "At least in Avalon we make amends. After life's fitful fever, we sleep well."

He patted them both on the shoulder. "Be happy to do the best you can; we ask no more than that." Stepping back, he placed the tip of his staff against the torque around his pupil's neck. "Here endeth the third lesson."

Gordon grabbed Grace's hand again, just to be on the safe side.

The adults laid out their picnic on the heights above Llangollen. The children had dug a plausible kind-of-a-hole and were busy filling it in again. The brassbound chest was safely in the car.

"Lunch is ready!" Edith called over to them. She knew that Gordon had come back from Avalon quite safely twice before, but her stomach was still in a knot. She thought Victor, Vivian and Elaine must be going through the same gut-wrenching emotions, especially as it was their first time. Zack, she noticed, was occupying Gordon's body with increasing confidence. There was something about that that tore at her insides, however hard he tried to reassure her.

Zack and Zoë stood with Miranda and Nick round the patch of just-turned earth. "I honestly think this is the best day of my life so far," Nick said. He stretched his hands out. "Let's swear on our lives that we'll always remember it, and keep our secret safe."

They joined hands. For at least two of them, there was more than one secret to keep safe.

"Oh wow!" Gordon said, breaking hold and heading for the picnic spread. "Something smells good. I could murder a tuna melt."

"Where are we? We didn't miss anything, did we?" Grace asked Zoë.

Chapter 10

Getting A Grip

They were into the last two weeks of the spring term, and school was whipping itself into a fervour over "end of term exams." These were enjoyed by those who were good at them, detested by those who were bad at them, and taken as they came by the majority of pupils.

For teachers, they were a mixed blessing. Exam conditions meant a few blissfully quiet lessons followed by a heavier marking load and the struggle to hold the attention of many children who'd lapsed into a bog-standard, post-exam stupor.

Mrs Peters' bump was more visible by the day. Grace jumped the gun when she asked her if she'd decided on a name for her yet. "We don't know if it's a boy or girl," Mrs Peters told her. "We're going to wait and find out in the old-fashioned way."

Grace was sympathetic. She knew what her form teacher was frightened of. Mrs Peters had miscarried three years ago. "Don't worry, Miss," she'd said, laying her hand on her tutor's arm. "I have a feeling that on the first day of the autumn term, you're going to bring your beautiful new baby girl into school to meet us."

She could have added that Maisie was a lovely name.

Every Monday, they had an extended a.m. registration for checking and signing diaries. It was a fairly relaxed half-hour. Quiet talking was permitted, although messing about was not allowed. However, some of the children in their tutor group were like puppies that had not been properly trained. Unless they were on a tight lead, they had a tendency to yap loudly, nip at each other's ears and get into mischief.

Miranda handed Grace, Gordon and Nick a little envelope each. It contained an invitation to her birthday party the following Sunday. Nick was genuinely moved, and Gordon was pleased to have another reason to spend some time with Grace outside school.

"I hope you can all come," Miranda said in a low voice. "I'm not inviting loads of people, only a chosen few."

Nick fought against the tears of gratitude that would have given him away. "I'd love to come," he assured her. He could rely on his mum to help him think of a good present. He was careful with his pocket money and had quite a bit saved up.

"I'd love to come too," Gordon said. He was willing to bet there were some good deals out there on books about horses and ponies.

"There are," Grace telepathed. *"I already looked."*

Gordon smiled quietly and turned his attention to his diary. He kept it meticulously and never forgot to get his mum to read and sign it. He could therefore be fairly certain of the weekly housepoint on offer for its proper use. He shut his ears to the persistent, predictable conversations Mrs Peters was having with those who didn't and couldn't. If he ordered something online tonight, it would be delivered by the end of the week, in plenty of time.

"Did your dad tell you which prison that murderer has been sent to?" Grace telepathed. She was attending to her diary as well, but it was a chance for a quiet chat.

"Yeah, I asked. It's H.M. Prison Manchester. He's also likely to be in solitary to stop other prisoners attacking him."

"I bet if you asked your ring it could take you there," Zoë suggested. "And we want to come too, don't forget."

The killer claimed to have an Alter-Ego who told him when and where and who to kill. That's what they wanted to check out.

"REECE!" Mrs Peters called out sharply. "MOVE!" She pointed to an empty chair on the other side of the classroom. "I've warned you twice; now you can move." There were two "naughty chairs" in their form room. They were used to separate people who persisted in messing about.

It could have been any of the four boys on that back table. Arthur, Dominic and Brian were just as bad. They scrawled on each other's work, broke each other's pencils, got into each other's bags, tipped each other off chairs …

Reece made great play with his reluctance, moving as slowly as he dared. Gordon fought against rising irritation. He knew it wouldn't stop there. Once Reece was on the other side of the room, it would simply mean broken bits of pencil and rubbers flying across the room whenever Mrs Peters' back was turned.

"Just ignore it," was Grace's advice, but Gordon found that very hard to do. Their tutor had her work cut out getting round all the diaries without all the time-wasting interruptions. He caught Reece's eye as he slouched past. Reece was really bad at reading words on paper, but quite good at spotting disapproval on another person's face.

"Who are you looking at?!" he demanded, puffing out his chest. It was meant to be threatening, but just looked ridiculous. Nick kept his head down. It was safer not to make eye contact with any of them.

"It looks and sounds like you, as usual," Gordon replied. He resisted the urge to hurl the posturing buffoon halfway across the classroom. Mrs Peters was beside Reece in a moment. "Sit where I told you to sit," she said. She pointed at the empty chair.

Reece resumed his crawl towards the other seat. "Why don't you tell HIM to mind his own business?" he said to her. "You never tell *him* off, do you?"

"He never gives me any reason to," Mrs Peters told him crisply. "Now make sure your diary is complete. And remember to write "None set" if you don't have homework for any subject on any day. I'll get to you in a minute." She went over to Gordon and gave him a reassuring smile. "I'll deal with it," she promised him. "Leave it to me."

Gordon nodded and turned back to his diary. Unfortunately, leaving it to her wasn't the ideal solution. She was a nice teacher - not one of the ones who tried to frighten you into behaving properly. Some kids took advantage, and she didn't have eyes in the back of her head.

The remarks started right after that. "Who do you think is the biggest "GOODY GOODY" in this class?" Arthur asked loudly.

"What, you mean who'd get voted "TEACHERS' PET of the Year?" Dominic said, at a volume calculated to reach everyone in the room.

"He means who's got the brownest nose," Reece chipped in. It wasn't a racist remark.

"Maybe we should vote on who's the biggest LOSER in here," Grace suggested to Miranda at roughly the same volume. "What do you think?"

"You'd be spoilt for choice," Miranda responded, nailing her colours to the mast. "We could have categories, though, like 'the thickest brick' and 'the most irritating idiot.'" There were a few "OOOOHs!" from some of the naughtier girls. Miranda looked at Nick, and he realised that the honour of their table was on the line.

"YEAH," he said. It was a start, and took more guts than he'd known he had.

"It *has* to be between Knickerlarse and the Gay Gordon," Brian announced to a chorus of titters round the room. This confrontation was far more entertaining than filling in gaps in your diary.

"That's ENOUGH!" Mrs Peters said sharply. "The next one with anything hurtful to say goes out of this classroom and into House detention. You know what you should be doing. Now DO IT!"

There was a temporary lull. "Do you want us to sort them out?" Zack asked. He was itching to wipe the smirks off their stupid faces.

"It would be no trouble," Zoë agreed. She looked at Grace with the eagerness of a hound waiting to be let off the leash.

"*No,*" said Grace. "*Miss said she'd handle it.*"

Gordon knew she was right. He got his reading book out of his bag: there were ten minutes still to go. He would rise above this childish nonsense and lose himself in a good story. He opened the book and tried to concentrate.

A sizeable rubber bounced off the back of his head. It had been thrown with considerable force. There was an explosion of giggles and mini-cheers from the corner of the room. A red curtain dropped in Gordon's mind, separating him from his better judgement. He slapped the surface of his table loudly with his right hand and swung round.

Brian was leaning back with a self-satisfied smirk. His two companions were patting him on the shoulders. The back legs of his chair suddenly shot forward - they'd apparently slipped on the polished floor – and he crashed backwards into a painful heap in the corner. He could easily have broken his neck.

Arthur's howl of laughter was cut short when the heavy science textbook in Dominic's left hand swung suddenly sideways with full force into his face. It knocked him right off his chair. Shocked and stunned, his head narrowly missed the corner of the neighbouring table. It could have taken his eye out.

Dominic leapt to his feet, staring at his left arm and the book. In doing so he seemed to catch the edge of their table, which slammed away from him into the wall. There was a howl of pain from Brian, who'd been struggling to get up out of the corner and had just grabbed the table for leverage. His fingers were still wrapped round the edge when it rammed into the wall. Two or three of those fingers would be severely bruised, if not broken.

Reece was rocking himself over his new table in explosive mirth, when he suddenly seemed to misjudge the distance between its surface and his face. There was a sickening thud as he apparently drove his own forehead into the tabletop with enough force to knock himself out. He slithered sideways off his chair in a crumpled heap, almost certainly suffering from concussion.

"WHOAH!" Zack called out, grabbing hold of Gordon's shoulders. "Easy, Tiger, EASY!" Gordon turned back to his book, closed his eyes and breathed deeply through his nose. He felt the red curtain lifting and noted that his hands were shaking. Oh dear, that had been several degrees over the top. He would definitely have to work harder on his self-control.

Mrs Peters sent for a first-aider. She would be arranging a meeting with their parents and the Head of House. This time, their nonsense had gone far too far. Somebody could have been badly hurt.

When he got home from school that day, it only took Gordon two minutes to discover that *The Complete Illustrated Encyclopaedia of Horses and Ponies: Authoritative Reference Care and ID Manual* was half-price online. It was by Catherine Austen, Sarah Gorrie, Pippa Roome and Nicola Jane Swinney. Gordon didn't know anything about the authors, but something told him there wasn't much they didn't know about horses and ponies; a bit like him and dinosaurs.

Maybe he could put together a *Complete Illustrated Encyclopaedia of Dinosaurs* one day. He wondered if there was any chance of taking a digital camera to the Jurassic Era and bringing back pictures of some real ones. How awesome would THAT be?!

Before placing the order, he checked with Grace. She was fairly certain that Miranda didn't already have it. She was also fairly sure nobody else was planning on getting it for her. Knowing Miranda's liking for quirky tee-shirts, Grace had found one that said "OMG! PONIES!" on the front. She thought it would make the perfect present.

Miranda's dad and new stepmum were giving her a course of riding lessons for her birthday. They were also forking out the fair amount needed for stabling and upkeep. She was a lucky girl.

He gave Nick a quick ring. Nick was leaning towards a digital photo keychain that stored up to one hundred pictures. His official reasoning was that Miranda could then have as many different pictures of her pony on it as she liked.

Unofficially, he was hoping that one of the photos on the key-ring might have him in it. He really liked the idea of being in Miranda's pocket. When Gordon rang, he'd been practising his dance moves in front of the mirror.

You can't blame a boy for dreaming.

Chapter 11

A God-Forsaken Place

"Are you really sure we want to do this?" Zack asked. He, for one, was having second thoughts.

They were standing outside a massive brick building. It occupied the whole of a city block. Its central portion looked curiously like a medieval fairytale castle. It was made out of red bricks and cream-coloured stones. Two round towers with conical tops framed a huge Norman arch, entirely filled with a solid wooden door. On either side the smooth high walls stretched an intimidating distance.

"It *is* a scary place," Zoë admitted. This was another world. A poet once said: 'stone walls do not a prison make, nor iron bars a cage'. Twelve hundred men in there would have disagreed with him, and a fair number would have given him a good kicking while they did so. Quite a number of them were category 'A' prisoners: people found guilty of the most heinous crimes.

"If only there was a way to recycle all this waste," Gordon muttered. That was yet another thought for yet another time.

Mabon's ring and Grace's stone had brought them this far. He and Grace were agreed; they needed to know. Their Alter-Egos were kind and good; Myrddin had called them "guardian angels." Had this red-haired murderer been cursed with a different kind? Was there some force for evil out there they didn't know about yet?

If they were on this planet at the same time and in the same place for a good reason, what about *him*? Was there such a thing as a guardian devil? H.M. Prison Manchester was a likely place to look for evidence.

"Let's get this over with," Grace muttered. They joined hands and closed their eyes. Red bricks and red hair, dark lords and demons, dreadful deeds and lost souls, 'What a piece of work is a man' ...

When they opened them again, they were in a dark corridor. A man in his late twenties or early thirties stood smiling at them. He was dressed in a white shirt and dark trousers – his own clothes. He didn't have red hair.

"You've come for the tour, I presume," he said with a Scottish accent and a faintly ridiculous air of self-importance. "Let me show you where I earned my claim to fame."

He led them a short distance along the corridor and into a whitewashed room lit by a single, dismal, neon tube. The wooden floor had a large trapdoor in its middle. Two stout planks were stretched across the trap, and a hangman's noose hung from the ceiling. It was coiled up out of harm's way.

"Nothing in my life became me like the leaving it," he told them proudly. He puffed his chest out. "This is where I swung for her. They recycled me in seven seconds, the all-time British record."

"Swung for whom?" Gordon asked in horror.

"For Alice Morgan," Zack said quietly. "James Inglis confessed to strangling her, and was hanged for it in May 1951. He claimed insanity, but the jury didn't believe him. The men they paid to carry out the sentence took him from his cell, stood him on that trap, prepared him for the drop and pulled the lever, all in seven seconds."

Grace gazed with sudden fury at the posturing buffoon. "How many seconds did it take you to 'recycle' Alice Morgan?" she asked him. The spirit shrank from her accusing gaze. Ghostly tears welled from the weak and hopeless face.

"They're changing guard at Buckingham Palace," it whined. "Christopher Robin went down with Alice." Grace grabbed Gordon's hand. "Get us away from him," she said. Gordon closed his eyes and counted on the ring ...

When he opened them again, they were in a cell about ten feet long and six or seven feet wide. A man was asleep in there on a narrow bed. The security light from the space outside shone in through the barred, square window in the metal door.

The head poking out of the regulation grey bedding was covered in distinctive red hair. Gordon made sure his dreaming body was between Grace and this self-confessed murderer of young women. Raising his ring hand, he let its light play on the man's eyelids. He saw them move; the man stirred ...

Grace retreated to the foot of the bed. Gordon took an involuntary step backwards to join her. The prisoner's eyes opened. It took a moment for his still-sleeping mind to register the fact that two children he had never seen before were standing in his cell. Was this a dream?

He glanced at the door to check that it was closed, and then raised himself on one elbow. From the level of the light he could tell it was still the dead of night. The only other sounds were muffled sobs from nearby cells. He stared at them. "Who are you? How did you get in here?" he asked.

"We travel in the wonderland of dreams," Gordon told him. "You told the police another person lives inside you and tells you where and when and who to kill. We came to see if what you said was true."

"How do you know what I told the police?" he wanted to know. "And what's it to you in any case?" He swung his legs out of bed and sat up. His eyes were cold and hard, his mouth set in a thin and selfish line. He stared at Grace with the stillness of a snake about to strike.

"There's terrible damage," Grace told Gordon. "but no demon, other than the one he conjures up himself." She stared at him with a mixture of compassion and loathing. "He was badly abused as a child. The adults who should have loved and cared for him killed all the good in him instead. Now there's just a dead thing where his conscience is meant to be."

The man hissed and coiled for the leap, only to find himself hurled back across his bed and hard into the wall. Zack and Zoë slid out to stand shoulder to shoulder with Gordon and Grace. Try as he might, he didn't have the strength to pit against the power that was pinning him to the wall of his narrow cell.

He stared at them and snarled, too far out for all his adult life in a sea of hate and rage. He had never waved and was always drowning.

"We're the children of the women you killed," Zack told him.

"We're the children of the women you can't now kill," Zoë said softly.

"We're the children who can help prevent atrocities like this," Gordon added sadly.

"It won't be easy," Grace admitted, "but we'll do our best."

They joined hands and faded from his sight, leaving him with his twisted, tainted thoughts, washed up on a barren shore.

Chapter 12

No Pain No Gain

"Isn't she beautiful?" Miranda breathed. Polly had thrust her head over the halter door and was nuzzling her neck. She stroked the pony's silky skin and blew affectionately into her nostrils.

"She certainly is," Grace agreed. It was Sunday 3rd April, Miranda's fourteenth birthday, and she was about to ride her very own pony for the very first time. The longing shone in her eyes.

Vivian and Elaine had driven them both to Polly's new base: an equestrian centre a few miles into Flint. The rates for stabling and lessons in Flint were cheaper than in Cheshire. Meanwhile, Miranda's dad and stepmum were getting everything ready for M's party later that day.

Grace was paired with a grey mare, the double of the one she and Zoë had found themselves riding in a fateful dream they'd had the month before they started secondary school. She was looking forward to feeling the Spring air in her hair and being at one again with the rise and fall of such a beast.

How powerful and compliant horses are, and how patient with the eager apes who ride them.

"Good girl," Grace murmured, stroking the muscled neck and finding acceptance in its docile mind. She gathered the reins with practised ease and swung herself into the saddle. It was the first ride of the day. She could sense its eagerness for exercise. "The world looks better from up here," Zoë murmured. Grace was happy to agree.

Miranda was less sure of herself. Polly was already saddled up. One of the stable hands had brought her into the yard where the dozen or so other riders were already gathered. Polly seemed to sense her new owner's uncertainty. She was skittish, shifting round as Miranda got her foot in the stirrup, forcing her to hop a little clumsily after her.

Another girl took Polly's head and steadied her enough for Miranda to clamber on. "You're not used to your new routine yet, are you Girl?" the stable hand said to Polly. She gave her a friendly slap and grinned up at Miranda. "Grip her quite firmly with your knees. Gather the reins in. Get her head up; show her you mean business."

Miranda gathered the reins and pulled a little too firmly for Polly's liking. The pony tossed her head and skittered backwards several paces.

"EASY!" the instructor called out. "She's got a very light mouth. I don't think she's been ridden all that much." She walked over. "Are you sure you can handle her? I can put you on Bella. Belinda could ride Polly until we've got her schooled a bit more."

Bella was a retired carthorse with a back as broad as a table. The biggest challenge when riding her was getting her to move at all. Belinda, on the other hand, owned a string of horses and regularly carried off trophies in the local gymkhanas. She'd already ridden in several point-to-points, and her sights were set on championship show-jumping. The look on her face said she would be more than happy to lick this wilful little pony into shape.

Miranda looked stricken. Polly was *her* pony, and this was *her* birthday. She most definitely did not want her precious new friend bonding with some other girl, especially one who could ride so much better than she could. She'd dreamt of this moment ever since she'd first been told of the wonderful present her Aunt Matilda was sending her. She wouldn't be denied now.

No, she and Polly would learn together. They would teach each other each other's little ways. "We'll be all right," she assured the instructor. "I want her to start getting used to me."

The instructor nodded understandingly. She checked the tightness of Polly's girth and the length of the stirrups. She made sure Miranda's hat fitted properly and the strap was secure under her chin. "Stay behind me," she said. "If she's too much of a handful, we can always put a leading rein on her."

Miranda sat proudly in the saddle while Vivian took several photos. Back straight, knees firm, heels down, toes pointing slightly out, beaming smile and only the smallest traces of nerves.

They set off at a brisk walk. The instructor was in front, then Miranda, then Grace. Belinda was on a gorgeous chestnut gelding and keeping a watchful eye at the back of the group. The pair of them oozed class.

Polly snuffed at the unaccustomed smells. Her ears pricked up at every passing sound. This was a new world for the quirky, strong-willed pony. All her senses were tingling. However, she followed the broad haunches of the bigger, calmer horse in front of her, and seemed to know her place in the line.

They moved along a rutted track that led down to the narrow country road, and then turned left on to the hard surface. "Trot on!" said the instructor over her shoulder. Her well-schooled horse broke obediently into the loping gait that would carry them to their next off-road track as quickly and safely as possible.

Polly needed no urging to follow suit. Her shorter legs clip-clopped at a considerably faster rate to keep up. "Up-up-up," Miranda muttered to herself through clenched teeth as she tried to time her rise to the rhythm of the high-stepping pony. It wasn't surprising that her falling bottom met the rising saddle more often than she would have liked. It was a jarring reminder of how much better it would be once she had got it right. No pain no gain. What was it Grace said? - "The path to knowledge is unfolded ... Ooh! Ouch!"

And then they were safely off road again and back to a walk. "Well DONE!" the instructor called over her shoulder. Miranda leaned forward and patted Polly's neck. "Good girl!" she whispered. The pony's right ear twitched and Miranda thought she could feel her pleasure. She decided this was definitely going to be the best birthday she had ever had.

Five minutes later they came to the field where the riding school horses were used to cantering. "Make sure you've got her head," the instructor warned Miranda. "Stay behind me." She broke into a measured canter.

Polly's response was immediate! She charged after the horse in front, apparently convinced it was a race. In vain Miranda did her best to haul her in, but the excited little pony had got the bit between her teeth. Nostrils flaring, breath snorting, neck flat out, Polly shot past the startled instructor and pounded along the field track at a full blown gallop.

Miranda's heart was in her mouth. She clung on for dear life ...

"*Zoë!*" Grace telepathed urgently, and Zoë was off like an arrow from a bow. A second later she was in the saddle with Miranda and had both hands on the reins, hauling the pony's head in. "WHOAH, girl, WHOAH!!" Zoë yelled, and Polly seemed to hear! Her head came up and she slowed to a canter, and then to a fast trot.

A hundred metres back, the instructor breathed a sigh of relief. Her priority had been to make sure none of the other horses followed suit. She'd been praying Miranda wouldn't come off at such a speed.

"*Great job, Zoë!*" Grace telepathed gratefully. "*Really great job!*" Zoë relinquished control of the reins to Miranda and raised both hands above her head in triumph. That was the moment, of course, when Polly's right front hoof went as far as her fetlock down a mole-hole. The pony stumbled forward, and Miranda went straight over her neck.

It could have been a lot worse. Polly had been slowing to a walk, and had been able to pull her hoof out of the hole without breaking any bones or straining any ligaments. Miranda's feet had come straight out of the stirrups, so she wasn't dragged and didn't damage her ankles.

It was over in a flash. She stuck out her right arm as the ground rushed up to meet her, and felt her wrist snap as it yielded to the force of the impact. Grace winced as the searing pain hit Miranda's nerve-endings.

"Wait here, everybody," the instructor said. She wheeled her mount and cantered briskly towards the trembling pony and the fallen girl. Grace cantered after her, ignoring Belinda's urgent "WAIT!"

"She's my best friend," she told the instructor by way of an excuse. They reached Miranda and dismounted at the same time. "I can help her!"

Miranda was sitting up moaning. Her hand flopped at an unnatural angle. "It's a badly broken wrist," the instructor said. "Are you hurt anywhere else? Did you bang your head?"

Miranda shook it to say no and to show that it was still working. It's just my wrist," she muttered. "Oh God, it hurts!"

"Let me see," Grace said gently. She took hold of the wrist with her right hand, supporting the weight of Miranda's hand with her left.

"Be careful," the instructor warned. "We need to get that to a hospital as soon as possible. I'm going to ring for an ambulance." She pulled a mobile phone out of her riding jacket.

"No, wait a moment," Grace said. "I think it's only sprained." Carefully she straightened Miranda's hand without relaxing her grip on her wrist. "That's better, isn't it?"

Miranda nodded, her eyes filled with gratitude and relief. "It's not hurting anymore. It just feels warm and tingly."

"Let me see," the instructor said. She squatted beside them, far from convinced. She'd seen enough broken wrists in her time, and that had been a particularly bad one.

"I just need to hold it a little longer," Grace said. "The horses are being very good, aren't they?" It was a simple but effective tactic, diverting the instructor's attention for those crucial extra seconds. Grace could feel the bones knitting and the sinews strengthening. The healing flowed through her like a river.

Zoë had gathered the reins of the two horses and the pony, and was whispering words of comfort in their ears. They stood together, their heads cocked as if listening. Wondering, the instructor went over and took hold of the reins. Grace stood up and helped Miranda to her feet.

Gingerly Miranda tested her wrist for movement and flexibility. She found that she had full rotation and control. "It doesn't even hurt," she said. "That's amazing!" She stared at Grace. "You have healing hands."

"Don't be daft!" Grace said. "It can't have been broken if it's OK now. You stretched the tendons, that's all - gave them a bit of a shock. It hurts for a while, but then it's all right. You just needed to hold everything in place for a minute." She turned to the instructor. "I've done it myself," she told her, by way of further explanation.

The instructor shook her head in wonder. It just goes to show: you can't always believe the evidence of your own eyes.

"Do you think you can ride," the instructor asked Miranda, "if I put a leading rein on Polly?" Miranda nodded. The best way to get over falling off is to get straight back on if you possibly can. The instructor beckoned the others to walk on and catch them up.

Polly stood stock still as Miranda climbed back into the saddle. "She's really sorry," Grace whispered, "...and she's very glad you're all right now."

Chapter 13

Holiday Plans And Déjà Vu

On the last day of the spring term Nick had a little surprise for them all. He waited until they were gathered under their favourite tree at the far end of the playground, and then dug into his pocket. "My mum reported our find to the coroner for North East Wales, and we handed the treasure chest over. He said the contents will go on display in the National Museum of Wales."

He held his hand out for them to see. Resting in its palm were four of the silver coins. "There were so many in the chest, and they were all the same," he whispered. "We thought it wouldn't do any harm to keep four of them as a little memento. Don't tell anyone!" He handed one each to Miranda, Grace and Gordon.

"Wow," said Gordon, "my very own 'piece of eight'. Thanks a lot, Nick!"

"You're welcome," Nick said, his eyes shining. "It's our secret. I'm going to keep mine forever."

"We all will," Miranda promised him. "Whenever we see or hold it, we'll think of us."

"The Awesome Foursome!" Grace grinned.

"Oy!" Zack protested. "What about Zoë and me?"

"*OK, the Super Six!*" Gordon agreed. "*We've skipped 'The Famous Five', but they must be getting on a bit.*"

"Into their eighties by now," Zack said. "I'm afraid Timmy must have turned up his paws a long time ago. He'd be about 500 in dog years."

"We've got some adventures to go if we're going to catch up with them," Zoë observed. "They had twenty-one, if memory serves."

"Promise me you won't worry," Grace said shrewdly to Nick, "about there being any curse on the Aztec silver."

"Course not," Nick said, almost convincingly. "That sort of thing only happens in stories."

The bell went and they made their way to their tutor room for morning registration. Oak House assemblies were on Wednesdays and this was a Friday, so there was no great rush. Mrs Peters had twenty minutes to deal with any individual or form business before the bell went for the start of period 1. There was no particular pressure to do anything anyway, it being the last day of term.

"Oh my God," Gordon said in a low voice as they settled round their table, "What are they *doing*?"

Three of the girls sitting on a table at the back of the class had plugged in some kind of contraption and were taking it in turns to run their hair through it. "They're curling tongs," Miranda informed Gordon and Nick.

Gordon put his head theatrically into his hands. "Just when you think you've seen everything," he muttered. "What'll it be next? - painting their toenails in class?"

Mrs Peters arrived with the register. "Put those away now, girls," she said crisply.

"Aww Miss, just two more minutes!" Chelsee Witherspoon wheedled, dangling the tongs. Debra Simpson was holding two mirrors at once, trying to see what her hair looked like from the back. Britney Clutterbuck was performing some kind of Goldilocks routine on it with a glitter-backed brush.

"NOW, or I'll have them," Mrs Peters insisted. "This is neither the time nor the place."

Gordon banged his head gently on the surface of the table. "Do you think," he asked Grace and Miranda, "there might be some difference in our DNA?"

"Never mind them," Miranda said. "Grace and I have got some news." She leaned forward, looking excited. Nick and Gordon leaned in dutifully to receive it. "You know my Aunt Matilda? – the one who married the Earl of Somewhere and Somewhere and they live in a sort of castle in the Highlands of Scotland?"

Nick nodded. "How's Polly?"

"She's great. I've got a load of pictures of her on my key ring, thanks very much."

Nick nodded again, playing it cool. He was totally delighted the key-ring present had gone down well, even though he hadn't made it into Miranda's pocket just yet.

"Anyway, she's invited me to stay with her and Uncle Fergus over the summer holiday. She says she wants to get to know me." She looked proud and pleased. "I've never been to Scotland, and I haven't seen her since I was five. She says I can bring a friend. Grace is coming with me."

"Wow!" Gordon said. "You should have a fantastic time."

"That's great," Nick said, smiling bravely. Grace looked sympathetic. She knew what he was thinking. In such an adventurous and romantic place, Miranda was likely to meet an interesting, slightly older, good-looking boy – probably the gardener's son – and that would be him out the window.

"I'll make sure she doesn't get into any mischief," she said, winking at Nick who blushed and looked away. Was it really that obvious?

"Your Uncle Fergus is an Egyptologist, isn't he?" Gordon said. "Away a lot looking for another Pharaoh in the Valley of the Kings."

"Yeah, good memory," Miranda confirmed. "I've never met him." She paused and looked puzzled suddenly. "At least, I don't *think* I've ever met him."

Grace shivered. "I just got a picture of someone in my mind. He looked like Lord Carnarvon – you know, the one who financed Howard Carter when they found the tomb of Tutankhamun."

"These are the voyages of the Starship *Velociraptor*," Nick chimed in, then looked amazed. "Why did that suddenly come into my head?"

"It feels like a collective déjà vu moment," Zack said.

"... which would connect it to one of our group dreams," Zoë added.

"How about that one none of us can remember?" Grace telepathed. She pulled the bunch of old keys out of her pocket and fingered them.

"We already know what one of those keys was for," Gordon thought back. "Maybe the others are for locks that lie ahead."

"Are you two going anywhere this summer?" Miranda asked.

"I'm going to Ireland," Gordon said. "We're renting a house in County Meath. It's near Tara and Newgrange. I really want to see the historic sites in the Boyne Valley. They're only a forty-minute car-ride from Dublin City Centre."

"That sounds interesting," Grace said. "Watch out for all the little people."

Gordon grinned at her. "Why else would I be going?" he asked. Nick and Miranda thought that was a joke.

"What about you, Nick?" Miranda asked.

"We haven't decided on anything yet," Nick said offhandedly. "We may end up staying put this year, and doing day-trips, mini-break type things." The others nodded.

"Nick's mum doesn't have much money," Grace told Gordon. *"They normally can't afford to go anywhere."*

That was when Gordon got the idea.

"Mum," he said when they were back home and on their own, "...could I ask Nick if he'd like to come to Ireland with us?" He'd already got a thumbs-up from Zack.

Edith was delighted. It was the first time Gordon had ever wanted to have a friend with him on one of their holidays. "Of course, Darling!" she said. "You'll be good company for each other. Let's mention it to your dad when he gets home."

Gordon poured himself some orange juice and got a chocolate digestive from the packet in the fridge. "The thing is," he said. "I don't think Nick and his mum have got much money."

Edith was sympathetic. She knew how much tougher it would be making ends meet if she were having to bring Gordon up on her own. It wasn't something she wanted to think about.

"Angela has her pride," she said. "She'll want to pay for his flight, but it's not much for a return flight from Manchester to Dublin. We're hiring the car anyway, plus there are twin beds in your room, *and* we're self-catering."

She grinned. "I'll tell her she'll be doing us a really big favour. You'll have a much better time if Nick comes with us." Edith knew that was only partly true: Gordon had had his best friend with him from day one. However, Angela and Nick didn't know that. "How do you feel about it, Zack?" she asked.

"Fine, thank you for asking. It'll be a laugh." Gordon didn't bother with the "he says" anymore. It was quicker just to relay the actual words.

Edith grimaced. "Let's hope so." Her concerns were understandable. She knew why Gordon wanted so much to go to Ireland this year. She'd asked him and he'd told her.

"You'll have to check his passport's up to date," she said. "They've still got time to sort it out if it isn't."

"Great," Gordon said. The idea was growing on him all the time. "I'll wait and see what dad thinks. If he agrees, I'll give Nick a ring and ask him."

An apple from the fruit bowl leapt into his outstretched hand. "Grace is going to Scotland with Miranda this summer," he told his mum, "to stay with Miranda's Aunt Matilda in a castle in the Highlands. They'll be there exactly the same time we'll be in Ireland. Isn't that a coincidence?"

Edith raised an eyebrow, and had the curious feeling that Zack was doing the same thing.

Chapter 14

Another Fairytale

On *The News* that night was yet more about the forthcoming wedding of William Wales to Catherine Myddleton. There were still three weeks to go, but the preparations were in full swing. The Media was gorging itself on all the incidental details: who'd had invitations and who hadn't, who'd be sitting where, what everybody would be wearing. They were especially interested in Kate, but her sister Pippa seemed to be catching the spotlight as well.

It is a truth universally acknowledged that nobody can put on a royal wedding (or a funeral, come to that) quite like the Brits. An estimated two billion people all over the planet were already looking forward to the "Kiss Me Kate" moment on the Royal Balcony: the sealing embrace above the heaving Mall. After all, it's what Britain is all about, when you get down to it.

Never underestimate the power of a fairytale.

"Let's hope they get it right this time," Victor commented. "It didn't work out for his father the first time."

"I think there's a good chance," Edith said. "She has to have a better idea what she's getting herself into."

Gordon looked from one parent to the other. "What are you talking about?" Victor decided Gordon was old enough to be brought into this particular conversation. Zack would have brought him up to speed in any case.

"In 1981, William and Harry's father, Prince Charles, married their mother, Lady Diana Spencer. It was the biggest, most spectacular Royal

Wedding of all time, a classic media event in front of a worldwide TV audience."

"It was gorgeous," Edith said dreamily. "She was so radiant and fragile under that veil. Her train was twenty-five feet long. We'd never seen anything like it."

"The beautiful princess married the handsome prince in order to produce strong healthy sons," Zack added. "They were needed to guarantee the stability of the monarchy and the line of succession into the foreseeable future. It's the nearest human beings can get to one of those fairy renewals."

Gordon nodded. "But they didn't live happily ever after, did they?"

Victor sighed. "They didn't, Son, no. As so often happens when human beings try to live a dream, reality intervened."

"Nobody bothered to tell Diana that Charles was married already," Edith said grimly. "That was their big mistake. We know it now. Hindsight is a wonderful thing."

She shook her head sadly. "Diana called it 'a crowded marriage', and unlike the fairytale princesses of yesteryear, she wasn't prepared to put up with it."

Gordon was puzzled. "He couldn't have married her in the first place if he was married already."

Victor reached for the wine bottle and poured himself another little slug. Edith put her hand over her glass, as he'd known she would. "You'll find that life can be a bit more complicated than that," he told Gordon. "The real irony was that Prince Charles turned out to be one of the most faithful men on the planet."

"He was already in love with another lady," Edith explained gently. "But they were young, and some influential people didn't think it was a suitable match; so, the other lady married someone else and had two children of her own."

She sighed. "After that – it was thought at the time – she couldn't ever be accepted as an eventual Queen Consort of England."

"The English throne thought it needed sons," Victor commented drily, "though it's recently got round to realising that the three most successful, longest-serving monarchs we've ever had have been daughters."

"Enter the blushing, innocent princess," Edith said, "apparently tailor-made for the part, and so willing to be swept off her feet by a handsome prince. She probably thought she was the luckiest girl in the world."

Gordon shook his head sadly. "Wouldn't it be better if we were like swans?" he asked. "Swans mate for life."

Victor took another warming sip of his rather good red. "You'd certainly think so," he admitted, "...but if you look at us and you look at swans, maybe Nature knows something we don't."

Edith grinned at him. "You're getting philosophical in your old age," she said. "I think the wine is helping."

"It certainly is," her faithful husband agreed.

"Why didn't he just say no to the whole thing?" Gordon wanted to know.

"So much easier said than done," Edith told him. "He's the heir to the throne of England, and he was handed the main part in a massive pageant. Remember the family motto: '*Ich Dien*'.

"It means: "I serve" Zack told Gordon.

"He didn't audition for it, and he certainly didn't write the script. The monarchy needed sons. The pageant cried out for a fairytale princess."

"It got both," Victor reminded them. "She gave us two great sons, and she never stopped being the people's princess."

"You should have seen her with ordinary people," Edith said, her eyes suddenly swimming, "especially children, and the old, and the sick. She was magic."

"For a while there, the 'Great British Public' almost decided they preferred the fairytale to the real thing," Zack said.

"And then she was gone," Victor said, draining his glass. "The candle burned out long before the legend ever did."

"Goodbye, England's Rose," Edith added as she got up to clear the table. "And life goes on. Hopefully, lessons were learned."

After dinner, Gordon phoned Nick and asked him if he'd like to come to Ireland with them. Nick was delighted at the idea, and said he'd ask his mum. Edith told Gordon to tell Nick to put his mum on the phone, and the mums sorted it out, as mums generally do. In ten minutes, it was a done deal: Nick was coming to Ireland with them.

Gordon found he was worried about Wills and Kate. "Are they going to be all right, do you think?" he asked Zack. He was climbing into bed at the time.

"You could always ask Zoë," Zack reminded him.

Gordon considered it. "I don't think I want to," he decided.

"Probably wise," Zack agreed. "There's not a lot you could do about it, in any case."

"Maybe not," Gordon admitted. Another idea occurred to him. "I could ask my ring to grant me another wish: that this time the prince and princess get to live happily ever after."

Zack beamed at him. "That would certainly be worth a try."

Chapter 15

Visiting Royalty

"I know this place!" Gordon said to Zack. "We've been here before."
He gazed once more across that sun-kissed valley. It was still a place
where sheep might safely graze. The deep, dark woods stood still on its
far side, with heavy rainclouds glooming over them. It all looked a little
smaller, though not by much.

They'd stood there almost ten years ago, two months before his
fourth birthday. Being taller meant he could see a little more of the
impressive castle in the distance beyond the wood. Its ramparts and
drawbridge, crenellations and guard towers all seemed to be in splendid
shape.

Gordon still felt a bit guilty about what had happened the last
time he was here. The fairies living in that castle had no idea that their
'dragon' had started life as the picture of a diplodocus that Nicholas
had made a mess of colouring in when he was two. They didn't know
that Gordon had dreamed up that ogre intent on destroying him *and*
their castle. It turned out to be a ten-ton Tom, the terror from next
door. Tom was a much nicer boy now, of course. There was no chance
of him ever coming back here.

"So what are we doing back here?" Gordon asked.

"I don't know," Zack confessed. "You're never too old for a fairy
story, I suppose. Maybe it was all that talk about fairytale princesses and
royal renewal ceremonies."

They were standing side by side looking over the valley and the
wood towards the castle. It was a bit of a shock when they heard Grace's

voice immediately behind them. "Look who's here!" it said. "Why am I not surprised?"

They whipped round to find Grace and Zoë grinning at them. "Do excuse us barging in like this. This is where the dream dropped us off. We hope you don't mind."

"Of course we mind. We'd much sooner be on our own, wouldn't we Gordon?" Zack said, playing along.

"Well tough," said Grace, "coz we're stuck with each other now. Any ideas where we are, or why?"

"We came here once when I was almost four," Gordon told them, "so we know it's Fairyland." He pointed to the castle in the distance. "That's the royal palace. You met the King and Queen two and a half years ago in the Forest of Arden, at their Renewal Ceremony."

Grace nodded. "Of course. I think I know why we're here now."

"Oh good," said Gordon gratefully. "We were just wondering if it had anything to do with what we were talking about last night."

"The Royal Wedding on 29th April," Grace said. Her ability to read minds quite often saved them time. "We saw stuff about that as well. Zoë and I got this really good idea, and I think that's why we're all here."

"OK," said Gordon. "Let's hear it."

"We were the first humans ever to be invited to a royal fairy renewal ceremony," she reminded them. "Remember the fuss that spiteful little knocker made about us being there?"

The other three nodded. A bunch of spying knockers in Gordon's back garden on Halloween had been one fairly direct consequence.

"So when we were watching all that stuff about our royal renewal ceremony, I thought: why don't we invite the fairy king and queen to attend?"

Gordon knew a good idea when he heard one, but at first glance he wasn't at all sure how they would manage it.

"That would be FANTASTIC!" he exclaimed excitedly. "But how could we do it? I mean, we're not invited ourselves."

"Yes we are," Zoë maintained. "We may not have invitations to occupy seats in Westminster Abbey, but we're all invited. The whole of humanity is invited! There'll be two billion people there, watching every single moment."

She beamed at them. "Think of all those hearts and minds and good wishes! And which is more important: the physical presence of the few or the spiritual presence of the many? I know what I think."

"Of course, you're right," Zack acknowledged. "Our bodies may not have been invited, but then our bodies won't be going."

"WOW!" Gordon said, as the implications sank in. "How exciting is that?! But will it work, do you think? Do we have the right to invite them?"

"If we don't, who does?" Grace asked. "Out of all the humans on the planet, we were the two they invited to their Royal Renewal. I think that makes us the only two who actually *can* invite their royal fairy majesties to attend our Royal Wedding. And it IS ours. They're *our* royalty."

"I'll bet if you gave Wills and Kate the chance to invite the fairy king and queen to their wedding, they'd jump at it," Zack suggested.

"It has to mean good luck for them," Zoë said. "I'd want as many good fairies as possible at my wedding."

"You're on!" Zack said. "In the meantime, I think we've got an important invitation to deliver. How's your flying coming along?"

"Last one to that castle is a fairy!" Grace said, and launched herself from the mountaintop.

There are very few sensations more exhilarating than flying in a dream.

Chapter 16

Dressing For The Occasion

They zoomed across the valley in a diamond formation. It made Gordon think briefly of the Red Arrows flying over Buckingham Palace. He stopped when he remembered that at that point they normally released red, white and blue streams out of their exhausts.

Grace was on point, synchronising their movements. They could see agitated figures fluttering between the crenellations. The castles alarm bells began to clang ...

With practised precision, the four swooped up into the air opposite the drawbridge and drifted vertically down on the visitors' side of the moat. It was more polite to land on the ground in front of the castle and wait to be invited in.

Gordon and Zack waved to the guards on the battlements, and were pleased to see several waving back. Clearly they had been recognised and judged to be friends. The drawbridge rattled down and the portcullis was raised.

An imposing figure emerged, dressed in solemn black and carrying a staff. Gordon remembered him banging it on the marble dais inside the castle's throne room to command the attention of those present. He was flanked by several important looking fairies dressed in the finest silks and satins. Their doublets were fringed with ruffled lace and adorned with splendidly embroidered buttons.

"Whoah," Gordon muttered, "mustn't let the side down." Instantly, all four of them were surrounded by twinkles. They rose a foot or two into the air while this was going on and Gordon could hear faint exclamations from inside each magic haze before they sank to the earth again and reappeared.

Zack was once more dressed like a fairytale prince in scarlet hose and a royal purple doublet trimmed with lace. On his head this time was a flat cap of hunter-green velvet, at least a foot in diameter. It was set at a very Zack-like rakish angle.

"Don't you look ... dashing." Zoë murmured.

"You're not half bad yourself," he replied. She was resplendent in a gorgeous tango dress made from passionate purple, rain-colour fabrics. Gordon had been taken with it on *Strictly Come Dancing*.

By contrast, Grace found herself rather more demure as a Grecian Goddess in spearmint green. Her dress was draped simply over one shoulder, bordered and fastened in fetching swirls by autumn-coloured braid and narrow bands of glittering gold.

Gordon was back in his lacy white shirt, gold breeches, and coat of many colours. Silver-buckles once more graced his knees, and diamonds winked coyly in the soles of his shoes. He and Zack were considerably taller than when they last wore these costumes, but all items fitted perfectly.

Some master tailor somewhere must have been keeping track of their personal measurements.

The reception committee crossed the drawbridge and stopped in front of them. The flanking courtiers cast admiring glances at the splendour of the visitors' garments while Black Rod delivered his message.

"Their Royal Majesties have bid me say Your Worships are right welcome in our lands. If it now pleases you to follow me, I will conduct you straight into their presence."

"Our grateful thanks," Gordon said with a respectful bow. Black Rod led the way back across the drawbridge and into the confines of the Castle Keep.

"I hope I don't have to walk far in these shoes," Zoë confided. *"Why did you give me such high heels, Gordon?"* She cast an envious glance at Grace's comfortable, gold-thonged, open-toed sandals.

"They go with the dress," Gordon replied. She was right, though. Those heels weren't made for walking. They were made for dancing.

"They do wonders for your calf muscles," Zack observed. He cast an admiring glance at Zoë's leg as it made its way through the slit in the dress at every stride.

"I'd sooner they were doing wonders for **your** *calf muscles,"* Zoë told him crisply. *"They're killing me."* She raised herself an inch or so off the ground and began to float instead. *"Oooh, that's better!"*

It felt altogether statelier approaching the cathedral at ground level. Its ornamental stone facade seemed to have been modelled on that of Westminster Abbey, or perhaps it was the other way around. Rose-coloured flagstones were set in a diamond formation all round it.

Shining black doors swung open to reveal the magnificent interior. Though taller now than the fairies who accompanied them, the teenagers still felt small as they were swallowed by the grandeur of the space.

And there was the crown, slow-turning above the marble dais, and the light still streaming through the great rose window, fractured in the cut-glass facets of the crown. The fairy king and queen beneath it were bathing in a magic rainbow glow.

Their majesties rose to greet them, he from his marble throne of green-veined stone, she from her high-backed, woven basket chair. "Sir Gordon and Sir Zack," the king said, smiling broadly, "we welcome you as always when you travel in our lands. My Ladies Grace and Zoë," - he extended his arms towards them - "...welcome too. We're happy to find you here in Fairyland."

Grace and Zoë curtseyed to the ground. Zack whipped off his medieval hat in a bow worthy of a French musketeer. Gordon contented himself with a respectful inclination of his head. "We're deeply honoured to be so received, and hope that all is well in Fairyland," he said.

He detected a sudden sadness in the King's smile, and a cloud crossed Grace's face. *"They're both really worried,"* she telepathed. *"Their children are behaving badly."*

Gordon turned his gaze to the Queen, and saw the hurt in her eyes. "If there's anything we can do," he found himself saying, "please ask."

The queen sighed softly. The king's mouth twisted in a wry smile. "Was it to make that offer that you came here now?" he asked. "Or had you something else in mind?"

Gordon swept his arm towards Grace. It was her idea after all. "You did us all great honour when you chose to welcome us to Arden's sacred groves," Grace said. "You made it possible for us to share in the renewal of your youth and power."

There was a fluttering of anxious wings among the watching courtiers.

"We came to ask if you would honour us again by accepting our invitation to attend the Royal Wedding of Prince William, Duke of Cambridge, to Catherine Middleton, Queen Consort on his succession to the throne."

The King took the Queen's hand. "It is you who honour us," he said gravely. "And gladly we accept. Fairydom shall hear of this. It is another step along our way to new beginnings, and a common cause."

He began clapping to show his appreciation of their plan. Immediately, the courtiers joined in, some - it seemed - more enthusiastically than others. The King held his hand up for silence. "The Queen and I would have some words with our distinguished visitors alone."

Again that slight fluttering of wings. Only when the outer doors had closed did the king and queen relax. They came down from their marble dais, wanting, needing and ready to confide in these children, whom they considered friends. The king lowered his voice almost to a whisper.

"Lately, we have seen a transformation in our children. Neither their exterior nor their inward selves resemble what they were."

This clearly was a very private grief. "They dress themselves in clothes of inky black," the queen murmured. "Their innocence and mirth has disappeared. They walk about as if in mournful dreams, not sharing their thoughts or worries with us. They show no interest in affairs of state." Her voice trembled; she looked at her wit's end.

"They sink in silence, lost in empty thoughts," the king added. "Their faces are chalk white, their lips are painted black. Heavy circles underline their eyes."

"That happens," Gordon said reassuringly. "We call them Goths in school."

"Stop the world, I want to get off," Zack added.

The king shook his head. "The children that we knew and loved are gone. They are replaced by changelings, alter-egos that are more dismissive, challenging and rude than ever our dear children would have been." He glanced grimly at his wife, who looked bereft. "We fear there is some calculating force corrupting them to undermine our throne."

Zoë's head shot up, her nostrils flaring like an eager hound. Grace closed her eyes. "There is something rotten drifting through here," she announced, turning slowly, as if trying to determine its direction. "It's a putrid mix of prejudice and spite."

She opened her eyes suddenly. "Wicked thoughts are coming from those woods!" Gordon flicked through the channels in his brain, like he had when Zack had been half a mile away in Kieran's house. He found it: an insinuating stench.

"There's something nasty brewing in that forest," he agreed. "We'd better go and find out what it is."

There was no way Zoë was going anywhere near a forest in a glittery purple tango dress and high heels. She looked meaningfully at Gordon, and he realised there was no way they could blend into a leafy setting in the special occasion clothes they were currently wearing. He decided on Lincoln green all round; after all, it had worked for Robin Hood. It took a few spangled moments for them to change, in time-honoured fairy fashion.

A minute later, with their majesties' fervent thanks and fondest wishes ringing in their ears, they were airborne and zooming through the marvellous rose window as though the lead-lined glass had not been there. Ahead of them lay the dark and murky wood. It was where the wild things were, and from where that evil wafted in a thick, pulsating stream.

Chapter 17

An Unfair Fight

The stench grew stronger, the nearer they got. By the time they reached the edge of the forest it was almost overwhelming. Gordon was on point this time. "Once more into the breach, dear friends, once more …"

They flew in low and landed in the outskirts of the wood. The dense bush provided immediate cover. Extreme caution was advisable. Gordon remembered something Zack had said in the Forest of Arden: "You're unlikely to see a fairy who doesn't want to be seen." It was time to get their bearings.

Over to Grace. She closed her eyes and shuddered. "So many hate-filled thoughts," she whispered, "coming from over there." She pointed towards a particularly dense tangle of twisted growth. Many of the ancient giant trees were dying in the grip of strangler figs.

Gordon felt those not-good-fairies vibes he'd first detected coming from the back of his house when he was eleven. They were so much stronger here. That almost certainly meant a gathering of sorts - the sort of gathering you could not just drop in on and be assured of a welcome.

"We need more effective camouflage," he thought to the other three. They needed to catch this coven unawares.

He closed his eyes and let his senses drift, involving himself with those limbed strangler roots wrapped round the trees through which they had to pass. He focused on a teen-sized fragment, willing it to move, just as he'd willed the movement of the pictures in the books he'd read with Tom.

When he opened his eyes again, Grace, Zack and Zoë bore a marked resemblance to twisted vines. They had turned into fine examples of nature's artistry in root. Their hair was moss on top of gnarled brown heads, their eyes swirled into knots. Their noses were little barked protuberances, their mouths small holes in which a wren might nest. Their fingers and their toes were trailing twigs.

Gordon looked down at himself and felt his neck crick slightly. He too had been transformed. He'd first imagined Entings years ago when reading *The Lord of the Rings*. He'd felt so sorry for Treebeard because all the entwives had been lost. It seemed really sad that there could be no more little ents.

In seconds, they were mingling with the vines and almost invisible among the writhen roots. Rapidly, they moved through the trees, approaching the source of the emissions. Gordon detected an additional smell, an unmistakable tang. They heard the crackling before they saw the woodsmoke wafting in the wandering warmth from a fire under a massive cauldron.

The cauldron hung from a spit in the centre of a ravaged area. To make the clearing, all the plants had been ripped out by the roots and stuffed in dying heaps between the surrounding trees and bushes. Effectively, the area was screened from the rest of the forest. The tangle made it impossible for anyone on the ground to see in or to approach on foot.

"Float slowly up towards the lower branches," Gordon telepathed. *"Be very careful. The vibrations are everywhere. The trees around that clearing are packed."*

Gnarled hand over knotted fist, they clawed their weightless way to excellent vantage points. Only feet from them, a motley assortment of nondescript fairy species squatted impatiently, muttering among themselves. There were knockers aplenty, cheek by jowl with what may have been disgruntled hobgoblins, malicious pixies, or even malevolent elves.

That's something you don't see very often: a hook-nosed knocker and a pigeon-toed hobgoblin on the same branch.

Sprawled around the edges of the torn-up ground were four lethargic forest trolls. The vandalising of the vegetation was clearly down to them. They had bits of broken twigs and torn leaves stuck in their hair and beards. Some still had sheaves of bashed-up bush clutched in their massive fists.

The clearing had obviously been made to order. Forest trolls don't normally take orders; not from anyone. They are famous for their non-cooperation, even with each other. Something must have been powerful enough to subjugate their wills.

A diminutive, goblin-like creature trotted methodically to and from the cauldron and from and to each troll. It was conveying a ladle full of the steaming, noxious liquid bubbling in the pot to the hollow gourds they were drinking from. Their great, craggy heads sank lower on their massive, muscled chests. The eye-watering stench confirmed it was a very potent brew.

If someone in the royal palace had been slipping even tiny quantities of that to the children of the king and queen, it would certainly explain the recent transformation in their personalities.

The goblin dropped the ladle beside the cauldron and swaggered over to one of the trolls. He clearly knew he had an audience, and was enjoying his moment. Clambering up the body of the beast, he drew back his tiny fist and smashed it as hard as he could into the troll's eye. The eyes and nose are the only remotely sensitive parts of a troll's body. "Get up and fight, you disgusting heap of steaming bat-droppings!" he screamed into its ear.

No reaction.

Jumping back to the ground, he snatched up a fairly stout stick, ran across to another of the trolls, clambered up its body as far as its massive shoulder and wacked the stick as hard as he could right across the bridge of its immense bulb of a nose. The crack it made sounded like a gunshot. "Come on, the lot of you! I'll take you all on!" the goblin yelled. He hadn't had this much fun in a hundred years.

Grace winced. It had made her eyes water just to watch. The goblin seemed eager to continue this humiliation of the stupefied giants, but his performance was cut short. A knocker dropped prominently from the trees and strode into the centre of the clearing. His self-important demeanour and distinctly wide-mouthed face was already etched in the memories of the watching humans.

"Thank you, Brother!" Groc called out to the little goblin, who looked enormously disappointed. Groc raised his fist in a gesture of triumph. "I now call to order the inaugural meeting of the National Fairy Front!"

Chapter 18

Working The Crowd

The trees all around the clearing disgorged their cargo of knockers, goblins, pixies, elves and goodness knows what else. It was difficult to believe that such a motley crew of misfits could be united about anything; but there they all were, dropping into the clearing, apparently prepared - at least for the moment - to listen to what their self-appointed leader had to say.

"In welcoming you all, Brothers – and Sister – to this first of many meetings," he announced, "may I begin by saying how heartening it is to see so many of you here."

His satisfaction oozed from every pore. He wasted no time in nailing his colours to the mast. "This tolerance we see today of every kind of deviance from the tried and trusted norms goes WAY beyond the bounds of common sense!"

"'ERE 'ERE!" yelled several well-rehearsed knockers in the crowd.

Grace was looking in vain for the solitary female apparently present somewhere in that throng. There was something fairly exclusively male about this kind of madness.

"So it is with great pleasure that I welcome you to the first annual conference of our newly formed but long overdue political party, THE NATIONAL FAIRY FRONT!"

There were enthusiastic cheers and raised fists from the knockers strategically scattered throughout the clearing.

"We offer a broad-brush manifesto, which I can summarise in a few words."

The cheering spread to the hobgoblins and the elves.

"With every fibre of its being, every nerve-ending, every strain of its sinews, the National Fairy Front is ANTI-HUMAN!"

The cheers rang out from every part of the crowded clearing. Groc was pacing the space he had round the cauldron in the centre, his face flushed, his voice ever more strident.

"Furthermore, we support the ETHNIC CLEANSING OF ALL UNDESIRABLES!!"

There was a collective roar of approval. The irony was not lost on Gordon, who was finding it difficult to imagine anything more undesirable than the collection of malcontents currently assembled below him.

"We say NO to all the liberal do-gooders who want to open our doors to anyone whose food smells funny! They would have us open our arms to everyone who looks or sounds different!" Groc spread his arms in a visual demonstration.

"They WET THEMSELVES in their eagerness to welcome anyone with funny foreign customs and funny foreign beliefs!" Fortunately, he didn't feel it was necessary to follow that point up with another visual.

"'Come one and all,'" they cry, "and help yourselves to our limited resources! Feel free to take all the houses and all the jobs and all the welfare you want!"

Groc was really getting into his stride. "You can say what you like about HUMANS!" he yelled, "AND I USUALLY DO" -

He paused for the inevitable guffaw from his appreciative audience.

"But their God the Father had the right idea. SODOM and GOMORRAH?! We were with him all the way on that one!" He pointed his right forefinger at the sky. "I will go FURTHER! Sod 'em ALL, I say, and let's not wait for tomorrah!"

He'd got them now, in his pocket, in the palm of his hand.

"And how brilliant was that FLOOD?! A MASTERSTROKE! If it hadn't been for Noah and his stupid ark, that would have been the whole problem solved right there, once and for ALL!!"

Hearty cheers and the wholesale nodding of heads.

"We advocate a return to the PURITY, SIMPLICITY and VIGOUR of Old Testament ideas. What has Nature always been about? - SURVIVAL OF THE FITTEST!"

That couldn't be denied.

"Since when did the meek inherit the Earth? Since NEVER!! We know what is right. MIGHT is right! And who knows that better than those of us who are ON the right?!"

He glared round the assembly and waved his little fist in a gesture of total defiance. "We say NO to this DISGUSTING notion of fairies consorting with humans. Can you imagine a planet polluted with fairman, humry HALF-BREEDS?!"

Several members of his audience could be heard being physically sick at the mere thought.

"WE say the Archbishop of Arden doesn't know his human BACK from his fairy FRONT!" Groc yelled. There were loud cries of "Right on, brother!" and "You SAID it!!"

"And what we ALSO say is that from now on he had better be WATCHING his back, because here comes THE NATIONAL FAIRY FRONT!!"

The cheers rang to the topmost leaves of the forest canopy.

"And as far as our liberal, bridge-building majesties are concerned, I tell you THIS!" He held his two hands out, as if wrapping them round the neck of an enemy. "Our tentacles are already inside their castle. We are tightening them, slowly but surely..."

He squeezed his hands into cruel claws. "...and we will go ON tightening them until we choke some sense into 'em. OR - better yet – get rid of 'em altogether, and replace 'em with some RIGHT-THINKING leader."

Grace knew just who he had in mind. And in amongst the laughter and the cheers, a growl of gleeful anarchy was growing.

"Let 'em eat cake for whatever time they have left!" Groc yelled. He raised his right fist and began to bang it against the air in front of him. "On YOUR behalf, this knocker is KNOCKING AT THEIR DOOR!"

The cheer they gave him nearly blew him away.

"And NOW," he bellowed, "the moment you've all been waiting for."

A shiver of anticipation went through the entire throng. Many a nervous glance was cast in the direction of the treetops. The occasion seemed to demand a roll on the drums, or the opening brass section of *Also Sprach Zarathustra*.

"I give you our mentor and rôle-model, the most powerful and distinguished force behind our movement! Please show your appreciation for MORRIGAN LAFAYE!!"

Chapter 19

Stone The Crows!

There was a sudden flapping of great wings, as an enormous crow took off from the topmost branch of the tallest tree above the clearing. Its wingspan must have been double that of an Andean Condor. It swooped across the open space with an ear-splitting CAW, and was big enough to blot out a lot of the light.

How was it possible for a creature that size to fly?

Once round the circle it went, enormous talons extended, apparently poised to tear the face off any creature foolish enough to glance up at it. Not until it was satisfied with the level of humility and terror beneath did it condescend to fold its wings and descend.

The turning, black blur came right down into the centre of the clearing to land beside the crouching Groc, by which time it had transformed itself into female fairy form. Statuesque and deathly pale of face, feathers lingered over her forearms and the lower extremities of her smoky black dress. Great black wings were folded along her spine. She drifted round the cauldron, just above the ground, and stared around the crowd with coal-black eyes.

Its members peeped out at her from under their raised arms. They were very careful not to catch her eye. Catch her eye and she caught yours. She was a Valkyrie: a chooser of the slain.

So this was the sister Groc had been referring to. It made a kind of sense. Grace tried to keep away from her terrible thoughts, but she glimpsed enough to know that the Morrigan's interest in the National Fairy Front was exclusively in the body count the policies of such a party would inevitably produce if put into practice.

"You see the power of my potion over these clumsy trolls," she rasped. Her voice reminded Gordon of fingernails being scraped against a blackboard. "It is time to remind your enemies just how powerful dark magic can be!"

Slowly she stretched out her arms. From beneath those black feathers, long, pale fingers emerged, tipped by cruel claws. A glowing ball of fire sprang from the forefinger on either hand and streaked into a potion-sodden troll on either side of the clearing.

The semi-conscious trolls combusted simultaneously. They burned with the ferocious intensity of petrol-dowsed tinder. Seconds of agonised thrashing and bellowing later, they subsided - mercifully soon - into charred heaps of foul-smoking embers.

She drew in a breath that rattled in her throat, like the warning of a snake about to strike. "Listen to GROC! Pay him heed, and follow him wherever he might lead!" She extended a wing towards Groc. He scuttled towards it, back bent, face turned away. "He is already using this potion to excellent effect. He has bewitched those closest to the fairy throne itself."

Her voice rose to a shriek that could shatter glass. "Seek out the children of your enemies and bend them to your will! Let them but sip my potion and they will be within your grasp. Confound their parents! Sorrow will bring them all low, and make them easier to overwhelm."

Her head shot up, her nostrils quivering. She had caught the scent of carrion on the breeze. "I am needed on a battlefield elsewhere," she rasped. But of this you may be sure. I will never be far from the NATIONAL FAIRY FRONT!"

She leapt into the air, her wings unfolding like the shrouds of death, beating the breeze into submission as she gained height. Once level with the top of the tallest trees, the terrible creature vanished into some other dark dimension, leaving behind a twisted wisp of mist.

There was a massive exhalation of bad breath from the membership, in many instances from both ends of their alimentary canals. They gazed with awe on Groc the Knocker, who had gone up perceptibly in their collective estimation. With the backing of a dark divinity like Morrigan LaFaye, how could he fail to command respect and loyalty?

There was no holding him back now. He puffed out his diminutive chest, and strutted round the cauldron. "The world is at our mercy," he yelled. "We have drawn up plans to poison the hearts and minds of our enemy's children EVERYWHERE!"

He pointed at the cauldron. "Give them this drug, and they will drive their parents to despair! Distracted, our leaders will lose their grip on world affairs. Then WE will rise out of the chaos and take CONTROL!"

They liked the sound of THAT all right. "We will RULE!" they chanted. "We will RULE!!"

"And the Empire that we build will last a thousand years!" Groc bellowed, his voice hoarse with triumph.

This was a nest of vipers. No – Gordon took that back; he had nothing against vipers. What the National Fairy Front was planning was pure evil. He felt that red curtain coming down inside his head again. So might was right was it? The ground opening up and swallowing whole cities of men, women and innocent children in fire and brimstone was something to be applauded? A flood drowning every land-based creature in its path that couldn't swim was a great idea?!

It came to him in a flash what he would do. It was time for a dose of their own medicine. How about a spot of Old Testament wrath? - a localised tornado, say, that would rip up everything in its path and wreak havoc like a pair of forest trolls? A whirlwind had to be right up their alley.

Above their heads, the heavy, storm-dark clouds were piling, as if assembled by some mighty hand. Gordon closed his eyes and the power ripped through him. The wind gained speed, narrowed into a spiral, and sent its full force down into that clearing. He was dimly aware of what passed for his hands being grasped. All four wove themselves into the vines while sending their strength as one into the fury of that blast.

The tornado tore into the ravaged space with terrifying precision. For anyone and anything in its path there was no escape. It touched down with a roar like the blur of a passing train. In a few splintering seconds of deconstructing chaos, the entire assembly became debris.

The hubble-bubble, toil-and-trouble cauldron and its dark-magic, child-bewitching potion was funnelled into a column of shredding wings and broken spells. Hurled hundreds of feet into the air, it spewed out of the top with a speed approaching that of the wrath of God.

And as quickly as it came the cyclone went. Its work done, it retreated to the clouds. The noise went with it, leaving the forest peaceful, unperturbed. All the bad vibrations had gone. The air smelt clean and fresh. Not a single wicked thought.

"How's that for a wind of change?" Gordon muttered. He opened his eyes to find that they were back in human form. Grace looked as exhausted as he felt. It was time for Zack and Zoë to get them home. There was nothing more that could be done tonight.

As Gordon felt his mind begin to slip into that dreamless region of deep sleep, he hoped the fairy king and queen would find the children that they loved so much had been returned to them.

Chapter 20

Tools Of The Trade

On the first day back after the Easter holidays, their year 9 English teacher, Mrs Earle, launched a unit on that particular use of language known loosely and not always helpfully as "poetry".

She began by asking them if they remembered what their "Ideas for a Billion Stories" booklet was designed to help them to do. That booklet had proved useful to all seven teachers in the School's Department of English. It was a handy reference point.

She waved Gordon's and Grace's hands down. "Not you two, nor you," he added, smiling at Nick and Miranda. "I know the co-authors of the booklet know. Come on, the rest of you." A few hands were tentatively raised. She chose one.

"It was to help us think outside the box, and come up with more original ideas in our stories."

Mrs Earle nodded. "Spot on. What I want to do now is to look at the tools of the poet's trade. Let's see if we can find ways of using them to come up with more original ideas in our poems."

Gordon had been waiting years for this discussion. His hand shot up. Mrs Earle had been expecting it. "OK, Gordon, kick us off."

"Probably the most obvious tool is rhyme." Mrs Earle duly wrote 'rhyme' on the board.

"Yep. Moon, June, soon, tune... What else?"

"Rhythm," Grace offered.

"Yep. Di-dah di-dah di-dah di-dah di-dah. That's just one pattern, of course. What else?" 'Rhythm' joined 'rhyme' on the board while everyone was thinking.

"Alliteration?" Miranda suggested.

"Excellent. Do we all remember what 'alliteration' is?" Nobody said they didn't, so he pointed at random towards the back of the class. This was a set 1, so no problems there. "Derek?"

"It's when words close together begin with the same letter."

"Indeed it is, well done," Mrs Earle said. "The mossy moor meandered round the mere." Zack gave her a little round of applause. "What else?"

Nick's hand crept up. Gordon nodded encouragement. "Assonance?" he suggested. The word had just popped into his head. He sort of thought he knew what it meant.

"Terrific. Remind us all what 'assonance' is."

"It's when you get the same vowel sound repeated inside words that are close together," Nicholas said fluently. He breathed a silent sigh of relief. He *had* known, after all.

"Now we're cooking with gas," Mrs Earle said. "That might have been a little clue, incidentally, what I just said. SO, 'assonance'. 'With a silent sigh I typed the final line.'"

"There's some alliteration in there as well," Zoë observed, "And some consonance."

"Hang on," Grace telepathed. *"What's 'consonance'?"*

"Assonance normally means repeating the same vowel sound within words. Consonance is the repetition of consonants, like the 'n' in 'silent', 'final' and 'line.'"

"Ooh, that's handy," Grace exclaimed. *"I hadn't noticed that."*

Gordon's hand was up again. "Go on," Mrs Earle said.

"Metaphor," Gordon said.

"METAPHOR!" Mrs Earle exclaimed. "The poetry train is finally leaving the station. What is my next question?" She pointed to a single hand that had just gone up.

"What exactly IS metaphor?" a puzzled boy had the guts to ask.

Mrs Earle beamed. "Got it in one!" she said. "The example I was taught when I was at school was 'The camel is the ship of the desert'." She unpicked it for them. "The camel is a principal form of transport across a desert. The ship is a principal form of transport across a sea. Obviously, a camel bears no other resemblance to a ship, any more than the elegant lady did who sailed across the room."

"So a metaphor is when you use a word or a phrase that normally means one thing to describe another thing that is similar in some way?" Miranda said. "I think I get it now."

Mrs Earle nodded. "We use metaphors all the time. We talk about someone exploding with rage or bursting with pride or having their feathers ruffled. Most metaphors are poetic when they start out, but once they become commonplace they lose their freshness and you don't even notice them."

That was certainly true.

"Once a metaphor becomes 'prosaic' like that, it's no longer much good to the poet, and he or she has to think of new ones." She looked round the class. "What's the other main way language has of linking ideas?"

Lots of hands went up. "Someone who hasn't spoken yet. Alice?"

"Simile."

"RIGHT!" 'Simile' joined the other words on the board. "Here's one from Seamus Heaney, a famous Irish poet:

"My father worked with a horse plough,

His shoulders globed like a full sail strung

Between the shafts and the furrow."

"WOW!" Gordon said, shivering suddenly. "That's *awesome*!"

"It's all there, isn't it," Mrs Earle agreed. "Subtle rhyme, strong rhythm, alliteration, assonance, metaphor, simile. Those are the important tools of the trade. But above all, when you read the whole poem, you'll see it has something important to say about life and the human condition."

She wrote SOMETHING IMPORTANT TO SAY in big letters on the board, and rapped it with the back of her knuckles as she swivelled to face them. "All good poetry has something important to say. That's what makes it life-changing. That's what makes it magic."

She glanced at the clock, walked back to her desk and sat down. "OK. A ten-minute discussion round your tables. Make a list of the things you think poets most often write about. Off you go."

The class settled down to their task. *"That definition you gave me back in October was spot on, wasn't it?"* Gordon said to Zack.

"Pretty much," Zack agreed. "All good poetry says something important in a powerful way."

"What oft was said but ne'er so well expressed," Zoë agreed.

"Poets write about love a lot," Nick observed. Gordon duly wrote it down. The role of scribe had become his. He liked doing it and he liked owning the notes afterwards.

"They write about death and loss a lot, too," Miranda said.

"They're the things people feel strongly about," Grace observed, "so it's about being young and growing old, joy and grief, life and death, right and wrong, love and hate, truth and beauty ..."

"Whoah!" Gordon said, "Slow down a bit."

"Things that make you cry," Nick added. He'd got it now. "Things that make you wonder, things that terrify you."

"That make you feel pity," Gordon said, performing the difficult feat of saying one thing while writing another. "Things that really make you think."

"All the things that make us what we are, the wonderful side of us - like love and honesty and sacrifice for others - and the terrible side, like hate and tyranny and injustice," Miranda said.

"Wow," Gordon said, throwing his pen down and massaging the writers' bump on his second finger. "That's some list." A new assignment was fomenting in his mind. "You know we put together that booklet to help people write good stories?" he began.

"Oh, oh," Grace said, grinning at him. "Are you thinking what I think you're thinking?"

Gordon grinned back at her, knowing perfectly well that she knew perfectly well exactly what he was thinking. "I was just wondering if there was any way we could put together a booklet that would help people write good poems," he confirmed.

There was a thoughtful silence. "Mmm, difficult," Zack mused. Not for the first time, he reminded Gordon of the Sorting Hat at Hogwarts. "There could be ways of helping people get into the right frame of language, I suppose."

The bell went. "I'll tell you what," Gordon suggested. "Why don't we all have a think about it, and see what we can come up with?"

Chapter 21

Now There's A Thought

"Where would you start?" Gordon asked Zack. They were up in their bedroom and the rest of his homework was out of the way.

"Well, we know pretty much what's important to us," Zack said, "so I think I would start with how to say it in a powerful way."

"Right," said Gordon. *"So what makes one way of saying something more powerful than another?"*

Zack started pacing up and down the bedroom in deeply thoughtful mode. "It's to do with the link between language and thought," he said.

"What link?" Gordon asked him. *"You think something, and then you say it, don't you?"*

"Oh, so you think language is spoken thought, do you?" Zack asked. He raised his eyebrows in polite enquiry.

"Isn't it?" Gordon said a little defensively. It seemed obvious to him.

"No," Zack told him. "It's actually the other way around. Thought is language which isn't spoken. A Professor of Linguistics once said to me: "Thought is most accurately defined as language arrested at the muscular level."

"WOW!" Gordon exclaimed, slapping his head. The implications of that switch hit him like a ton of bricks. *"That is a pretty SIGNIFICANT difference."*

Zack nodded his head. "It explains how thoughts can be re-shaped and re-energised. How often have you heard someone say 'I never thought of it like that'? Changing the language changes the thought."

He smiled sadly. "Make the language more powerful and you make the thought more powerful - that's what poets do. On the other hand, make the language more neutral and you take the sting out of the thought. That's what spokespersons, liaison officers and politicians do."

"*Right,*" Gordon said, hanging on to Zack's coat-tails (metaphorically speaking).

"Spokespersons, liaison officers and politicians can turn 'innocent women and children blown to pieces' into 'regrettable collateral damage', Zack explained, "whenever civilians are killed in a war zone."

"*Does that explain why it's important to learn as many words as you can?*" Gordon asked, getting his head round it, "*because the deeper and richer your experience of language, the deeper and richer your thinking becomes.*"

"Absolutely," Zack agreed.

"*But how does that help us write better poetry?*" Gordon wanted to know.

"OK," said Zack. "That's to do with the way language works. On an everyday basis, words normally operate in what is known as a "field of reference". There's a metaphor right there."

"*What's a 'field of reference'?*" Gordon asked. He was beginning to see why Zack had said "Mmm, difficult," when he'd suggested an *Ideas for at least a Billion Poems* type booklet.

"It just means that any word is likely to have a certain number of other words associated with it, words you'd expect to find in its company. For example, Miranda's just got a pony."

With him so far.

"The field of reference for 'pony' would include 'trot, canter, gallop, stumble, saddle, reins, stirrup, bit, hoof, fetlock, mane, tail, shoe, blacksmith, stable, paddock, hay, mash, brush, comb, ride, jump, groom, snicker, whinny, snuffle, shiny, coat', not to mention 'field.'"

"Loads of pony and horse words, I see," Gordon said, nodding. That was easy enough to understand. It was pretty obvious, now Zack had pointed it out.

"So if I wanted to find a fresh new way of describing rain, say, in a poem," Zack went on.

"Is rain important?" Gordon asked.

"It might be," Zack pointed out, "if your poem was about what forty days and forty nights of it might have washed away."

"Ooh, yes," Gordon acknowledged. That would be another kettle of fish – to use another metaphor.

"I could write something like "The scattered pitter patter of the gleaming, moonlit rain was like a shiny pony trotting down a country lane.""

"You could," Gordon said, *"but it isn't very good."* He had high standards. Zack had been quoting Shakespeare at him for the last thirteen years.

"Agreed," Zack said, "but it's on the way. It has rhyme, an easy rhythm, assonance, consonance, and quite a fresh simile. But suppose instead I wrote "Along the lane, the rain came trotting with the night on its back"?

"OOH!" Gordon said. *"That's better."*

"It is," Zack said. "'Trot' and 'back' are pony words, not rain words, so their use is metaphorical. They 'ponify' the rain. They change the way we think about it. And that isn't all. There's an internal rhyme – assonance and consonance rolled into one - and the rhythm is like a rising trot. 'Along the lane the rain came trotting, with the night on its back.'"

"I see, I think," Gordon said slowly. *"From simile to metaphor."*

"I could floodify the rain as well," Zack said, "and bring in the notion of Old Testament wrath, just by adding one word."

"Go on then," Gordon said.

"Along the lane the trotting rain had the night on its bibled back.""

"I think I'm ready for bed."
"Me too."

Chapter 22

The Good, The Bad And The Ugly

"How'd you get on?" Grace wanted to know in school the following morning.

"Sure but slow," Gordon told her. "We got as far as how you go from simile to metaphor."

Grace grinned at him. "That was a little poem right there, what you just said!"

"That's called a 'found' poem," Zoë told her.

"Who's 'we'?" Nick wanted to know. Oops.

"I asked my mum what she thought," Gordon told him.

"So did I," he said. "We didn't get past rhyme. 'Hey diddle diddle, the cat and the fiddle.'"

"Not poetry though, is it?" Miranda pointed out. "That's why it's called a nursery rhyme, not a nursery poem."

"Rhyme is where I always go wrong," Nick confessed. "I try to find a rhyme, and reason goes out the window."

"I know what you mean," Miranda agreed. "With the royal wedding coming up I googled 'royal wedding poems' last night." Gordon groaned and Miranda giggled. "I wrote some down," she said. "I knew you'd like them." She fished a sheet of paper out of her bag.

"William and Kate, have set the date,

They've chosen, as the day they will marry.

April 29, for the second in line

To the throne, (just in front of Harry)."

Gordon closed his eyes in mock suffering.

Miranda's face was alive with mischief. She continued to read.

"I wonder who will wear the biggest hat.

No-one will care along as no-one is fat."

"AAARRGGHH!" Gordon yelled. "No more! It's torture! I can't take it!"

"I asked my mum as well," Grace said, taking her lead from Gordon. "We came up with making separate lists of the nouns, verbs and adjectives we could use for any given subject. Then we read up and down the lists to look for unusual combinations."

Zack nodded appreciatively. "Good thinking."

Zoë grinned at him. "Thanks."

"There's only one problem with that," Nick observed.

Grace raised an eyebrow. "Which is?"

"You have to know the difference between a noun, a verb and an adjective," he pointed out.

"That does help," she was forced to agree.

"We made a list of words as well," Gordon said, "but we didn't go on to divide it into nouns, verbs and adjectives."

"What was your list about?" Miranda wanted to know.

"Pony words," Gordon said.

"OOH," Miranda exclaimed, immediately interested. "Why?"

"We were thinking about the noise of raindrops on hard surfaces and wondering about similes, and we came up with a trotting pony. So then we made a list of pony words and got as far as "Along the lane the rain came trotting, with the night on its back."

"Good start," Zoë said.

Zack grinned at her. "Thanks."

"And then the rain made us think of a flood, and flood made us think of Noah's Flood and God's punishment for sin. So we changed it to "Along the lane the trotting rain had the night on its bibled back."

"*Seriously* good start," said Grace approvingly.

Nick looked a bit despairing. "You see, that's the difference between you and me," he said. "My mind just doesn't work like that. I only wish it did."

Gordon put an affectionate arm round his good friend's shoulder. Nick hadn't had a Zack to bring him on. "Of course your mind works like that," he assured him. "You just need to let it know it works like that."

"Oh, oh, look out," Grace murmured.

Gordon looked up to see what looked like a delegation heading their way. It was made up of all the liveliest, naughtiest, noisiest boys and girls in their form. He felt Nick's shoulders stiffen, and removed his arm.

"This should be interesting," he said. "Maybe they want us to help them write better poetry."

On they came: Arthur Sykes, Brian Michaels, Reece Parker, Dominic Delaney, Chelsee Witherspoon, Debra Simpson and Britney Clutterbuck. Gordon and Grace eased themselves imperceptibly further forward to make a line of four in front of Nick and Miranda. Of course it didn't look like that to anyone else.

The Maleficent Seven came to a halt in front of the Awesome Foursome, or more accurately, the Super Six. Gordon folded his arms and smiled, which never went down well with the opposition. Arthur opened the batting. "You got us into a lot of trouble at the end of last term," he said.

Gordon cocked his head slightly. He let pretend puzzlement play with his eyebrows. "I'm interested to know how you work that out." he said.

Reece pursed his lips and looked down the bridge of his own nose, while affecting a posh voice. "I'm interested to know how you work that out," he minced in mocking repetition. "You smarmy, self-satisfied little git."

There was an overloud shriek of laughter from the Chelsee/Debra/Britney trio, designed of course to egg Reece on. Gordon looked back at him and appeared to notice something for the first time. "You know, your face looks a lot better since you flat-packed it into that desktop," he said.

Reece wrinkled his lips back in a snarl and started forward. Dominic laid a restraining hand on his arm. "We came to talk," he reminded him.

"We're listening," Grace said.

"All our parents got called in. There was a meeting with Peters and Davies about our behaviour. That was down to you." Mr Davies was the Head of Oak House.

"How was that down to us?" Gordon asked. "What did we do?"

"What you always do," Brian said. "You interfere. You look at us like we're something the cat dragged in. You pass comment. You're always judging."

"He speaks up for the decent majority," Grace said. No way was she leaving Gordon out there on his own. "They're our lessons as well. It's our form as well. Why should you be allowed to spoil it for the rest of us?"

"It's the teachers' job to control us, not yours," said Chelsee, "you snotty cow!"

"Watch your mouth!" Gordon said. He was suddenly more serious; his red curtain had just twitched.

"Leave her to us," Zoë advised him. "We're looking forward to it."

"I've been meaning to ask you," Grace said, looking Chelsee straight in the eye. "All this walking round the playground covered in fake tan with your bits hanging out. Is it meant to be attractive?"

Chelsee's face flushed scarlet under the fake tan. "You are seriously heading for a slap," she said, but she made no attempt to administer one. Maybe she had more sense than they had previously given her credit for.

"We're giving you fair warning," Dominic said. "Stay off our case from now on."

"Is that an ultimatum," Gordon asked, "or are you open to negotiation?" He looked from one to the other. "That's a serious question."

"What do you mean – negotiation?" Arthur demanded. "What's to negotiate?"

"Well, the way you behave annoys us, and the way we behave annoys you. So maybe if we talk about it, we can both change the way we behave."

"We only have a laugh!" Brian said. "What's wrong with having a laugh?"

"Nothing. It's when your 'having-a-laugh' spoils the lesson for the rest of us that there's a problem."

"We can't all be goody, goody teachers' pets all the time. We're not all like you four: good at everything," Debra said.

"Never putting a foot wrong," Britney chimed in. "It's not normal."

"We have a laugh," Nick said. "We're always laughing. But we also come to school to learn."

"We come to learn as well, you nerd," Arthur said dismissively.

"SO far," Gordon said, "you have called me a smarmy self-satisfied little git, Grace a snotty cow, and Nick a nerd. What have we called you? Have the words 'loser', 'bully', 'retard' or 'wrecker' passed our lips?"

"You SEE?! THAT'S what you do right there!" Brian said. "Just because you're clever about the way you do it doesn't mean you don't do it."

"That's a fair point," Gordon conceded, "but when did we ever throw anything across a classroom? When did we ever interrupt a teacher when they were trying to tell us something? When did we ever muck about so much that we took the focus of the lesson?"

"You expect us to be just like everybody else in the class and let you get away with it," Miranda said. "That's what gets up your nose. We're supposed to be scared of you, and we're not. We never will be."

"We're not scared of YOU, NEITHER!" Britney said loudly.

"We don't want you to be," Miranda said calmly. "You stay out of our faces, and we'll be happy to stay out of yours."

"THAT seems fair," said a new voice. Tom had come across the playground, and was now standing shoulder to shoulder with Gordon. "Anyone got a problem with that?" he asked, into the sudden silence. He stared at Arthur, Brian, Reece and Dominic. "Any one of you? Any two of you?"

"Come on," Arthur said to his mates. "We've made our point." He turned and walked away, followed closely by the others. Chelsee waited until they were ten or twelve paces away before whispering something to her two tangoed mates. It provoked their corporate trademark shriek of laughter.

"Thanks, Tom," Gordon said. He was genuinely touched.

"No problem," Tom said. "See you." He walked off. The bell went for a.m. registration.

Chapter 23

The Usual Suspects

"OK," Victor Bennett said. The final member of his anti-riot team had just made it through the door to his office, muttering an apology and clutching a scalding plastic cup of the muck called 'coffee' on the front of the machine in the corridor. "What have we got?"

D.S. Elaine McIntosh handed him a piece of paper with four names and four photos on it. Each name was typed under a grainy photocopy of an image taken from a CCTV camera.

"Most of the hardcore activists kept their faces well hidden. A lot of them had been bussed in from other cities. We got the impression they'd done this before. But these four are home-grown."

Victor glanced at the sheet and grimaced. The shaven heads, snarling faces and facial tattoos were hardly a subtle disguise. Having "Made in Blacon" tattooed across your forehead was a bit of a giveaway for a start. Blacon was an area in Chester lived in by a fair number of families spilling out from poor areas of Liverpool.

The so-called protest march had taken place last Saturday in one of their surrounding districts. Word had got out that a large empty building in Dutton was about to be bought by a Muslim business man with plans to turn it into an Islamic Cultural Centre. Local opinion was divided. An educated, tolerant minority were for it, an Islamophobic minority were against it, and the vast majority had more important things to think about.

The EDL – *'English Defence League'* - had had little trouble mobilising the street army that turned up for what was supposed to be a local protest march. It is never long before a right-wing hate-group enlists the support of anyone in that particular area who gets a kick - in more ways than one - out of using violence. With effortless ease, the football hooligan will lend his support to any cause that gives him a chance to kick someone's head in. Just tell him where the bovver is likely to be, and he'll be there.

The trick is to tell him that he's NOT a mindless, tribal, ignorant, racist thug. Tell him instead he's a true-blooded Englishman fighting a just cause for his country against the liberal lefties promoting an insidious, relentless infestation of aliens and illegal migrants. Tell him that, and he's over the bloody moon.

Change the language and you change the thought.

This was doubtless why Ronnie Sparrow, Johnny McGivern, Frankie Sharples and Stevie Snellgrove had given the so-called protest march their unfettered support. It had rapidly turned into a riot when the EDL faction broke through the barriers the police had erected to keep them away from the Antifa supporters who had turned up ready to confront them.

The local police were well aware that this was likely to happen. There'd been similar protest marches in Luton, Leicester, Stoke and Bradford. Reinforcements had been bussed in from the surrounding areas. The police were equipped with riot gear, dogs, photographers and additional CCTV cameras. The idea was to identify as many of the perpetrators as possible.

They were now engaged in the time-consuming business of picking out those hailing from their particular patch. Victor and his team were considering what to do about the four definites they'd picked out so far. "Have we got anything we can do them for?" Victor asked.

D. C. Peter Medway took a sip out of the plastic cup of scalding liquid and grimaced. "Nope, given that it's not illegal to shave your head, stick your feet in laced-up bovver boots and stick two fingers up at a police camera while screaming abuse at the forces of law and order.

The cameras never caught them dancing on any vehicles or smashing any shop windows or hurling any bricks."

"They've all got form," Elaine told him. "Expelled from school, ASBOs, causing an affray. Sparrow and McGivern were both done for common assault last year. The CCTV camera outside Rosie's Night Club showed them attacking a couple of harmless blokes on the assumption that they were gay. They're all from problem families - harassment of neighbours, a string of complaints. The younger siblings are nearly all headed in the same direction.

Victor sighed. "And then they stomp along our streets waving England flags and accusing decent Muslim families of being vermin."

"The world's gone mad, Boss," Peter informed his chief cheerfully.

"It's always been mad," Victor informed him. "And it gets madder in a recession. The devil finds work for idle hands." He stuck the photographs on his notice board. "We don't have the resources to follow them around with a pooper scooper, so let's make sure everyone of us out there knows those faces and puts the right names to them."

They turned to go. Victor added one more thing. "Get word to any officers in the vicinity of that social club building. There's only one sure way of making certain it won't ever be turned into a Muslim Community Centre."

After they'd gone, he retrieved the photos from the noticeboard and made another couple of copies. It wouldn't hurt to see if they prompted any time-travelling. They could do with some incriminating evidence.

Chapter 24

Regional Operations HQ

Frankie Sharples was the last one to slouch through the doorway into the front room of the McGivern family residence. He was dressed in his trademark combat fatigues, tucked into his Dr Martens black, 8-eyelet boots. The hand clutching the half-drunk can of Special Brew had the letters Y O U R tattooed on the third joint of each finger. The hand clutching the empty plastic ring and the other 3 cans in the four-pack had the letters N E X T tattooed in similar fashion.

The lettering aped the Fraktur typeface favoured by Hitler's National Socialism Party: 'Nationalsozialismus' or 'Nazi' for short. Those knuckles told you quite a lot about him.

The other three young men in the room used the number one clippers once a week. Frankie, however, shaved his head religiously - to use the word metaphorically - every other day. He was proud of the word "England" tattooed in the same German Gothic lettering across the back of his head. It was underneath a square St George's flag that sat more or less on top of his thick, bony skull. He didn't want any stubble obscuring his banner.

You could understand it really. It saved him the trouble of having to explain his views to anyone. It was as good as carrying a placard saying "I am a racist thug with psychotic tendencies." You could see him coming, accurately assess your chances of reasoned debate, and take whatever avoidance strategies were available to you at the time.

"Nearly tripped over a couple of penguins on the stairs up to your landin'," he growled. "Probly on their way down the Social for another 'and-out."

Ronnie Sparrow snorted. He was sprawled over one end of the crimson velour sofa purchased from the ever-present DFS Ultimate Sale: £1,999.99 down to £399.99 + nothing to pay the next twelve months, after which low monthly payments over 36 months at the competitive rate of 29.9% APR).

"Since we were in here last week," he said, with the tip of his tongue curled up towards the roof of his mouth to produce the classic English impersonation of an Indian accent, "another ten of our relations have moved in. We need a bigger flat, and if you don't give us one straight away you are a dyed-in-the-wool racist."

His Ben Sherman shirt was tucked neatly into his shrink-to-fit Levi 501s, which were tucked neatly into his wine red, Vintage, 10-eyelet Doc Martens. He'd mugged a fair few nerds to get the money for those, and very proud of them he was.

He took a deep drag on his 23rd fag of the day. The fingers of his right hand were heavily stained a similar colour to the curtains and paintwork of the room he was in. His knuckles read G U N S and A M M O. A pair of Waffen SS runes was tattooed on his forehead.

"I'm no bleedin' racist," Johnny McGivern protested. "I just think they should all eff off back where they came from, that's all."

"I heard there was a million shacks to let in Bangladesh," Stevie Snellgrove quipped. "There's so many of 'em over 'ere."

His knuckles said B O O T B O Y S, which seemed appropriate, not only because of their footwear but also because all four young men seemed to be suffering from the same severe case of arrested development.

"They ain't never goin' back there!" Ronnie Sparrow assured him. "It's under water half the time. They got all the jobs and houses and hospital beds goin' over 'ere. Why go back to a stinkin' bog?"

"That protest march was a right laugh, though, weren't it?" Stevie said eagerly. Ever since that afternoon, he'd found himself reliving the joyful experience of being swept along in an army of like-minded skins, all yelling abuse at anyone who looked as though they might be an immigrant.

Then they'd caught sight of those long-haired, bearded UAF paedos shoutin' "RACISTS!" at them, jus' becoz they woz standin' up an' defendin' England and all she stands for from all this foreign filf. All 'ell 'ad broke loose then. Those barriers 'adn't lasted long. They'd've killed the lot of them if them riot police hadn't got in the way.

He'd wanted to see them university weirdoes smashed to the ground under a tide of rampaging skins. He had ached to feel his boots thudding into their faces as they grovelled in the dirt. They thought they were better than him. They looked down on him from a great height. They thought they knew everything when they couldn't see what was goin' on right under their bleedin' noses! Their noses'd be bleedin' all right, if he'd been able to get a punch or six in.

The first line of a Pink Floyd song went through his head. "We don't need no edge-u-cay-shun," (Dumb da-dumb, dumb dumb). Stevie fancied himself as a bit of a spokesperson for the movement. How much use would the UAF be in a war? Tell him that! It was people like him that made us great - swelling the army and fighting for Queen and Country - not the whingeing liberals, the conchies.

Hitler had been right: get rid of the intellectuals, the perverts, the gyppos, all the foreigners with their stinkin' food and weird religions makin' a bleedin' mess of their own countries and then coming here to crap all over ours. Flush the bloody lot of them down the toilet, and let's get back to what made us great.

"It was good," Ronnie agreed. "It would've been better if I could've got my bat round some 'eads."

"Worry not. Lads," Johnny grinned, "because what I have 'ere," - he held up a key - "is a 'assle-free way into the back of that social club." He grinned evilly. "We might not 've kicked any 'eads in last Saturday, but we're the ones given the honour of making sure there's never goin' to be any Islamic Centre in that particular buildin'."

"YESSSS," Frankie hissed. He downed the rest of the open can of special brew and cracked open another. "'Ow'd yer get it?"

"Connections," Johnny said smugly. "I volunteered us for the job, and we was selected. The cans of petrol are already inside under a load of dustsheets. He smirked at his mates. "The painters and decorators are supposed to be startin' next week. The petrol's gone in inside paint and varnish tins. I even have ..."

He unfolded a large piece of paper and spread it out on the table. "... a plan of the building. We go in 'ere," - he pointed to a door at the rear that had been circled in red - "then we set the fire 'ere, 'ere, 'ere, and 'ere."

His finger stabbed at the red crosses drawn at various strategic locations. "The kitchen with its gas stove, an upstairs storage room close to the roof timbers, load-bearing beams and ductin' straight up to the roof."

"Sufferin' Jesus!" Ronnie muttered. "It's like we're the bleedin' SAS." He gazed at Johnny with renewed respect.

"That's what we are," Johnny told him. "We're 'Special Forces'. Get this right and there'll be plenty more chances for us in the movement. It's growin', and we're growin' with it."

He was totally confident. "Money's no object, I've bin told. An' if the government can't or won't keep the immigrants out, maybe the likes of us can burn 'em out."

"WICKED!" Stevie breathed, which was no more than the truth. "When are we goin' in?"

Johnny glanced at his Action-Man watch with the camouflage strap. "Tomorrah night, midnight, after the neighbourhood watch 'as gone boe-boes."

Chapter 25

Rhyme And Reason

It came as no surprise that in their next lesson with Mrs Earle she challenged them to come up with a poem of their own. Her advice was to start by thinking of something worth saying, something they thought was important in some way. They had their notes to fall back on there.

Once they knew roughly what they wanted to say, they needed to find the most powerful way they could of saying it. For that they could call on striking similes, ground-breaking metaphors, subtle rhythms and internal or external rhymes in different patterns. They could make their poems prance in a pretty dance of alliteration, or flow with the slow and soothing tones of cloning assonance.

Last, they should expect it to take at least an hour. It would need lots of polishing on its way to the absolute best each pupil was capable of doing at that moment in time. For that reason, she advocated using a word-processor if at all possible. She further advised against using the internet to find someone else's poem and claim it as their own.

"Believe me," she assured them, "I will know."

That was much less likely to happen with a set 1 class, but she had come across it often enough further down the sets. Her favourite example was when a twelve-year-old boy in a bottom set had proudly presented her with a poem he claimed to have written himself about a mouse. It began:

"Wee, sleekit, cowrin, tim'rous beastie,

O, what a panic's in thy breastie!"

Zack decided what his poem was going to be about on the way home in the car. Edith had *Steve Wright in the Afternoon* on Radio 2, and Pink Floyd's *The Wall* came on. It's a really catchy song, but its message drove him ballistic.

"Those are TERRIBLE words!" he fumed. "I'm sorry Roger Waters had such an awful time when he went to school, but that's no reason to get a choir-load of London kids to sing "We don't need no Edge-u-kigh-shun". That's like saying "We don't need no Laura Norder" because one or two policemen crossed the line.

"He's right about the dark sarcasm though, isn't he?" Gordon pointed out. *"And we certainly don't need thought control."*

"No, we don't," Zack conceded, "but he seems to be saying all teachers use dark sarcasm to control your thoughts. How many teachers have you met who did that?"

"None," Gordon admitted. *"In fact, I wish a lot of teachers were better at thought control than they are. That way, we might get better behaviour in the classroom."*

"It's shocking that anyone with influence over young people should try and turn them against their schools," Zack insisted. "Doesn't he know how hard it is for kids growing up in our inner cities? Education has never been more important than it is today."

"OK," Gordon said, *"so that makes it a suitable subject to write a poem about."*

Once they'd got home and Gordon had kept their strength up with a chocolate biscuit and his usual glass of orange juice, they went up to their bedroom to make a start. Zack had his first draft ready by supper time. They had to share the keyboard, but Zack was a really fast touch-typist and didn't need it for long. They printed out his first draft and he polished it with a pencil.

Gordon went on staring at the screen, moving words and lines around, getting new ideas every time he read his poem through. They were both amazed how quickly bedtime came round.

They discovered they'd each spent around three hours striving for the best poem they could possibly write. It was a good job there wasn't any other homework that had to be done that night.

Gordon yawned and stretched. His eyes burned, but he was pleased with his final draft. He'd done it entirely himself, Zack having been completely wrapped up in his own poem. *"Let's see yours first,"* Gordon said. They had agreed they were finished, and had printed out both efforts.

"OK," Zack said, "but you've got to sing most of it. You know the tune."

The Wall

"'We down' need now edge-U-kigh-shun'
[Dumb da-dumb (dumb dumb), dumb da-dumb (dumb dumb)],
Roger had those schoolkids chant.
[Dumb da-dumb (dumb dumb), dumb da-dumb (dumb dumb)].
How wrong was that? A moaning rant
From a tortured soul on a narrow ledge
is one thing, all in all blaming baby
For the dirty waters in its bath.
But isn't that entangled, hard-won path
To knowledge beset with thorns enough
In our inner cities? Does he know how tough
It is just to survive? I wish he knew:
What a difference schools are making.
[Dum da-dum (dum dum), dum da-dum (dum dum)],
The time and trouble teachers take.
[Dum da-dum (dum dum), dum da-dum (dum dum)],
How many of them in those classrooms
[Dum da-dum (dum dum), dum da-dum (dum dum)]

Strive to keep kids' dreams awake.
Dumb, da-dumb (three four), dumb da-dumb (three four)
Dumb da-dumb - HEY! ROGER!
Keep them dreams awake,
Dumb, dumb-dumb diddle-um (What a pillock),
All in all, you put a
-nother brick in their wall."
Gordon chuckled. He read on.
"We all need much better school songs,
[Dum da-dum (dum dum), dum da-dum (dum dum)]
Some of us, clearly, more than most,
[Dumb da-dumb, dumb dumb, dumb da-dumb, dumb dumb)]
To try and right the many birth-wrongs
[Dum da-dum (dum dum), dum da-dum (dum dum)]
That tie us to the sticking post.
Dumb, da-dumb (three four), dumb da-dumb (three four)
Dumb da-dumb - HEY! WATERS!
Love them kids the most
[Dumb, dumb-dumb diddle-um (What a pillock)]
All in all, you told them
How to build their own wall.
Zack had then stipulated that the chorus was to be sung by the
Islington Green School Choir, as it was in the original recording.
WE ALL NEED AN EDGE-U-KIGH-SHUN!
[Dumb da-dumb (dumb dumb), dumb da-dumb (dumb dumb)],
To help us thrive and tyke controwl.
[Dum da-dum (dum dum), dum da-dum (dum dum)]
The charnce is right there in those clarserooms.
[Dum da-dum (dum dum), dum da-dum (dum dum)]
Please down't leave us kids alowne.
Dumb, da-dumb (three four), dumb da-dumb (three four)
Dumb da-dumb - TEACHERS! PLEASE DON'T

Leave those kids alone.
(Dum dum dum, diddle-um-diddle-um-dum)
All in all poor Humpty
Must have had a great fall
(Dum dum dum, diddle-um-diddle-um-dum)
After which the Numpty
built his own bloody wall.
Zack Rampant

"*That's strong!*" Gordon said when he'd finished laughing.

"Thank you," Zack said. "I feel better for having written it. Let's have a look at yours."

"*It started off simple,*" Gordon said, "*and then it got more complicated.*"

My Plan

In simple ways I want to make the world
A better place. If I can, I will count
Myself lucky, and with amazing grace
There's a chance I might. A wizard once told
Me that I was his heir. To be fair
He also said I had a lot to learn.
And as my knowledge of the world unfurls
I realise what an enormous amount
There is for me to do to keep pace
With everything that's wrong. Could I be bold
Enough? Could I care enough? If I dare
To love, will people love me in return?
It won't be easy. Sometimes you are hurled
Into a pit of doubt and fear. The Mount
Of Olives is desecrated, the face
Of evil smiles. That's when you have to hold
Fast. I'm so aware that hope, not despair,
Is what matters. We *can't* let the world burn.

Gordon Bennett

"Whoah," Zack said. "That's an ambitious rhyme scheme you've gone for there."

"I know," Gordon confessed. *"I didn't start out with it. Then I got interested in what would happen if I went for it."*

"It took you to the Mount of Olives," Zack grinned.

"It did. I like that bit. But do those questions work in the second stanza? It was keeping to ten syllables a line that gave me those. And I'm not sure about the last three lines." He looked uncertain. *"The internal rhyme in the penultimate line pushed them into that shape. Do you think it's awkward?"*

Zack read stanzas 2 and 3 again. "No, I like it," he told Gordon. "The questions highlight the struggle. The imperatives emphasise the need for determination. I think it's good."

"I'm glad," Gordon said, *"because I'm too tired to do anything more to it tonight. My brain hurts!"*

Zack nodded agreement. "Most poets will tell you they put a new poem aside for a week or two and see what they think of it after that."

Gordon did an enormous yawn. *"Good for them. They don't have to hand it in for homework."*

Chapter 26

Of Love And Loss

"Let's see then," Grace demanded. Gordon, Zack and Nick had only just got through the school gates. She and Miranda had already swapped theirs while they were waiting.

"I'll bet mine isn't nearly as good as all yours," Nick said. He rummaged in his bag looking nervous.

"I'll bet it's brilliant," Gordon said supportively.

"I dedicated it to you," Nick said. "I hope you don't mind." He handed it over. "I don't want anyone other than us and Mrs Earle reading it. It's personal."

Gordon held it while the others clustered round to read it at the same time. As his eyes travelled down the poem he felt tears pricking at them. He was gobsmacked!

For Gordon

I'm only frightened now from time to time.
If I could be enlightened as to why,
I would climb out of this fear pit. I try
To find the strength. I'd go to any length
To find an answer. Tell me where to look.
I'll listen to advice, read any book.
Do you know anything about coping
Strategies? I'm hoping you can help me
With the here and now bit, and the terror.
Is it possible there's an error
In my makeup? Or is it trickery? -
A gimmick – like that Indian rope thing?

If I had a dad, he'd teach me to fight.
Or a guardian angel who'd be right
There for me through thick and thin.
But hang on! I HAVE got someone I rely upon:
My absolute best friend, who's never scared
Of anything. He's always been prepared
To see my monsters off. And when they go
They're gone for good! Perhaps I'll never know
How he does it, but now my life is fun.
Without him, I don't know what I'd have done.
Nick Robinson

"I think that's the bravest poem I ever read," Miranda said. She gave Nick's arm a little squeeze.

"Gordon was right," Grace told him. "It IS brilliant. It's so honest it hurts."

"Do you really think so?" Nick said eagerly. "I tried ever so hard. It took me ages."

Gordon stuck his hand out. "Thanks mate," he said huskily. "I don't know where I'd be without you, either." Every ship needs a pilot officer as well as a captain.

Miranda took Nick's piece of paper and started reading it again. "You said that when you look for rhymes the sense goes out the window," she said. "It hasn't done in this poem. The rhyming is really smooth - rhyming "coping" with "Indian rope thing". She shook her head in admiration.

"Yeah, well," Nick grinned, "I don't think I'd ever tried to write a poem about something important before. And there aren't too many words that rhyme with "coping". I'd already used "hoping" and I wasn't getting anywhere with "loping", "moping", "roping" and "sloping".

"I like the way the "here and now bit" in line 3 of the second stanza picks up the "fear pit" in line 3 of stanza 1," Grace said. "That's a pretty slick trick, Nick."

Nick laughed delightedly. With friends like these, his enemies could get stuffed. "Not too gimmicky, then," he joked, "like that Indian rope thing?"

Miranda handed Nick his paper back and dived into her own bag. "You mention not having a dad," she said. "Mine is about losing my mum, and then getting a new step-mum." There are very few things in life more important to write about than that.

Rest In Me

I lost my mum when I was eight.
It was really hard. She asked me
To look after my dad. To date
I've done the best I can.

  When he

Was lonely I took his hand so
We could remember together.
She was there too, ready to go
That extra mile for us, whether
We laughed or cried.

  Then came the time

He told me that he'd found another mum
For me. By then I was ten and could mime
Acceptance, knowing I would come
Round to it if I tried.

  It was what she

Would have wanted for him. I do know that.
"Look to the future," she'd have said. "Be free
From grief at last. Put out a welcome mat
To happiness. Be glad for him."

It's nice

That he knows his own mind, and if she's kind
To him why not? I've my own life to find.
Only ...
I can't bear the thought of losing her twice.
Miranda Lansbury

A tear trickled down Grace's face. Miranda saw it and wrapped her friend in a hug. "Don't!" she said. "You'll set me off. I wept buckets writing it. I felt as though I'd been wrung out by the time I'd finished it."

"Your mum would have been proud of you," Gordon said gently. "You'll never lose her. She'll always be in there with you."

"I know," Miranda said. "I didn't know, because I hadn't really thought about it. Writing that poem made me realise that I hadn't lost her, not completely." She smiled sadly. "I slept really well last night, and I had a lovely dream about her. I woke up this morning feeling as though a weight had been lifted off my shoulders."

"'The props of my affection were removed, and yet the building stood, as if sustained by its own spirit,'" Zack murmured. Zoë nodded sadly. Wordsworth had been through something similar.

"I love the way the sense runs over the end of your lines," Nick said. "You hardly notice the rhyme because the sense runs through it, even from one stanza to the next."

"That's called 'enjambment,'" Zoë said, "in the trade." Zack nodded approvingly.

"I noticed Seamus Heaney doing that in *The Follower*," Gordon pointed out. "Do you remember?

'At the headrig, with a single pluck
Of reins, the sweating team turned round
And back into the land.'"

Nick shook his head. "How do you DO that?" he asked Gordon. "No wonder you're clever. You remember everything!"

"No I don't, not everything," Gordon lied. He turned to Grace. "What's yours about?"

"It's brilliant!" Miranda declared stoutly.

"I was taking that for granted," Gordon assured her, smiling.

Grace handed hers over, a little bashfully. "It's like Miranda's," she said. "Hers is about losing her mum. Mine is about never having known my dad."

My Father

My father hides from us. I've looked for him
All my life. Sometimes I close my eyes and
Try to find his thoughts. They're out there
Somewhere, on the other side of time.
There seems to be no rhyme or season in
His absence. It makes no sense to me.
I look for him in spring, when daffodils
Might have taken the winds of March
Out of his sails and slowed him down.
In summer, I hope to see him striding
Through the ripening corn, his face alight
With joy at finding us still looking.
In autumn, when the leaves drop from the oak
I glance up at its forlorn branches in
Case there's a chance I will find him hiding,
Hoping to surprise and entrance us both.
But then winter comes, and I find myself
Wondering through my window at the frost
Whether somewhere in deep space he got lost
On his way back to mum and me.
I know he loves us. We may see him soon.

He'll fly through a magic window
On the other side of the moon.
Grace Forrester

"Nice," Gordon murmured. "All that assonance and internal rhyming bind the first two stanzas together, and give the rhymes in the last stanza more emphasis." He looked up. "Is it just me, or did anyone else have a 'déjà vu' moment when they read that last sentence?"

Grace shivered. The bell went for a.m. registration.

"Zoë's done one as well," Grace telepathed to Gordon.

"So has Zack," he told her. *"His is strong, and it's funny."*

"Zoë's is strong, and ... thought-provoking," Grace told him. Gordon picked up a trace of anxiety in Grace's voice and in her eyes.

Zack and Zoë were of course party to anything they said to one another - telepathed or otherwise. They slipped each other copies as soon as they got the chance. Gordon tucked his into his English folder, and was able to read it while ostensibly reorganising some of the loose pages of notes and drafts.

Sense and Sensibility

I'd much prefer the pleasures of the flesh,
The sweet scent of cinnamon or the fresh
Tang of citrus on the tongue. I would stroke
A young puppy and let it lick my face
Or roll in some icy snow then soak
In a nice hot bath. To let my pulse race
At the thought of another would be good -
To feel his touch, or let my senses swim
In the soar of a cathedral choir. Should
I get the chance I would watch the stars dim
In the light of dawn, just before the sun
Blinded me with brilliance. To smell fresh bread

I'm told is amazing. It would be fun
To run until my lungs hurt.

　You once said

You sometimes thought you would like to be me -
A guardian angel no-one can see -
and be free of the shocks flesh is heir to.
That's interesting, 'cause I'd rather be you.
So let's swap - any time that you care to.
Zoë Nobody

Ooh – there was food for thought there all right. Zack was unusually quiet for quite a while after reading that.

Chapter 27

The Fires Of Hell

Johnny McGivern led the way over the back fence. It was a cloudy night, and very dark away from the main road. The Social Centre had a couple of motion-sensitive security lights to the rear. He'd been reliably informed they'd been switched off.

This was a residential area. Nothing stirred. The dial on his watch glowed midnight. Churchyard yawning time: time to breathe out a little contagion to this part of the world.

Last year, at considerable expense, Johnny had had the Reichstag eagle tattooed on his back. It flew from the nape of his neck to the width of his hips. Its spread wings stretched the length of both his arms. He felt the night air rustle its black feathers and shivered in anticipation. "This one's for you, Adolf," he promised his bird of prey.

The task-force flitted across the unlit concrete, unlikely phantoms through the night-cloaked space. They scuttled as quietly as their combat boots allowed towards the rear door, which was set in an alcove and surrounded by wheelie bins. Johnny found the keyhole and inserted the key. It turned noiselessly in the freshly oiled lock. Seconds later, all four of them were inside.

The painting and decorating supplies were exactly where he'd been told they'd be: set up on some trestle tables at the back of the main hall. There were piles of cotton twill dust sheets, and five litre cans of stain, varnish and white spirit. There were also several gallons of what was supposed to be brilliant white emulsion and gloss.

"Ronnie, you pick out the paint tins with a white blob on the lid," he whispered. "Get the lids off. Stevie, grab the dustsheets and pile them in the kitchen round the units and the gas stove. Soak 'em with white spirit. Frankie, get up them stairs and pile all the furniture up. We want the roof well alight before the brigade can get 'ere."

"Jawohl mein Kommandant," Frankie growled. Skinheads don't normally take orders, not from anyone. They are famous for their non-cooperation, even with each other.

The acrid stench of petrol filled the volatile space. Ronnie and Johnny grabbed a tin each and set off in different directions to either side of the hall. The idea was to pile dust sheets and furniture round the two most combustible locations, dowse it, then lay a petrol trail to the rear door they had come in by. By then Frankie should have soaked the furniture upstairs and left a trail down the stairs.

Stevie would have turned all the cooker gas taps on and splashed some of that white spirit back out of the kitchen as far as the petrol spilt in the hall. One match on the way out, and inside five minutes the whole hall should be burning like the fires of Hell.

There were a number of reasons why this particular best-laid plan might gang agley. All four of them had had a few jars in the run-up to the event, to pass the time and give themselves a shot of what is often referred to as "Dutch" courage. Consequently, their balance and steadiness of hand was less than perfect.

In their enthusiasm, whoever had filled those cans with petrol had failed to err on the side of caution. Consequently, their contents had begun slopping and spilling as soon as they were picked up. Boots and trouser bottoms were doused as their carriers tried to move at speed across the dark space.

The moment they were inside, a prearranged signal had alerted the forces of law and order. They had been provided with inside knowledge from somewhere, and were quietly parked in a neighbouring street. The police would have piled in already, had it not been for the presence of all those combustible materials. Instead, they'd phoned the Fire

Brigade, and taken up positions at the rear and the front of the building. The engine was less than a minute away.

Whoever had used the hall last had not stacked the furniture. Consequently, the odd bench had been left on the hall floor, just waiting to catch a skinhead unawares if he was trying to move at speed without enough light to see where he was going.

The fumes from the spilt fuel were making their heads spin, befuddling them even more. The words "Burn, baby burn, disco inferno," were running at volume through Johnny's head as first one shin and then the other made painful contact with an invisible bench. He did a spectacular face-plant on the other side of it, soaking himself in petrol in the process. Ronnie heard the crash and the curse and skidded to a halt, while looking back in the direction of the noise.

He couldn't see anything, but the shiny floor was already wet with slopped petrol. It wasn't surprising that his feet shot from under him and he crashed painfully on to his back. The tin he was carrying shot up into the air on the end of his hand, and its remaining contents hit him full in the face before he'd had the wit to let it go.

Gordon could not be certain where the ignition came from. Maybe there was an electrical fault somewhere. Maybe one of the tins struck a spark against a metal stud in a skinhead boot. He just knew that at that moment of chaos he thought he saw a black blur descend into the centre of the hall with the beating of cruel wings. He felt the rush of displaced air ...

Glowing balls of fire sprang from a spot in the centre of the hall and streaked into the petrol-sodden skinheads on either side. The semi-conscious skins combusted simultaneously with the ferocious intensity of petrol-dowsed tinder. Seconds of agonised thrashing and bellowing later, they were subsiding into charred heaps of foul-smoking embers.

At such a ferocious temperature, human flesh melts.

The front door exploded. Firemen with breathing apparatus and foam extinguishers dashed in, dowsing the flames in jets of foam. Gibbering with terror, Frankie and Stevie bolted out of the back door into the arms of waiting policemen. It would be a further hour before the firemen would let anyone else in the building. A quick examination confirmed that the two heaps of body-shaped foam were beyond human help.

That one was for you, Adolf.

Maybe the sudden flaring of flame had seared Gordon's eyeballs, but just before he felt his senses drift and let his guardian angel get him home, he thought he saw two crimson, burning eyes up in the ceiling rafters. Up there, the darkness hovered as thick and black as the wings of a giant crow.

Chapter 28

Learning From Mistakes

Gordon stirred and opened his eyes. For a second the stench of petrol and burning flesh was still in his nostrils, but his next breath filled his nose with the safer fragrance of freshly washed bed-linen.

He was in no hurry to move. Today was a special holiday in honour of the wedding of William Wales to Catherine Myddleton. Gordon didn't need to be at the Abbey before 10.00 a.m. He hoped that Grace hadn't been too traumatised by yesternight's events. Watching those trolls burn in the Easter holidays had been upsetting enough.

He'd heard her cry out as the flames erupted, then everything happened so fast. In seconds, those two young men had been beyond the help of even her healing hands. He shuddered, remembering how he'd felt when he'd first seen someone being burned alive: outside his bedroom window in Cornwall, just before his eleventh birthday.

Such a lot had happened since then.

His dad appeared in his bedroom doorway. "Oh good. I was hoping you'd wake up before I left. "How'd it go?" He didn't have the day off, and would get a report in any case once he got to the office, but an eye-witness account would be handy, especially from one of the only two people to have seen everything.

"Two of them burned to death, Dad," Gordon said. His voice trembled a little. "The firemen got there too late to save them. The building is mostly OK, just superficial damage."

His dad closed his eyes. "Christ," he muttered. "I'm really sorry, Son. It should never have come to that."

It wasn't his patch. He'd merely passed the intelligence on. He supposed the local coppers hadn't wanted to go in early for fear of alerting those who'd prepped the job for the four lads. If police activity had been spotted beforehand, the job would have been called off, and the next time, they might not have had a heads-up.

Of course, there were risks in not going in until after they were inside and covered in guilt. Something can always go horribly wrong, and clearly something had.

Victor walked over to his son and squeezed his shoulder. "I wish you hadn't had to see that."

"It's OK, Dad," Gordon said bravely. "It was really quick. The fireman covered them in foam, but there was nothing anyone could have done, not even Grace."

"Oh God, of course," his dad said. "How's she taking it?"

"I don't know, yet, but I'll find out soon," Gordon said.

"You saved the building," Victor reminded them, "and all the surrounding buildings. A hundred families could have been put at risk if that building had exploded." He ruffled Gordon's hair, and turned to go. "I'll get off," he said. "Thanks again, Zack."

"You're welcome," Gordon said automatically.

"I suppose the lesson is we should always show pictures like that to Zoë as well as to me," Zack said. "If she'd seen those photos, we could probably have stopped that happening."

"Right," Gordon said. Learn from your mistakes. 'The path to knowledge …' He swung his legs out of bed. "Best get some breakfast," he said. "We've got our own mission to attend to this morning."

By now, Gordon trusted Mabon's ring: it hadn't let him down yet. It had taken him into the sacred Forest of Arden, where he and Grace had played their part in a Royal Renewal ceremony. It had taken him to Her

Majesty's Prison Manchester when he had asked it to. It had taken him to Fairyland before he'd known that's where he needed to be.

As far as Grace was concerned, her dreamstone had shown itself capable of transporting her at will. It had coordinated her movements with Gordon's. Because of that, they'd been able to deliver their invitation together. So there seemed no reason to doubt that they would all meet as agreed outside the Great West Door of Westminster Abbey at 10.00 a.m..

It was Friday 29th April 2011.

The wonderful sound of the London Chamber Orchestra drifted from the Abbey. Gordon and Zack found themselves standing on the red carpet leading from the cars and carriages to the Great West Door. The Abbey clock showed 10 a.m. precisely.

With simultaneous precision, Grace and Zoë appeared next to them. They were all, of course, invisible to non-magic, human eyes. So far, so good.

The atmosphere was electric. Many in the crowd had been waiting for days. For more than an hour they had been cheering and clapping as the vast majority of the 1,900 guests entered the Abbey through the Great North Door.

The really special moments were now close at hand. Very shortly, the protagonists would be arriving with similar precision at the Great West Door. Most of the males would be in high-ranking military uniforms.

"Let's have a look inside," Gordon suggested. "We've got time."

"Ooh yes," Grace said eagerly. "I can't wait to see what everyone's wearing."

"Along as no-one is fat," Zack reminded them wickedly. Gordon groaned.

The first things to catch their eye were the trees. There were six field maples and two hornbeams spreading their lush young foliage twenty-five feet into the air on either side of the nave. There were wonderful flowers everywhere, too. Around 30,000 fresh blooms had been brought from Windsor Great Park's Valley Gardens to dress the Abbey for this great occasion. "I think their Fairy Majesties will feel at home in here," Grace murmured.

The majesty of the building regularly dwarfed any event taking place in it, but at eye-level, the glittering array of designer dresses, spectacular hats, sparkling brooches and the smartest of shoes on their very first outings (as evidenced by the number of unmarked soles) was truly impressive. The leading fashion houses of Europe must have thought all their Christmases had come at once.

There was much waving, hand-shaking and chatting while ushers patiently guided everyone to their allotted seats. Gordon, Grace, Zack and Zoë spent ten minutes floating through the space spotting famous faces on all sides, and then it was time to be outside again.

Their fairy majesties weren't arriving until 10.40 a.m., but there was no way Grace and Zoë were going to miss the arrival of Princes William and Harry at 10.15 a.m..

Preceded by a single police motor-cyclist with blue lights flashing, the custom-built Bentley came smoothly to a halt at the red carpet. Its huge windows and extended glass panels to the rear and in the roof afforded spectators the best possible view of the occupants from all angles.

"The Queen has two of those," Zack observed. "They're 40 inches longer than the standard model, and they sit on a 151-inch wheelbase. There are no others like them in the world."

Trust Zack to be in possession of such recondite information. Grace and Zoë could not have been less interested. They had eyes only for the young princes, resplendent in their magnificent uniforms.

"Don't bother giving us the detail about those uniforms, badges, medals and insignia," Zoë advised him. "We'll just look at them."

Gordon's eyes were drawn not to the red of Prince William's uniform, but rather to the simple dress of the lady in red who floated out of the car behind her two sons. Age had not withered her, nor custom dimmed the sadness behind those extraordinary eyes. She showed no interest in the cheering crowds. Her attention was focused proudly on the two splendid young men her sons had become. As she drifted past Gordon, Grace, Zack and Zoë, however, she shot them a secret smile.

"Do you think Myrddin made that possible?" Grace telepathed to Gordon. They watched the spirit of Princess Diana wait patiently for her sons to greet those waiting for them at the door, before all three disappeared inside.

"I don't know," Gordon murmured back. He thought of Miranda's poem. "Maybe he didn't have to. I don't think your mum ever goes away. When her own body stops working, she just moves in with you."

Chapter 29

Under The Mistletoe

At 10.35 a.m., they zoomed to the top of the towers over the Great West Entrance. From there, they had an uninterrupted view of their Fairy Majesties' flight path, while still keeping at least one eye on events unfolding below.

"Here they come!" Zack announced, two minutes later. He had caught the first gleam of the sun's reflection on the glittering, sky-born carriage coming over the western horizon. Its approach was preternaturally rapid. Gordon briefly remembered the images he had had as a child of Father Christmas galloping through the heavens on a crimson sleigh piled high with sacks and pulled by snorting reindeer.

That image was soon replaced by the lightness and beauty of this royal coach. It was drawn by two small, perfect unicorns and surmounted by the turning crown that glinted in the sun. The carriage was pumpkin shaped, and made from curiously pale and interwoven vines. It was bedecked with crimson roses and leaves of deepest green.

It circled the spire of Big Ben and made a faultless descent on the roof of Westminster Abbey, bringing a bloom and freshness to the pinnacles of stone.

His Fairy Highness sat on a purple cushioned seat with his back to the unicorns. Dressed in crimson and gold, he remained youthful in appearance. The Queen sat opposite him on a cushion of white silk. She seemed to float in a dress of pansied pinks. Wreathed in those roses, leaves and twisting vines, the beauty of her perfect, gentle face still had the power to take your breath away.

Gordon and Zack bowed low, while Grace and Zoë sank into deep curtseys. Two attendant fairies in livery of purple and gold braid steadied the snorting unicorns. They all admired the way the harnesses and horns of those fabled creatures had been picked out in bright gold.

The king leapt from the coach in excellent spirits. "All hail, Sir Gordon, and the brave Sir Zack," he called out cheerfully. "My Ladies Grace and Zoë, how content we are to find you here as planned. The sun smiles bravely on this day's affairs, I think."

"Indeed it does, Sire," Gordon said, tearing his eyes from the queen and the unicorns. "May we believe that you have had a hand in blessing London with this clear blue sky?"

The king laughed heartily. "Why not, why not? You yourself have power over the elements, when occasion serves. And it may be that other hands than ours have taken time to wave away the clouds. They could not be allowed to frown on such a scene as this."

He held his own hand up for the queen to take, and she dismounted with a radiant smile. "We owe you all our heartfelt gratitude," she said, "for returning our dear children to us. We know not what you found in those dark woods, but whatever it was, it is dispelled." A great weight had been lifted. "Our children are the gentle, loving souls they were before. Their clouds of gloom are gone, and fortune once more smiles on us."

Gordon bowed in acknowledgement, but his smile had gone. "We had reason to hope that might be the case," he said. "But Your Majesties should know you are ill-served by at least one member of your household with access to your children." He was deadly serious. "We may have scotched the snake, not killed it."

The king looked grave. "We suspected as much," he said grimly. "But talk of this must wait for another time." His smile returned. "For see, their royal majesties below arrive to lend the day their special grace."

And thus it was that the King and Queen of Fairyland came to be hovering protectively above the bride and groom throughout the ensuing ceremony. Those who had taken it upon themselves to issue their majesties' unique invitation kept careful watch from a respectful distance above the choir screen.

William slipped the ring of pure Welsh gold on Catherine's finger. When the Archbishop of Canterbury blessed the newly-wed couple, their fairy majesties joined hands to add a blessing of their own. They made their sign of the endless knot with sprigs of sacred mistletoe, cut with Arden's blade.

The blessing conferred and the ceremony concluded, the purpose of their visit was fulfilled. In advance of the human procession, their fairy majesties fluttered unobtrusively along the Abbey nave and smiled between the avenue of trees before flying out of the Great West Door.

Behind them, Grace linked with Gordon and Zoë with Zack, making a little procession of their own. Outside was a sea of waving flags. Cheering, happy onlookers soaked in the magic of the moment.

Above them all a riot of bells broke out, the start of a full peal - over 5,000 changes, yet still the same peal - taking more than three hours to complete. Back on the roof, the unicorns looked eager to be away.

"What amazing beasts," Gordon thought to himself (normal conversation was impossible).

The king smiled. *"Bred specially in the Shetlands for the royal coach,"* he told him telepathically. *"They are 42 inches from their withers to the ground, broad in the body with plenty of heart room, and powerful thighs for long journeys. There are no others like them in our world."*

The coach-fairies waited for the royal command. The queen held up a pair of acorns.

"Your prince and his bride chose to plight their troth in the nearness of trees," she said. *"It is a good sign. We will plant these acorns in the woods*

of Windsor Great Park's Valley Gardens. Their trees waved to us as we passed."

The king nodded. *"All Fairydom shall hear of this great day, and of you four. You are a force for good. Perhaps at last we'll find a common sense in common cause and save our planet from the greed of fools."*

The unicorns leaped upwards. Weightlessly the wonder-coach rose with them, rapidly gaining speed in a loop around Big Ben before accelerating through the clear sky to the west. Soon, it had dwindled to a gleaming dot over Windsor Castle. Gordon and Grace went on waving until they were completely out of sight.

"What lovely people they are," Grace murmured. *"I'm so glad their children are all right again."*

Gordon smiled. *"I know what you mean,"* he said. *"They may be fairies, but they're our kind of people."* Beneath them, the newly married Duke and Duchess of Cambridge were climbing into the state landau, made for the coronation of Edward VII in 1902. It was drawn by four Windsor greys, each pair guided by a liveried horseman.

The duchess still carried her bouquet, which contained a sprig of myrtle from the bush grown from the original myrtle in Queen Victoria's wedding bouquet. Continuity and renewal; their fairytale was just beginning. Gordon, Grace, Zack and Zoë joined hands and wished them the best of British luck, before whizzing off home to catch the rest on telly.

Chapter 30

Coincident Alley

It was a sunny Saturday morning in mid-May, and Edith was going shopping in Chester. There were very few things Victor loathed more than shopping, and this time the garden came to his rescue. Edith was the first to admit it was screaming for attention. Not having been into town for ages, however, Gordon and Zack decided they would go with her.

As usual, she parked the car in the Tesco car-park, and they made their way into Eastgate by cutting through BHS. They'd do their food-shopping on the way back, spending enough not to have to pay for parking. Edith headed right - across the top (or bottom) of Frodsham Street and under the clock into Foregate Street - towards the Grosvenor Shopping Precinct.

"HELLO!" Vivian called out. She and Elaine emerged from the crowds of shoppers and tourists thronging the area. "That's a coincidence. We haven't been into town in ages."

Grace and Zoë were swinging along behind them, arm in arm, and looking very grown-up. Grace had recently started experimenting with make-up, and was noticeably taller in her weekend heels. She was fourteen going on seventeen. Catching sight of her, Gordon suddenly felt a bit young and shabby. She grinned at him. *"Fancy meeting you here,"* she telepathed, *"all footloose and fancy free."*

"You two are looking very ... eligible," Zack said. Zoë fluttered her eyelashes in mock allure.

"There's a limit to how eligible you can be when you're following your mums around the shops," she told him.

"We'd just decided it was coffee time," Elaine told Edith.

"OOH," said Edith, brightening at the thought of a cappuccino and an almond croissant. A thought popped into Gordon's head from nowhere.

"Have you been down Coincident Alley yet?" he asked Grace.

She and Zoë looked interested. *"No, I've never heard of it,"* Grace said. *"Sounds quirky. Where is it?"*

"Mum, while you three are getting coffee, Zack and I thought we'd show Grace and Zoë a little place we know near here."

Edith glanced at Vivian and Elaine who nodded happily. They were more laid-back than she was when it came to their children going off and doing things without them. Edith was getting there, but it was taking time. "All right, Darling," she said. "I don't need to worry, do I?"

Gordon grinned. "No, you don't. I know you will, but there's really no need. We'll be back in half an hour. If you've moved on, we'll buzz your mobiles."

How did we ever manage without mobiles?

Elaine grabbed Edith's arm and steered her away. "Have fun!" Vivian called over her shoulder.

"Oh, I think we will," Gordon said. He was suddenly excited.

"So, tell us more," Grace said.

"It's only two minutes from here. Come on, we'll talk as we walk."

The Chester Rows are covered walkways at first floor level. They contain shops and cafes, and date from medieval times. They are unique. Nothing quite like them exists anywhere else in the world, which is, of course, what 'unique' should always mean. The children crossed Foregate and climbed the steep stone steps to the row opposite Browns.

"I found it by chance about four years ago," Gordon told them. "I'd been wondering about witches and wizards floo-powdering themselves all the way to Diagon Alley, and thinking how ridiculous that was. I mean, London can't be the only place witches and wizards go for stuff. There have to be outlets in the provinces."

They came to the gap in the row leading to Godstall Lane. "So one night, when Zack was well out, I nipped into town on my own. There was so much psychic energy pulsating around Godstall Lane you couldn't miss it."

It had been a daring thing to do at that age.

"And there it was – Coincident Alley. I only had a quick look round. I didn't want Zack to wake up and be worried."

Zack snorted. "I didn't even find out he'd dreamed off somewhere without me until we were in Cornwall for his eleventh birthday. Two racing brooms turned up! Gordon had hired them from a place in this Alley."

Ahead of them, Godstall Lane threaded its narrow way towards the cathedral. Gordon, however, had stopped and turned to face a solid, white-painted, brick wall. "There," he said. "Can you feel it?"

Grace frowned. "I feel ... something," she said. "I don't know if I'd have noticed it, if you hadn't said."

Gordon held his hand out. "Let's all hold hands. Concentrate on the wall."

As soon as Grace gripped Gordon's hand, her head shot up eagerly. Zack's and Zoë's did the same. "Oh WOW!" she said.

The wall in front of them was dissolving, and a round Norman arch, no more than six feet high, was coming into focus. Witches and wizards were a good deal shorter in the old days. Beyond it, a narrow, cobbled street stretched the length of the row, almost as far as Northgate Street. On either side of it were half-timbered buildings with bottle-glass windows and interesting shop signs.

Gordon led the way through the arch into Coincident Alley.

Rhedyn's Rent-A-Broom was the first shop on the left. Gordon noticed it was looking considerably smarter than it had when he was here last. Business was clearly booming.

"HEY!" Grace said, pointing at the freshly painted sign above the shop. In quite large letters (gold on a dark green background) it said *'By Appointment to Myrddin's Heir'*.

"WHOAH," Zack said. They clustered round the window. Two familiar-looking brooms were prominently displayed in the centre of it: a GSX1300R Hayabusa and a ZX 750 F Turbo. The sign underneath them read "ridden by Myrddin's Heir and his attendant spirit on the night that Mabon's Cairn gave up the Tara Torque. Book now for first available dates in 2013."

"How much did she charge you for renting them?" Zoë asked him.

"She didn't," Gordon said. "I was standing outside the shop, just looking into the window, when she rushed out and pulled me in. She said they had a special offer on: ride any two brooms for a night free, and choose your own night.

She gave me a little tin whistle and told me all I had to do was blow on it and the brooms would find me. I took the whistle just to get out of the shop, to be honest."

"The questions are," Zack said: "how did she know you were Myrddin's Heir before he'd even told you? And how did she know you would need two brooms?"

"I don't know," Gordon admitted. "Maybe she sent two to be on the safe side, or to give me a choice."

There were other possibilities. The brooms had spotted him and were jiggling up and down with excitement. "Let's keep moving," he suggested. The last thing he wanted was to attract any attention.

At least he now understood why Rhedyn had inveigled him into riding her brooms. He was glad the signs didn't mention his name. Clearly his status in the witching and wizarding world was enough to have created a two-year waiting list for those particular brooms.

"How many witches and wizards come here to shop, do you think?" he asked. There were quite a few people moving in and out of the shops and scurrying up and down the Alley. They looked like perfectly ordinary people, but he noticed they turned away from one another as they passed, as if they didn't want to be seen doing whatever it was they were doing.

Was this a place not to be seen shopping? Or was being a witch or wizard something you wanted to keep secret, even from other witches and wizards? It was a relief that no-one even spared them a glance.

"I don't know," Grace said. "People come from all over the North West to shop in Chester. It's heaving out there."

"There are a lot of shops down this Alley," Zoë pointed out. "They may not be paying rent to the Duke of Westminster, but for them all to stay in business they must get customers."

"I'm keeping an eye out," Zack said, "...for anyone we know."

Yes, of course; he had a point there. How many witches or wizards were there actually living in and around Chester? Where did their children go to school?

The next shop along was *Heulwen's Handy Hardware and Health Foods Emporium*. If the window display was anything to go by, it stocked a range of goods that weren't widely available in the world he knew. *Lakeland Plastics* didn't do cauldrons anywhere near that size.

There was an offer on some ingredients that he'd only ever come across before in the play-that-must-not-be-named. There wasn't much call for newts' eyes, frogs' toes and dogs' tongues in *Holland and Barrett*. The prices in the window were in euros. Maybe they made that switch when Ireland joined the euro zone.

Gordon spotted a sign at the far end of the Alley, on their right. "Ooh," he said, pointing. "Can we just pop into that shop?"

Chapter 31

A Matter Of Choice

Wynfor's Wonderful Wands, the sign read. Its bow-fronted window contained a large number of slim, rectangular boxes, tastefully arranged in three tall pyramids, which meant you could see through the display into the shop. Similar rectangular boxes were stacked inside on shelves from floor to ceiling. The notice in the window said "Wands for Every Occasion. Exceptionally Stable and Eager to Please. They practically wave themselves!"

"Does that mean some wands aren't stable and eager to please?" Zoë wondered.

"Maybe they're like people," Zack suggested. "They choose somebody and think they're going to live happily ever after; then something goes wrong, and they get moody and stressed out."

"Imagine having an argument with your wand!" Grace giggled. "What if it had a nervous breakdown, or wanted to go off with another witch or wizard? You could find yourself up a creek without a paddle!"

"There are plenty more wands in the wand shop," Gordon pointed out, "so either witches or wizards have lots of children reaching wand-waving age, or wands do need replacing from time to time."

"What do you want to go in there for?" Zack wanted to know. "Were you thinking of getting a wand?"

"OOH!" said Grace, to whom the idea had not previously occurred.

"No," said Gordon. "You and I seem to be managing pretty well without one. Myrddin hasn't said anything to me about wands." While he was speaking, the shop door had given a welcoming tinkle and opened of its own accord. Courteously, Gordon waved Grace and Zoë over the threshold first. He and Zack followed them in...

The shop appeared to be unattended. The inside was Tardis-like in its inner proportions. Shelf stacks stretched away on either side. The long counter was bare, save for a circular lump on one corner with a prominent button sticking out of it. The sign beneath it said 'Please Ring For Attention'.

Behind them, the shop-door locked itself. The open/closed sign on it flipped over. Simultaneously the window and door blinds came down.

"Whoah," Zack muttered. That was his trademark 'possible incoming Exocet' sound. Instinctively they circled the wagons, back to back, eyes on all points of the compass.

When nothing else happened, Gordon decided to ring for attention. He pressed the prominent button. The sound that rang out was out of all proportion to the situation. It resembled the beginning of a full peal of the bells at Westminster Abbey. Maybe the sound that bell made depended on who pressed the button.

After about ten seconds it ceased as quickly as it had begun. They became aware of another sound, a rattle, growing in volume and intensity. It seemed to be coming from the rectangular boxes behind and in front and to the sides of them. It was as if all the wands were trying to get out at once.

The rattling sound drowned out any noise the ladder platform behind the nearest rack might have made, for it slid suddenly and apparently silently into view. Perched on top of it was a man of mature age, bearing a marked resemblance to the actor John Hurt. It could have been his twin brother.

"I wondered when I might be seeing *you*, Mr Bennett," he said, softly. Goodness me, he even sounded like him.

"Pull the other one," Grace said softly. "It's got bells on."

Mr Wynfor – for presumably this was the Wynfor of Wynfor's Wands – grinned. "Just my little joke," he said, with a broad Welsh accent nothing like John Hurt's. "It normally raises a smile."

He scrambled down the ladder and came over to them, by which time, he was shorter, rounder and squinting through a pair of unusually large spectacles with disconcertingly thick lenses. Reaching under the counter, he drew out a wand that looked a little too long for him and waved it at the rattling boxes.

"Ffyn Hud, Distaw!" he commanded. The rattling subsided, a little reluctantly. "They *all* appear to 'ave chosen you, Boyo," he said. "That's one to tell my grandkids, and no mistake."

"Are all your wands Welsh-speaking?" Gordon asked him. "Or do they speak more than one language?"

Mr Wynfor looked highly indignant. "What do you think this is yere, some kind of backwater establishment?"

He put his hands on his hips. "'Ow far would I get now with a shop full of wands speakin' only Welsh when the bulk of my customers wouldn't know a Bara brith from a sausage roll?"

His mock indignation was replaced with genuine pride. "Highly educated these wands are - speak anythin' you like. Their Latin might be a little rusty, mind. Dead language, see."

"I didn't come here for a wand," Gordon said. "Not just now, anyway." Mr Wynfor rolled his eyes. "Given that all I sell is wands," his expression seemed to say, "why the blue blazes else would you come in here?"

"I'll bet you know all there is to know about wands, Mr Wynfor," Grace said winningly. Her soothing tone and deferential manner seemed to have the required effect. Mr Wynfor beamed.

"Well, yes, Miss Forrester, that is the normally accepted view of things. I'm not a man to boast mind, but it 'as been said that what I don't know about wands cannot possibly be worth knowin'."

Grace swung her eyes back to Gordon. *"Go on, then, ask him,"* she telepathed.

"What I was wondering," Gordon said, "is when did wands become the size they are now? The old wizards – like Moses and Prospero – carried rods or staffs, which are much bigger. Myrddin has a staff, Gandalf had a staff. When did they shrink to these smaller pieces of wood?"

The shopkeeper's eyes narrowed. "Mmm, 'ighly intelligent question, that one. In all my years as a wand-master, nobody 'as ever asked it. Put your finger on a conundrum there, you 'ave, Boyo. 'Ardly surprising though. Myrddin wouldn't 've nominated a pea-brain to be 'is heir, now would he?"

He looked from one to the other. "I'll answer it the best I can, but can I ask the smallest favour in return? Rhedyn there at the other end of the Alley - always been an astute businesswoman ..." - His fingers tapped out a little nervous tune on the base of his wand. "'Er enterprise 'as never looked back, see, since she 'appened to mention that you'd ridden 'er brooms."

His eyes took on an eager, pleading look. "Would you mind if I were to, you know, put a notice in my window sayin' that you were frequenters of my establishment? Perhaps a photo of you smilin' and wavin' one of my wands? No, no, of course not, several steps too far that!" he added hastily, as he saw the expressions change on their faces. "Discretion, discretion, never my strong point."

"We don't want to advertise our names or faces," Gordon said kindly, "but if it would help your business in any way to say something like "visited and valued by Myrddin's heir and his close friend and associate", I think we'd be OK with that, wouldn't we?"

He looked at Grace, who nodded willingly. Both Zack and Zoë turned away slightly, trying to hide their smiles.

"Gracious, most gracious that," Mr Wynfor said. "It's very grateful I am, I can't tell you. And of course, in return, anythin' I can ever do for you. Free wands of course, any time, in return for the usual endorsement."

He put his own wand down, rubbed his hands together in his excitement, and then remembered the question. "The rod and the staff, yes, let me see. "Yea, though I walk through the valley of the shadow of death, I will fear no evil, for thou [art] with me. Thy rod and thy staff they comfort me." Psalm 23 of course."

His eyes took on a dreamy look. "They were giants, those old wizards. Gods, even, you might say, that's 'ow good they were. All the magic they 'ad then, see - ran through them like a river."

Those were the days of miracle and wonder.

"Your wands nowadays, diminutive, aren't they, pale imitations. Couldn't 'andle the old rods and staffs, most of your modern witch-and-wizardry." His voice became more animated. "Very interestin' what you can channel, of course, through eleven inches of supple holly, 'specially if a skilled wand-master 'as incorporated a phoenix feather. Not easy to get your 'ands on, certainly don't come cheap. Where was I?"

"At 'closes in the consequence'," Zack muttered drily.

"Ye-e-ss," Mr Wynfor recalled, "the old rods and staffs, very comfortin', in the right 'ands. Massive pain in the proverbial, mind, in the wrong ones. Blood under the bridge, that - long stories, ages ago."

He swung his gaze back to Gordon. "In a nutshell, lost, most of them. All of them, for all I know. We do our best, mind - a very good best, in the circumstances. Be lost without my little wand, I would indeed. But what anyone would do nowadays, look you, with one of the *old* rods ..."

He broke off, leaving the question hanging, and stared at Gordon as though something momentous had only just occurred to him. "It would take a giant," he murmured, "to 'andle one, now as then. Very dangerous, I would imagine, in the wrong 'ands, but in the *right* 'ands ... Now there's a thought, indeed it is."

Gordon backed towards the door. "That's been very helpful, Mr Wynfor," he said. "We need to be going now. No doubt we'll see you again. You've been a great help. Thanks very much."

Behind him the blinds flew up and the sign flipped over to open. The door unbolted itself and swung open. There was another customer standing on the step looking distinctly irritated. He was clearly not used to being kept waiting. "Whoops," Zoë murmured as she caught sight of him.

He was as long and thin as Mr Wynfor was short and stout. Julius Caesar would certainly have identified that look as lean and hungry. His fingers reminded Gordon of the claws of a crab. The kindest thing that could be said about his eyes was that they were ... unkind.

He strode imperiously into the shop. Unlike the other people they had seen in Coincident Alley he stared straight at them, piercing Gordon and Grace with a penetrating glance. Grace hissed suddenly and put the tips of her fingers to her temples. A pain had stabbed through her brain like a thin-bladed knife.

"Well, well, *well*," he drawled, "what exalted company you keep nowadays, Wynfor." The tone of his voice gave the distinct impression that he was talking to a dog. Grace left the shop immediately, her forehead creased with pain. Gordon followed her after smiling apologetically at Mr Wynfor, who appeared not to notice. His attention was entirely focused on his latest customer. His expression reminded Gordon of a frightened rabbit.

As they began the short walk back to the Alley entrance and Godstall Lane, they heard the sound of the blinds dropping and the door bolts slamming into place. Gordon had the distinct feeling that the shop would be shut for some time.

Chapter 32

The Good Samaritans

"Are you OK?" Gordon asked. Grace massaged her temples gently. Zoë put a comforting arm around her shoulders, and Zack looked concerned. Gradually the creases in her forehead smoothed themselves out, and her eyes cleared.

"Yes, I'm fine. I suddenly had a really bad headache. It's gone now."

"It came on when that sinister-looking bloke walked into Wynfor's," Gordon said. "Was that the face that sank a thousand ships, or what? Did you try to read his mind?"

"I don't normally," Grace said. "At least I try not to, but sometimes it just happens. I think he's got some kind of anti-probe missile system on intruder alert. It felt like a steel rod had been fired into my brain!"

"Forewarned is forearmed," Gordon said grimly. "We'll know what to expect when we see him again."

Grace looked alarmed. "Do you think we'll be seeing him again?"

"'Well, well, *well*,' Gordon drawled, in a frighteningly exact imitation of the man's voice and demeanour. 'What exalted company you keep nowadays, Wynfor.' I'd say there's a better-than-even chance. He's going to want to test us out. He needs to find out what kind of force he might have to reckon with."

Grace stared at him. "Can you read his mind?"

Gordon closed his eyes. His mind's eye was back in the wand shop, watching the terrified Wynfor cowering behind his counter. "No, my Lord, no, please no!"

"But of *course* you must be punished, Wynfor. Disloyalty must always be punished." Gordon felt the cruel pleasure behind the soft tone of voice. It was the merciless enjoyment of watching a struggling fly, having pinned it to the table. It was the relish in the moment before pulling its wings off.

"But I've done nothing disloyal, my Lord! I 'ave always done as you commanded."

"Indeed you have, Wynfor," the voice drawled. He pronounced the man's name with the same disdain that he might have pronounced the word 'Vermin'. "Otherwise, as we both know, you and your daughter would both be dead. But did you do it, I wonder, for the right reasons?"

"I did it, my Lord. Is that not enough? Please, my Lord, don't punish me! You know I can't bear it! Why must you PUNISH ME?!" His voice was rising almost to a scream.

"Because you entertained a disloyal *thought*, Wynfor. Just now, when I found your shop closed and you were talking to that boy, I read your pathetic little mind. You need reminding where your loyalties lie. I have always found a little pain most helpful when 'conditioning' a servant."

The crab-like hand turned and opened its fingers. A wand of twisted wood that looked like strangler fig was suddenly in its grasp. It was tipped with a blood-red crystal. Gordon saw the tip begin to glow. He heard the hopeless, begging cries of the defenceless wand-master. Wynfor was anticipating the agonies he was about to endure ...

The door of his shop suddenly resounded under the beating of an urgent fist. "MR WYNFOR! Are you there? Sorry to bother you. Can you let me in for a moment please? I won't keep you long." It was Gordon's voice, and he obviously wasn't going to go away.

"MR WYNFOR, COO-EEE!!" That dratted girl was out there as well, the one who'd had the damned effrontery to try and probe his mind. With a tight smile, he re-sheathed his wand. No matter; the pleasures of Wynfor's punishment could wait for another time. It would give him time to think up something even more exquisitely unbearable with which to torment him.

"Our business can wait. Get up man, stop snivelling. Compose yourself. It appears you have customers." The window and door blinds shot up and the bolts shot back. The door swung open and Gordon and Grace clattered back into the shop.

"Sorry to disturb you again, Mr Wynfor," Gordon said innocently. "Do finish your business with this gentleman first."

"Our business *is* finished," the 'gentleman' said crisply. "I know you will give the matter further thought, Wynfor. We'll speak again, *soon*." Wynfor bowed his head as the man swept out of his shop. He did not raise it again as the door closed.

"Oh, Mr Wynfor, I'm so sorry," Grace whispered. "Would you mind awfully if I held your hand for a moment?" Without raising his helpless head, Wynfor put both hands on the counter. Grace took one and Gordon the other.

"We'd like to help," Gordon said gently. He felt the river within him begin to run through his hand into the hapless little man. He knew that Grace was doing him the same service. When Mr Wynfor looked up again, his eyes were filled with tears.

"You're very kind," he said. "Very kind, indeed you are. But please don't concern yourselves. You're young, lives stretching ahead of you out of sight, isn't it, and the brightest of prospects? The very best of luck to you, but I'm not worth the trouble." A tremor passed through him. "You make your bed in this world, and then you have to lie in it. Not to worry, mind. It's only for life."

Since when did the meek inherit the Earth? Since NEVER.

Gordon tightened his grip. "Myrddin wants to see the world a better place before he dies," he said urgently, "a better place for the likes of you and us. Grace and I are going to do our best to help make that happen, and we'll do our best to help you now. We know that you're a good man, and that you'll help us in return."

Mr Wynfor shook his head, but he didn't let go of either hand. He seemed to be getting stronger. That might even have been a little flicker of hope that Gordon caught a glimpse of, behind his eyes.

"A better place for the likes of you, certainly, and well deserved I'm sure," he murmured. "Too late for me, I'm afraid - not worthy, see? Too weak, fallen from grace, given in to pressure, done some things ..." The shudder that ran through him threatened to shiver him into small pieces.

"The quality of Myrddin's mercy is not strained," Grace said. "We've been to Avalon. We know."

Wynfor stared at her. "You've *been* to Avalon?" he whispered. "The Tara Torque then, it still works? It's true – that there may be hope, after all?"

Gordon grinned at him. "Now there's a thought, Mr Wynfor. Indeed it is."

Chapter 33

Resurrection

Gordon's mobile rang. "That'll be my mum, worrying about us," he said apologetically. He dived into his pocket to take the call.

"Must be nice 'avin' someone to worry about you," Mr Wynfor muttered. He released their hands and recovered his composure. He was putting his recent narrow escape behind him, for now.

"From now on, you can rely on us to worry about you," Grace assured him.

"Hi, Mum. Yes, we're fine. OK, I'll ring you when we're ready to find you. Yes, of course. We will. OK, bye." He slipped the phone back into his pocket.

"I didn't expect the pleasure of your company again, so soon," Mr Wynfor said briskly, his barriers once more securely in place. "What did you come back for? Changed your mind about tryin' a wand, perhaps?"

"It's OK, he's gone," Zack said. Zack and Zoë had followed Wynfor's tormentor to see where he went from there, but now they were back the shop. "Marched straight down the Alley as if he owned it, and out through the arch."

"Who was that man, Mr Wynfor?" Gordon asked.

"Man? What man? Oh, *that* man - just a customer. Not very 'appy about his last purchase. 'E said the wand showed an unacceptable level of reluctance to do as it was told. He could 'ave just 'anded it over, of course. I'd 'ave been 'appy to exchange it. But that's not his way."

There was a quiver in his voice. "Instead he snapped it in front of me. Broke its back, useless to anyone now. 'Served it right', he said, 'not fit for purpose'." Wynfor's lower lip trembled. "I'd put a lot of work into that wand. Brought it up right, trained it personally."

"He doesn't seem like a very nice man," Grace prompted.

"Nice? No, 'nice' is not a word I've ever 'eard anyone use when speakin' of ... Not that anyone does speak of ... Let's say no more about it, eh? That would definitely be best."

"Where is your broken wand now, Mr Wynfor?" Grace asked.

"It's here, in the bin." He bent down and retrieved the broken pieces. "I'll give it a decent burial of course - last rites, add it to the other things on my conscience."

"May I hold it for a moment?" Grace asked.

"Yes of course. A break like that - terminal damage. At least it was quick. He could 'ave held a flame under it, burned it slowly, made me watch." He closed his eyes and shuddered again.

Grace took the pieces and turned them carefully in her hands. She saw how the snapped pieces slotted together and pushed them gently into place so that you couldn't see the join. "Hold it like that, will you?" she said to Gordon.

He took it from her carefully. As soon as he was holding it steady at both ends, she wrapped her right hand round the join and closed her eyes.

"There's no way," Mr Wynfor insisted. "There's no ... Oh, great heavens! No, no, I don't believe it."

A glow had surrounded Grace's hand. It shimmered and was spreading slowly along both halves of the wand. The shimmer reached Gordon's fingers and the brightness of the glow increased. Sparks began to shoot along its length. Back and forth, back and forth ...

The wand gave a sudden, violent shudder and began to hum, softly at first but increasing in volume until it sounded like the chord of C major on a cathedral organ. Mr Wynfor threw his head back and added a melodious G above it in a surprisingly pure tenor. It was a glorious fifth, to celebrate the reunion of the wand with its creator.

Smiling, Grace nodded to Gordon, who let go. She turned her hand over and opened it. The song subsided. The wand lay in her hand, contented and whole again. "I would not 'ave believed that," Mr Wynfor breathed, "'ad I not just seen it with my own eyes. I don't suppose, if I may ..." He held his hand out uncertainly.

"Of course," Grace said, handing it to him. "You have to be sure that it wasn't a trick, or a gimmick – like that Indian rope thing." Gordon laughed with delight. She really *was* amazing.

Mr Wynfor held it delicately between his thumb and the first two fingers of his right hand. He closed his eyes and began to wave it gently, as if conducting a wonderful piece of music. The strains of the Vienna Philharmonic Orchestra began to fill his shop. It was the opening of the Blue Danube Waltz, by Johann Strauss Junior.

The sound swelled as the piece developed. The harmonies were subtle and sweet, every instrument perfectly in tune. Then, just when you thought it couldn't be more perfect, the willowy figure of a nymph in flowing white sprang from the tip of the wand. She turned in the air in a weightless dance of points and pirouettes. Her arms waved like fronds of seaweed in the ebb and flow of a tide.

She was joined by another, and another, until there were nine, filling the shop with the wonder of their dance. Mr Wynfor brought the piece to a fading moment of perfect peace and stillness. The nymphs slipped back into the wand, their performance for the moment at an end.

He opened his eyes. "And that," he said, "was a bloody miracle if ever there was one." He handed the wand back to Grace. "It's yours now. Take it. It can never be anyone else's."

She took it uncertainly. "I wouldn't know what to do with it," she said. "And I can't walk around Chester with a wand in my hand. It's too big to go in my bag, and I haven't got any pockets."

Mr Wynfor laughed with delight. "Where 'ave you been all your life, Girl?" he said affectionately, "...walkin' round with a talent like that and knowin' nuthin' about wands!" He beamed. "That wand owes you its life and more. It couldn't even play the piano before. There's nuthin' that wand won't do for you. Not that you'd ever ask it to do anythin' untoward."

He shook his head vigorously. "No, no, of course you wouldn't. A much better home that wand's gone to and it knows it." He gazed affectionately at her. "You just tell it 'Stand down!' and it will secrete itself about your person. You won't know where it is, could be anywhere, doesn't matter. Then, if you feel the need of it, or you just want to get to know it better like, when you're on your own somewhere …"

Zoë looked thoughtful. Their lives had just got a little more complicated.

"You just say 'Wand to me!' Talent like yours, you could probably just think it. There's very few can do that nowadays, I don't mind tellin' you."

Wynfor had entirely recovered his good spirits. "Don't know what the world's coming to, both parents out at work all the hours God sends. Nobody's got time to teach their kids anythin' any more. Manners, morality, out the window. Where was I? Oh yes," - he shot Grace a gleeful glance - "…'wand-to-me!' and there it will be, in your 'and, ready to do the business."

Grace looked down at the wand nestling contentedly in her hand. "It does feel .. right," she said. The wand disappeared. "Oh wow!"

"It's not gone far," Mr Wynfor said smugly. "Go on, get it back. Have a little go."

The wand was suddenly back in her hand. She laughed with delight. "That's fantastic. Thank you so much, Mr Wynfor. As long as you're sure."

"Sure? Of course I'm sure. Never been so certain of anything in my whole life. Mind you, I 'aven't been certain of many things in my life. It's an uncertain world, and these are uncertain times."

He shook his head slightly, as if to clear it. "More important though, the wand's certain. It's a match made in 'eaven that is. Till death do you part, perish the thought. Long time to go yet, though, yes indeed."

"There's just one more thing, Mr Wynfor," Gordon said. "How will we know if you need our help again?"

"Bless the boy," Mr Wynfor muttered, throwing his eyes to Heaven. "Why did we 'ave to wait so long for 'im, eh? Tell me that! Why did we 'ave to wait for things to get in the right state they're in now?!"

He looked grim and resigned. "Don't you be worryin' about me, Boyo," he said. "I'm nuthin' and nobody. You've got far more important things to worry about than me."

"No, I haven't, Mr Wynfor," Gordon said, "You and people like you are the most important things I have to worry about. You're not 'nothing'. You're everything, and it's high time you inherited the earth."

Gordon was suddenly fierce. "People like that wand-breaker have had it for too long, and they're killing it. We need to give it back to the people who'll nurture it. People like you."

Mr Wynfor stared at him for a moment, and then as if on impulse stretched out his hand. "Will you shake my 'and?" he asked.

Gordon reached out and shook it. "Gladly!" he said.

The tears were back in the little man's eyes. "The wand will know," he said.

Chapter 34

High Noon

"Well," Zack said, as they walked through the arch and back across the row into Foregate Street. "That was an eventful 'alf 'our. Never a dull moment with you, is there? I've said it before ..."

"You had a Welsh lilt, then," Gordon pointed out, laughing. "Accents are catching, aren't they? You sounded just like Mr Wynfor."

"What a character!" Zoë said. "Straight out of Dickens. Come to think of it, that whole alley was straight out of Dickens - full of old curiosity shops."

"I take it from the phone-call that our well-coffeed mums are hitting the shops?" Grace said. Gordon nodded.

"Tell you what," Grace suggested. "They don't need us for the moment. Why don't we go into Grosvenor Park and find a quiet spot? I'm quite keen to start finding out about this wand."

It was a warm day - just right for a stroll in a pleasant park in pleasant company. It seemed like a great idea. They ambled down St John's Street, turned left past the Roman amphitheatre, and were in the park in five minutes.

It was a pleasant place, with tidy municipal flowerbeds, green open spaces and a number of mature trees. "Once the oaks in the dell start producing acorns," Gordon said, "we should plant a couple in this park." It seemed like a good place for the renewal of energy.

Zack and Zoë whizzed off to do a quick recce. The park was never very busy, and this morning seemed pretty typical. There was a jogger or two, a few mums with toddlers and push-chairs, and a pensioner on one of the benches enjoying a leisurely look at his newspaper. A couple strolled hand in hand with eyes only for each other.

Their Alter-Egos were back in seconds. "There's a pretty secluded spot over there with nobody in it at the moment," Zoë said. She pointed towards some tall trees and luxuriant bushes.

"Perfect," Grace said, and then shivered. She glanced up at the sky, but there were no clouds currently near the sun. "Funny," she muttered. "I suddenly got the chills then."

"Maybe somebody walked over your grave," Gordon said lightly, then remembered how he'd felt when Zack first introduced him to that expression. "It's what people say when ..."

"I know," Grace said. "I think it had more to do with who just walked into the park."

The park had many ways in and out. Four young people – two boys and two girls – had just entered it at the far end. Even at that distance their demeanour suggested they owned it. They stood for a moment sweeping haughty glances the length and breadth of the open space. Then their eyes converged on Gordon and Grace.

The taller of the two boys said something, and the other three laughed. With no particular hurry, they began walking straight towards them. Gordon used his bionic lens to zoom in on the advancing group.

The taller boy was slightly in the lead. As far as Gordon could judge, he was about sixteen. His skin was very pale, as if he spent most of his time away from natural light. His eyes were pale too, more grey than blue.

His nose was beakish, and held at an angle that suggested he was avoiding a bad smell at the level of the vulgar, whom he'd rather not be anywhere near. His mouth was thin and ... 'mean' was the word that popped into Gordon's head. The overall impression was that he was doing the ground a bloody great favour by walking on it.

"Todd Mortlake," Grace's voice sounded in his head. *"That was his father we saw in Wynfor's shop. He's been sent to test us. He thinks it'll be no contest."*

"Whoah," Zack growled. Gordon grinned. *"Easy, Tiger,"* he telepathed. That was the advice Zack had given him, the last time a group tried testing him.

Just behind Todd was the other boy. Shorter and wider, he was probably the same age. His hair was thick and black and flopped low over his forehead, giving the impression he was more about brawn than brains. Dark brown eyes, beetle-browed, nose somewhat flattened having been broken at least once, possibly in the front row of a scrum.

"Carter Cromwell," Grace said, *"named after Charles Carter, a famous American stage magician. His family claim direct descent from Oliver and indirect descent from Thomas."*

"He looks like he may have inherited some of the family traits," Zack muttered. Zack's loins were definitely girded for battle! The oncoming quartet had already covered almost half the distance between them.

Gordon concentrated on the girls. *"Oh my God,"* Grace giggled, *"you're not going to believe their names."*

"Come on," Gordon said. *"We don't want them to think we're unreasonable. Let's meet them half way."*

He and Grace began walking towards them. Out of the blue he had another thought and looked at his watch. It WAS! One minute to 12 p.m..

High Noon.

"Go on, then, test my credibility," Gordon said. They were rapidly narrowing the gap. His bionic zoom was no longer necessary.

"The one nearest to Todd is Petronilla Aquitaine," Grace said. *"She gets Petra, or Tron sometimes."*

Zoë snorted. "How about 'Nil'?" she suggested. There really was very little of her. She was almost as tall as Todd and pencil-thin, skin and bone really. Her knees stuck out like knots, and her eyes seemed unnaturally large in that skeletal face. She looked anorexic, haunted. You'd wonder she had the strength to walk around, much less be a threat to anyone.

"Looks can be deceptive," Grace reminded them all. *"The other one is Astrid Aragon."*

"Don't tell me," Zack said. "Their families trace their ancestry to European royalty."

Grace grinned. "What else?"

Astrid was trotting along beside Carter. She was shorter and wider than he was by roughly the same number of inches. Gordon's dad would have said she'd been at the back of the queue when looks were given out, but she looked as though she could pack a punch. Behind those darting eyes, Gordon thought he detected barely suppressed rage.

"What do you think, guys?" he asked the others. "Is this the 'A' team?"

"No way," Zack muttered. "All the same, keep your wits about you."

The two groups came to a halt about ten feet from one another. Gordon folded his arms and smiled, well aware of the effect this normally had on his opposition. The leader of this latest team looked down on him in every sense. They may have belonged to the same species, but they came from very different worlds.

"Well, well, *well*," he sneered, "the latest claimant to the title of 'Myrddin's Heir', whatever that's supposed to mean." He looked Gordon up and down. "Doesn't look like a mega-wizard to me. Looks more like something that's been dragged up in a slum and parcelled out to the nearest rag-tag-and-bobtail comprehensive."

Gordon's expression didn't change. "'Well, well, *well*'?" he repeated. "Have you got any verbal mannerisms of your own, Todd?" he asked, with an air of genuine enquiry. "Or do you copy your father in everything?"

The expression on all four faces changed. Astrid's eyes narrowed into slits. Petronilla's eyebrows went up in surprise, making her eyes look even more as if they had once belonged to a bush-baby. Carter glanced up at his leader, and a flicker of uncertainty crossed his face.

Todd's lips wrinkled back in a wary sneer. "What could a gutter-rat like you possibly know about my father?"

"Oh, you can tell quite a lot about fathers from the way their children behave. Judgemental, dismissive, arrogant, ignorant, supercilious, deeply prejudiced, spiteful, cruel. How am I doing?"

"How DARE you!" Todd snarled. "We're going to show you what your proper place in the scheme of things is, you little worm. It's time you learned to respect your elders and betters!"

Zack and Zoë took up positions on either side of the delegation. The four envoys clearly had no idea they were there. It would have been funny, if it hadn't been pathetic.

"WE?" Gordon repeated innocently. "Why is it 'we', Todd? Was the job of disciplining a couple of gutter-rats from the local 'rag-tag-and-bobtail comprehensive' judged too big for you to handle on your own?"

His face was suffused with sorrow and sympathy. "Doesn't Mortlake Senior have much confidence in his son? Does he doubt your ability to take care of family business?"

A muscle in Todd's right cheek began to twitch. *"You hit the nail right on the head there,"* Grace telepathed. *"He's going to try a muscle-cramping curse on you."*

"If he pulls a wand, take it off him," Gordon beamed to Zack.

A second later the words "Wand-to-me!" hissed through Todd's gritted teeth. He whipped up his right hand, ready to direct his curse. A smooth, slim stick with a diamond tip leapt into it. A microsecond after that, the wand was apparently floating in mid-air. Zack had it in his left hand, and Todd had doubled over gasping for breath.

Zack had punched him in the solar plexus, just for good measure. The punch hadn't been in the brief, but Zack used his initiative from time to time.

Gordon held his hand up and the wand whizzed over to him. He caught it cleanly, folded his hand around it, and introduced himself. "This is not a happy wand," he told Todd. "Not surprising really. Nobody would mistake you for 'The Happy Wanderer'."

"GET HIM!!" Todd wheezed. He was too busy catching his breath to do it himself. Up came two of the three other wand-hands Todd thought he had at his disposal. Curiously, Carter hesitated ...

Zoë snatched Petronilla's and Astrid's wands before their fingers had time to wrap round them. She transferred them to Grace in the twinkling of an eye. Grace's hands were clasped innocently behind her back. It happened so quickly that Petronilla and Astrid had no idea where their wands were. It was quite comical the way their jaws dropped simultaneously. They whirled round looking for them. Grace and Gordon hadn't moved.

"Wand-to-**me**, NOW!" Petronilla shrieked, holding out her hand.

"Wand, get BACK here!" Astrid growled menacingly. She curled the chubby fingers on her right fist.

"They don't want to," Grace telepathed. *"They'd rather stay with me."*

"Try telling them to stand down," Gordon thought back. Meanwhile, Carter had caught his eye, and the briefest of winks told him two things. Master Cromwell had no intention of drawing his wand. Furthermore, he wouldn't be letting the other three know he still had it.

Grace's hands were now hanging by her sides. They were visibly empty. A little smile of satisfaction played with her lips. Having three happy wands contentedly secreted about her person felt nice.

"Give it back NOW!" Todd demanded. His eyes were on the wand still nestling in Gordon's hand. There was a quiver in his voice. Gordon could almost smell his fear.

"I didn't hear the magic word," he said.

Todd drew in a shuddering breath. "Give it back," he said slowly, "or my father will make you wish you had never been born."

"He's terrified of his father, and of what he'll do to him if he goes home without his wand," Grace told Gordon.

"Here's what we'll do, Todd," Gordon said. "The wand chooses the wizard, right? Why don't we let the wand choose?" He opened his hand. The wand lay there. "Call it."

Todd stared at Gordon, then at the wand in his open palm. They could see his jaw muscles grinding. Gordon waited, his face expressionless, his eyes fixed on Todd.

"Wand-to-me!" Todd commanded suddenly. He stretched out his open right hand in an imperious gesture. Gordon felt the wand shiver, but it stayed where it was.

"Wand-to-**me**, NOW, you TRAITOR!" Todd yelled. This time his desperation was evident. The wand didn't even flinch. Then it wasn't in Gordon's hand any more.

"I'll deck him," Astrid rumbled, deciding she'd resort to more traditional methods. She ducked her head behind her massive fists and danced forward on the balls of her feet. She was quite agile for such a solid lass. An impressive right hook streaked towards Gordon's exposed jaw ...

It never got there.

The fist stopped in mid-air about a foot from his face. Astrid spun round, and the punch got going again. It still had all her weight behind it, but now it was travelling in the opposite direction, while the rest of her body was arcing over an invisible obstacle.

The obstacle seemed suddenly to gain in height while she was curving over it. She flipped in mid-air and landed flat on her back with a smack that knocked all the wind out of her sails. A considerable amount of wind it was too.

"Looks can be deceiving," Grace told her, "but not in your case." Gordon never moved. He ignored Astrid completely. His eyes had never left Todd's face.

"Do you think your wand knew you were planning to snap it and put all the blame on Wynfor?" he asked. Todd's twitches had multiplied, and he seemed close to tears. Gordon began to feel sorry for him. What must it be like to have a father like that? What must it be like to have to face him with an admission of failure?

He addressed them all. "This is what you do," he told them. "You go together to Todd's father. You tell him that you all did your best. Tell him Todd took the lead and did everything he'd been told to do, but it was no contest. We were too strong for you."

His eyes raked round them all. "Astrid Aragon, Petronilla Aquitaine, Carter Cromwell, tell him that I knew all your names. Tell him your wands deserted you for me, and there was absolutely nothing you could do."

Astrid was picking herself up. Petronilla kept darting glances at Todd. He was rooted to the spot and speechless. Carter kept his eyes on Gordon. He didn't move a muscle.

"Tell him that if he has anything he wishes to discuss with me, I will be happy to meet him personally at a place and time of his choosing."

"WHOAH! Are you sure about that last bit?" Zack said, suddenly alarmed.

"*Yes I am,*" Gordon beamed back. "*I don't know why, but I am.*"

"Fair enough," Zack said. Gordon had apparently undergone a growth burst that morning. Given the circumstances, it was probably just as well.

Todd turned and began striding back the way he had come. Petronilla scurried to catch up with him. Carter waited for Astrid to get moving and then fell into step beside her. Throughout the encounter he hadn't uttered a word.

They had gone about twenty yards when Gordon was suddenly in front of them again. Todd gasped and stopped. Petronilla stumbled against him and stopped too. Astrid and Carter drew level. All four waited in a silent line, watching Gordon the way one might watch a lethally venomous snake.

"Tell him if he ever sends anyone else to do his dirty work, he needn't worry about finding me again, because I will find *him*. I don't like bullies."

And then he wasn't in front of them anymore. They spun round. He was standing just where they had left him.

"Gordon Bennett!" Carter thought grimly.

Exactly.

The retreating figures disappeared through the gate at the far end. "What will we do with four wands?" Grace asked nobody in particular.

"They're going to come in handy," Gordon said.

"OOH!" Zoë breathed.

"You've just been to the future, haven't you?" Grace said to her. Zoë's eyes were shining. She was looking at Gordon with undisguised admiration.

"Keep it as a surprise," he said, winking at her.

"Keep it as a surprise from ME?!" Grace said incredulously. "You've got to be ... HEY! – You've hidden it! I can't find it in your head."

"I just learned how to keep a secret," Gordon said. The technique was so simple it had come as a real surprise. It wasn't the only thing he'd learned, while he'd been inside Octavius Mortlake's brain.

With one accord, they turned and headed back to the city centre. It was time they retrieved their mums. Grace was coming to terms with the fact that Gordon and Zoë knew something that she and Zack didn't. She was actually looking forward to finding out what the secret was!

She'd never had that feeling before. What with that and the fact that she was now sheltering three wands (she could feel their little hearts beating), life had just got even more interesting.

"I'm puzzled about Carter Cromwell," Zack said. "He didn't draw his wand, and he didn't try to attack us."

"That's because he's on our side," Gordon told him.

Chapter 35

Preparing The Ground

Shortly after Gordon and his mum had lugged the shopping from the car to the house, Grace got in touch. He'd been expecting it. There was no way Zoë could keep a secret from Grace for long.

She was beside herself with excitement! They discussed it, and agreed to arrange a rendezvous at his house the following morning. She would contact Miranda and he would contact Nick.

Miranda and Nick's parents were to be told, for the moment, that they had a poetry project for English and wanted to work on it together. Gordon's mum would do the collecting, around 10.30 a.m.. They'd have lunch at Gordon's. Edith would bring them home, after they'd finished the project.

Miranda and Nick were not to be told yet what the real reason was for them getting together. Tomorrow morning would be soon enough, when Gordon and Grace would be on hand to help them cope.

Gordon sat his mum and dad down Saturday evening and told them. They hadn't signed up for any of it, of course, other than by having what they fondly imagined would be a normal child.

"Oh my giddy aunt," his dad said heavily. "Are you sure?"

Gordon nodded. "I'm certain. I should have realised ages ago. But to be fair, I haven't really had anything to do with witches and wizards anywhere near my own age." He looked from one parent to another. "So far it's been more about ghosts, gods and fairies than witches and wizards. Even though Myrddin told me I was his heir, it still didn't really click."

Victor gave a massive sigh. "So not only am I contending with reprobates, thugs and criminals of every description, there's a whole other dimension of wicked witchcraft and wizardry out there, probably pulling a lot of the strings."

Gordon smiled bravely. "Yes, but look who you've got on your side."

His dad nodded grimly. "I'm the first to admit that's a really big plus, Son. But I worry for you, and so does your mum." Edith shuddered. If anything terrible were to happen to Gordon, she didn't know how she would be able to cope. Impulsively Gordon gave her a hug.

"I've got Myrddin on my side, Mum, don't forget. I wouldn't be much use to him if anything terrible happened to me, now would I?" Edith's eyes filled as she hugged him back. She was getting used to the fact that he could read her mind now.

"No, of course not, Darling." She didn't remind him that Gods had been known to sacrifice their heirs, supposedly for the greater good of mankind.

Gordon grimaced. "This is a steep curve I'm on now," he said. "But the dreams were a big clue. The dreams should have made me realise."

Edith readily agreed to do all the ferrying tomorrow. What Angela would say when she found out, she had no idea. Edith didn't know anything about Nick's father, she now realised. Maybe Angela knew more than she'd ever let on. It's not something you can really talk about. And Miranda's parents? How would they take it?

Oh well. '*Qué será, será.*'

Chapter 36

Breaking It Gently

The following morning Gordon made preparations. He carried a couple of empty wooden boxes out of their garage into the rear garden and placed them close to the fence. He put some empty cans and plastic containers on them. He checked the sight-lines to make certain that that part of their garden wasn't overlooked.

His mum was back around 11 a.m. with a car full of excited children. They took their orange juice and chocolate biscuits into the garden. Edith and Victor left them to it.

"OK," said Miranda. She looked at the boxes apparently set up for some kind of target practice. She wouldn't have thought that was Gordon's thing. "What's going on?"

"We're all agog," Nick said jovially. Whatever it was, he was looking forward to it.

"*You start,*" Grace telepathed to Gordon. She stood where she could watch Miranda's face.

"You know you're our best friends," Gordon began. "But there's something about us that we've never told you. It's something only our parents know."

Nick's face fell. "Why are you telling us now?" he asked. He was worried that some awful secret was going to spoil things. Grace's heart went out to him, even though she knew he wouldn't be worried for long. At least, she hoped not.

"We're telling you now because of something that happened yesterday. Grace and I met some people. As a result we came into possession of certain ... artefacts. It made me realise something I should have spotted a long time ago."

He looked from Nick to Miranda and saw the apprehension on their faces. "I discussed it with Grace, and we agreed it would be a good idea to get together this morning and put our cards on the table."

There was a pregnant pause. "Well," Miranda prompted, "spit it out!"

Grace grabbed Miranda's hands and looked her full in the face. "There's no easy way of saying this. You're a witch, Miranda."

Miranda snatched her hands away and jumped back. "You said I was your best friend!" she cried out, the tears blurring her vision.

"You *are* my best friend, apart from Zoë, my best friend in the whole world."

"Then how could you say such a thing to me?!"

"Because it's true, and because it takes one to know one."

Miranda wiped her eyes with the back of her hand and stared at her friend. "What do you mean?"

Grace gave her a bittersweet smile. "We're *both* witches. I've always known I was a witch, but I thought it was just me. Then I met Gordon, and things really started happening. Yesterday, we realised that you had to be a witch too."

"And you, Nick, have to be a wizard, the same as me," Gordon said. "Well, maybe not quite the same as me."

"Thank God for that," Nick interrupted feelingly. "I thought for a minute I was going to be left out. But what does it mean? How do you know?"

Gordon grinned at him. "How do I know what? – that I'm a wizard, or that you are?"

"Both," Nick said. "No, wait, you first. How do you ... WHOAH!" (He'd picked that exclamation up from Gordon). His eyes widened. "All those bullies you've sorted out over the years. I never knew how you managed it. Is it because you're a - you know," - he dropped his voice to a conspiratorial whisper - "a wizard?"

Gordon nodded.

"I *knew* it," Nick said triumphantly. "I knew there was something different about you. You always denied it."

Gordon shrugged. "I had to, Nick. Zack and I agreed it'd be best if I pretended I was just like everyone else."

"Who's Zack?" Miranda asked. The jury was still out as far as she was concerned. This could be some weird game Gordon and Grace were playing. This could be like that time when Grace went all funny on her: sounding and acting differently for a while before going back to normal.

"His imaginary friend," Nick explained. "He had an imaginary friend when he was only ... OH!" It was to be a morning of realisations.

"WHAT?" Miranda asked him.

"When Gordon first came to nursery class, these three boys tried to bully us. One of them asked Gordon if he'd brought his imaginary friend with him, then he jumped about a foot in the air, and Gordon said "What's the matter Tom? Did my imaginary friend blow in your ear?"

"See?!" Gordon laughed. "I'm not the only one with a good memory."

"SO?" Miranda said, a bit impatiently. She was a bit like Gordon's dad - she wanted proof!

"He *was* with you," Nick breathed. "He *did* blow in his ear. You didn't just imagine him."

"No I didn't," Gordon agreed. He's always been with me. He's here now."

"What is he, a spirit?" Nick asked. "Do you get one if you're a wizard? And if so, and I'm a wizard as well, why haven't I got one? Harry Potter didn't have one. None of those other witches and wizards had one."

"SLOW DOWN!" Miranda said. "Let me get this. Gordon is a wizard, and he's got a ... What have you got?"

"We're not quite certain," Gordon told her. Myrddin calls them our 'guardian angels.'"

"STOP RIGHT THERE!" Miranda commanded. "Who's 'we'? Who's 'Myrddin'? You said 'our guardian angels'. There's more than one?"

"The 'we' is Gordon and me," Grace said quietly. "The other guardian angel is mine. Her name is Zoë."

"Myrddin is the most powerful wizard our two worlds have ever known," Gordon told her. "His names are many, but the power is one. You're probably familiar with his English name – Merlin."

"Is Zoë here too?" Miranda wanted to know. Let's have some order here. First things first. Grace nodded. "OK," Miranda said. "Now I'm not doubting you or anything ..."

"No, of course not," Grace said evenly. "But you'd like her to show herself in some way – because obviously you can't see her."

Miranda folded her arms. "Wouldn't you, in my shoes?"

"Blessèd are they that have not seen," Zack murmured.

"I just knew you were going to say that," Gordon told him.

"OK," Miranda said. She rubbed her ear and exchanged a speculative glance with Nick. "So you each have a guardian angel." The demonstration had been simultaneous. Zoë and Zack took up position and blew in unison on the count of three. "That's pretty amazing, but does it have anything to do with me being a witch?"

"Not as such," Grace said. "It was the dreams that told us – once we started to put two and two together." She'd seen Gordon was right as soon as he'd made her think about it. "It's one thing to dream about somebody; it's quite another for the person you're dreaming about to have the identical dream at the same time in every particular."

Gordon and Grace's paths crossing had been the catalyst. "Since Zoë and I met Gordon and Zack, we've started dream-travelling to different places together. We just assumed we could do it because of our special powers."

"Because you're a witch and a wizard, you mean?" Nick interrupted. He wanted to be sure he was keeping up.

"Yes," Gordon said. "At least, we think 'yes'. But there may be another reason why our powers are as 'special' as they are. We won't go into that now." He looked from one to the other. "We honestly don't know if other witches and wizards can do it or not. We've got so much to learn."

He looked thoughtful and excited at the same time. Learning was his favourite thing.

"We've only just found out that there *are* other witches and wizards. There seem to be different sides to the power. Or maybe there are just different stages of development. There are lots of 'maybe's'. It was that that started me thinking."

"Thinking what?" Nick wanted to know.

"That if you and Miranda could travel in our dreams with us, you must have some kind of special power too. And then I thought about Polly, and the treasure chest."

He transferred his attention to Miranda. "You must have noticed that you happened to write a story about being invited to a place you'd never been. In the story, you were taken up to 'the big hoos' in a trap pulled by a gorgeous black pony called Polly."

He grinned at her. "And hey presto, you're invited to that very place, and your aunt has sent you a gorgeous black pony called Polly for your birthday! What's the betting that when you and Grace get there this summer you're met by a guy called Duncan?" His eyes twinkled. "I've got a feeling the inside of that house will be strangely familiar."

Miranda sat down with a thump on the freshly cut grass. Victor had not wasted his time while Edith and Gordon had been in Chester the day before. "It's been scaring me," she admitted. "I keep seeing it - the outside and the inside. I see the sweep of the main staircase, the long corridors and the room Grace and I are going to share. There's a narrow flight of stairs going up to my uncle's workshop and observatory."

"The stairs you're never to go up," Grace added. "But you don't need to, because of the secret corridor behind a panel in our bedroom. I've been there too, but I can't remember when."

Miranda stared at her. "Oh my God!" she said. "It's true! We *are* a couple of witches."

"That may have been the dream that none of us can remember," Gordon added. "That bunch of old keys turned up in Grace's pocket. One of them unlocked the treasure chest Nick dug up in that dell in Wales. We each keep getting snatches of it."

"YES," Nick said. He joined Miranda on the grass, his eyes lit up by the wonder of it. "I was at a space academy, training to be a starship pilot." He looked up at Gordon. "You were there! You had a Vulcan with you. His name was Mr Zack."

Gordon nodded. "Something did its best to wipe that dream from all our minds. We were all in it together at one stage, I think."

"The starship *Velociraptor*," Nick said. "A treasure chest."

"Uncle Fergus," Miranda whispered. "What's going on? Why did I say that?"

Gordon turned his attention to Nick. "In year 7, you wrote a story about Francis Drake hunting down a Spanish treasure ship. Then recently you had a dream about finding a treasure chest hidden by Sir Edward Kitchin, Drake's cabin boy."

"That's right," Nick exclaimed excitedly. "I hadn't remembered that bit! How did you know that? Oh sorry," he grinned shamefacedly. "You're a wizard; I keep forgetting."

"You're a wizard too," Gordon said gently. "How come that rainbow came down in that very spot in the dell? Who had been wishing he could find a pirate's treasure chest?" He spread out his hands. "And suddenly there's one there, at the end of the rainbow? Give me a break! You said yourself: 'What are the chances?' I don't know why it's taken me so long to realise."

He grinned at them both. "Welcome to the club," he said. "We don't have jackets, but it's early days."

Nick and Miranda looked at one another. Their worlds had just been turned inside out – in a manner of speaking. "So what happens next?" Miranda asked.

"We thought," Grace said, "that you might like to try out some wands we happened to have got hold of yesterday."

Chapter 37

The Proof Of The Pudding

"Yeah!" said Nick, before being overtaken by understandable self-doubt. "Only don't expect me to be brilliant at it or anything."

"We're all complete novices," Gordon said. "When we went shopping in Chester yesterday, we didn't know we were going to be coming home with magic wands."

"Where did you get them," Miranda asked, "the Disney shop?" Grace looked reprovingly at her. Miranda giggled. "Well you have to laugh, don't you?" she said in her own defence. "You'd cry otherwise."

"For now, it doesn't matter where we got them, or how we got them," Gordon said. "Let's find out if two of them will work for you."

"OK," Nick said, rubbing his hands eagerly. "Where are they?"

Gordon looked at Grace and nodded. Three wands appeared in her right hand, as if by magic. When Miranda and Nick had finished gaping, they noticed that Gordon was holding one as well. Grace put two on the grass and stood back. The wands that she and Gordon were holding disappeared again.

"How did you do that?" Nick said, admiringly. "That's better than Paul Daniels that is."

"We'll soon show you," Gordon said, "provided this next bit works."

"We need to find out if these wands are willing to choose you," Grace said. "And if they have a preference."

"They're bound to prefer Miranda over me," Nick said. "It stands to reason." He couldn't help being under her spell. He was growing up.

"No they're not, and no it doesn't," Miranda said stoutly. "What do we know about wands and how they make choices? One wand might go for a quirky, strong-willed girl like me, and another might go for a kind and sensitive boy like you."

Nick looked down and blushed to the roots of his hair.

"Kneel down together," Gordon suggested. "Hold one of your hands over the wands."

They did as they were told. Immediately both wands started jiggling about in excitement, like little dogs anticipating a walk. That was a good sign.

"Now concentrate on the wands. See if there is anything that draws you to one rather than the other. Open your hearts and beam your thoughts to them."

Miranda stared at both wands, and then gave a little gasp of recognition. Nick did exactly the same. You could tell they weren't influencing each other's behaviour. It looked as though each had suddenly forgotten that the other was there. Every fibre of their being, every particle of their attention, was focused on the wands beneath their hands.

Gordon could feel the energy. The hair went up on the back of his neck. Miranda's and Nick's eyes snapped shut at the same time. Nothing else existed for them at that moment. The wands rose together an inch or two off the ground, straining towards the open palms.

"Now say 'Wand-to-me'," Gordon said softly.

"Wand-to-me!" they said simultaneously.

They opened their eyes and shouted for joy. Each held a contented wand in the palm of their chosen hand.

"What now?" Nick asked. His eyes were shining. He was ready for anything. The urge to give his new wand a wave was almost irresistible, but he was scared he might wreck Gordon's garden.

"Lesson two," Grace replied, "which incidentally is as far as we've got. Tell it to stand down."

Nick held the wand in front of his face so that they could look at one another. "Stand down! – please," he added, out of force of habit. The wand had already disappeared, but using the magic word wouldn't have done any harm. It might conceivably have done some good: nobody likes being taken for granted.

He looked at Grace and Gordon, suddenly bereft. "Where's it gone?!"

"It's secreted about your person," Gordon told him. "You won't know where it is, could be anywhere, doesn't matter." He said that last bit with a trace of Welsh accent.

Miranda was still cradling hers, as if she didn't want to let it go. "It's so wonderful," she murmured. Impulsively, she gave it a little kiss before telling it to stand down. It was gone in an eye-twinkle.

She waited a couple of seconds.

"Wand-to-me!" she said again, wanting to be absolutely sure. There it was, nestling in her hand again. "THAT IS ... something else," she muttered. "Oh my God, my very own magic wand." A pony **and** a magic wand! What more could a girl want?

"Yesterday, a bad wizard murdered his wand by snapping it," Gordon told Nick and Miranda. "Grace brought it back to life."

"I *said* you had healing hands," Miranda exclaimed triumphantly. "You always denied it. My wrist was smashed on my birthday, wasn't it? You mended it in seconds!"

Grace looked shamefaced. "I had to deny it," she said. "I couldn't let that riding instructor think I was some kind of miracle-worker."

"The queue would stretch from here to Lourdes," Gordon said, quoting his dad. "Anyway, the point is that after she'd brought it back to life it was much stronger. The wand-master said it couldn't play the piano before. Now it can replicate a symphony orchestra and a company of ballet dancers, all at the same time."

"Wow!" Miranda blurted out. "Could it do *Take That* live at the City of Manchester Stadium?"

"The point is," said Gordon again, a little more firmly, "Grace was able to make it more powerful by holding it and beaming power into it."

"You were holding it as well," Grace pointed out.

"OK, so I think we should find out what your wands can do now." He pointed at his little practice range. "Then we'll see if Grace and I can make any difference to their level of performance."

Miranda and Nick looked at one another and nodded. That seemed fair enough. They took up positions about twenty feet from the target. "Your wands speak whatever you speak," Gordon said, "which saves you having to learn some kind of dog-Latin."

Nick blew through his lips in a happy-pony expression of relief. Miranda wasn't sure which she would have preferred, but she had to admit it made life easier not having to worry about the difference between leviOsa and levioSAR.

"Miranda, why don't you take the can on the left? Nick, you take the squeegee bottle on the right. See if you can knock them off from here."

Miranda focused on the can and imagined it flying backwards off the box. "Strike!" she said, bringing the wand down with a flourish. The can obligingly pinged off the box and collided with the fence behind it. She blew on the end of the wand and looked round at the others in triumph.

"Don't be nervous, Nick," Grace said encouragingly. "You can do it. We know you can."

Nick grimaced. He was apparently the only one who wasn't too sure. Fear of failure – he'd struggled with it all his life. Maybe the wand would lend him a bit of confidence. He glanced at the target and pointed his wand in its general direction. "Strike!" he said half-heartedly.

Even so, the wand did its best. A little chip of wood flew off the fence panel, just to the right of the squeegee bottle and up a bit. "SEE?" he said, resignation and defeat written all over him.

"That was terrific!" Gordon said. "You saw that chip of wood! Now imagine you're Special Forces. You've got a laser beam trained on the bottle. Can you see that red dot, right over its heart? Aim the wand and squeeze the trigger."

Nick closed one eye and sighted his shot along the barrel of the wand. "Bang!" he said. The wand obligingly let out a crack like an air gun and the squeegee bottle smashed into the fence.

Gordon ran over to it and brought it back. There was a small round hole in it. Nick's shot had gone right through the middle. "Dead-Eye Nick," Gordon said. Miranda gave him a little round of applause. Nick glowed and cheered up perceptibly.

"Right," Gordon said briskly. "Now hold out your wand Nick. Keep hold of it." Nick did as he was told. Grace and Gordon each wrapped a hand round its remaining length and closed their eyes. Nick tightened his grip and did the same.

A glow spread outwards from Grace's hand. It grew brighter as it reached Gordon's and then washed over Nick's. Nick shivered, but kept his eyes shut. He concentrated on the feeling of the wand getting warmer in his hand.

He heard the sound first from far off - like a high-speed train. Nearer and nearer it came until he imagined a Virgin Express was actually hurtling through the garden. He felt the displacement of air pushing him backwards and mussing his hair.

He opened his eyes to see Grace and Gordon letting go. The sound began to recede as rapidly as it had approached. The door in the French windows behind them banged open and Victor hurtled out.

"What in God's name was THAT!?" he exclaimed. He scanned the sky for a UFO, or at the very least a low-flying police helicopter.

"It's OK Dad, sorry!" Gordon said apologetically. "We didn't know that was going to happen."

His dad looked mystified and annoyed at the same time. "It's not going to happen again, is it?"

Grace and Gordon looked at each other. Miranda and Nick looked diplomatically away. "It might happen again," Gordon admitted, "but we'll be ready for it next time."

Victor's voice took on a pleading tone. "Keep it down if you can, Son. The whole house shook. We don't want any of the neighbours reporting an earthquake." Shaking his head slightly, he turned and went back into the house.

"What are we going to do now?" Grace asked, giggling.

"OK, next time, when it starts to happen, we'll relax and control the flow a bit. We'll take a bit longer." She nodded agreement and Miranda struck the pose. Having seen what happened last time, Miranda decided to close her eyes in advance. She didn't see Grace and Gordon grasp her wand, but she felt the warmth spreading up from her hand. It suffused her whole body with its energy. Maybe it wasn't just the wand that was getting a power-boost.

This time the sound began like the moaning feedback of an electric guitar plugged into a powerful amplifier. It grew slowly, controlled but intense. The upper harmonics began to kick in ...

And suddenly she was staring at the roof of Buckingham Palace. Brian May was standing there alone, with big hair and flowing clothes, like some Old Testament prophet. He had his head bent over a gorgeous guitar, and was caressing the National Anthem out of it. Somewhere, unseen, a full orchestra was miraculously adding its layers of sweet sound.

Grace and Gordon must have let go, because too soon it faded - before any of the neighbours had time to tell them to turn it down. Miranda opened her eyes, and there were tears in them. Gordon and Grace were staring at each other in wonder.

"I've never had this feeling before," Nick admitted. His chest swelled and he looked at his arms as if seeing them for the first time. I feel like I could do anything." He ran three steps and launched himself into the air. Luckily Gordon's elm tree got in the way. Otherwise he would have been ploughing up some neighbour's turf.

"WHOOHOO!" they heard him shout from somewhere amongst its branches. He was completely hidden by its dense foliage. They ran over to it and looked up. He was twenty feet off the ground!

"EASY, Nick," Gordon called up to him. "It'll take a bit of getting used to." He had some sympathy though. He remembered how far up in the air he'd gone after planting his acorn in the dell. "Can you get down?"

"Does the Pope have a balcony?" Nick called back. This was suddenly a different boy. They saw him swish and flick. "Float!" he said, then "WHEEE!" They could see him hovering, apparently weightless.

"Featherlight!" he commanded, and began to drift slowly down through the still, warm air. "Stand down," he said, as his feet touched the ground. He strolled out from under the tree, grinning broadly. "I think I'm getting the hang of it."

They walked back to where Gordon had replaced the targets on the top of the boxes. "Let's see if there's any difference in the wands' performance," he said. "Be pretty careful. They could be a lot stronger."

Nick and Miranda stood in the same spots. They were both aware of how different it felt this time. They'd best be pretty careful.

"Try saying "wand-to-me" under your breath," Gordon suggested. Their wands leapt into their hands on full alert. "Remember," he said again, "we're being careful."

"STRIKE!" they said simultaneously, pointing their wands at the target.

Cans, plastic bottles and the two wooden boxes exploded in a deconstructing blast similar to a serious gas explosion. All four children crouched instinctively, arms wrapped round their heads in a shower of descending debris. They weren't hurt. None of the pieces was bigger than a matchstick.

The French doors flew open. "IN, NOW, ALL OF YOU!" Victor shouted. All along their street people were coming out of their houses, trying to see which one had just had the back blown out.

Nobody had told the wands to be careful.

Chapter 38

A Wand Can Work Wonders

Nick didn't tell his mum at first. He wanted to find out what being a real wizard with his very own wand actually meant, before he said anything. And find out he did, with surprising speed and assurance.

He led the way when it came to finding out what his wand could do. He was the first to discover that the command 'Power on!' activated the wand without having to hold it. That meant you had both hands free, which was really handy.

Against all the odds, Nick discovered he had a real flair for wizardry. His initial leap into the tree followed by his defiance of gravity and his ability to float were fair indications of unusual aptitude. And that was only the beginning - in more ways than one.

His mum had got him a punchbag two Christmases ago - a male relative had thought it might help toughen him up a bit. They'd screwed a big hook into a joist in his bedroom ceiling and hung it up. Nick had not made much progress. He'd tried punching it for a while, but he didn't know if he was doing it right and it hurt his hands.

So his mum had got him some boxing gloves. He danced around the punchbag for a while after that. He ducked and weaved, fooling no-one, least of all himself. The whole exercise seemed futile. The bag hadn't done anything to him. More significantly, it couldn't hit him back.

He'd woken up in the middle of the night a few times and been terrified there was someone in his room, after which, his mum gave it up as a bad job. She took the punchbag down and tucked it away in the corner of his wardrobe. That's where it had been ever since.

He got it out again now, and hung it up. Once he'd powered on and said 'Lift!' he found it weighed almost nothing. He concentrated on his fists, muttered 'Punch!' and hit it. The bag leapt away from him. It swung and juddered like a mad thing. His fist had buried itself, and it hadn't hurt at all.

So he got stuck in.

His mum came running up the stairs. What was making that tremendous thudding noise? She could feel the shockwaves all over the house. She was pleased as well as surprised. Maybe the punchbag hadn't been such a waste of money after all.

He moved on to manoeuvres. He developed commands like 'Sway', 'Duck', 'Whirl', 'Block', 'Twist', 'Turn' 'Kick', 'Weave', 'Shove' and 'Throw'. He found that in each case he was much faster, stronger and more agile than he would ever have believed possible. Within a couple of days, his mushrooming methods of attacking his punchbag were threatening to wreck his bedroom and demolish the ceiling.

Angela parked her car on the driveway and moved the punchbag into the garage. Nick rediscovered an old weight-training bench and some weights in there that had belonged to his dad. He pulled them out, got his back on the bench under the bar, muttered 'Lift!' and bench-pressed 60 kilos straight off! The unarmed combat sessions got really serious after that.

Some of his carefully-saved pocket-money went on a few more items of basic equipment, and the garage became a power gym. He spent at least an hour a day in there after school, and in no time he was looking a lot more solid. Maybe there was some wand-assisted muscle-building going on as well. He needed all of his latest blazer now, and more.

Obviously his mum couldn't fail to notice these dramatic changes in his demeanour, appetite and daily routine. He expected her to ask him about it. He'd even worked out what he might say when she did.

Curiously, she said nothing. He supposed she was pleased to see him standing on his own two feet at last.

Gordon was a bit worried that Nick might be overdoing it, but he could understand his best friend's new-found enthusiasm. It must have been so liberating finally to climb out of that fear pit. He was certainly coping a lot better with the here and now bit.

A couple of weeks after that fateful Sunday – Monday, 30th May, for those who like to keep track of these things – Grace, Gordon, Nick and Miranda were as usual among the first to enter the form-room when the bell went for morning registration. Mrs Peters wasn't there, which probably meant that staff-briefing was overrunning by a minute or two. It happened occasionally.

What almost never happened, however, was that Reece was early too. He could normally be relied upon to be late. He'd been warned about it several times, but there'd recently been a case-conference and he'd agreed to try harder to get up when his mum told him to. Consequently, he was on time for once.

There was a downside to this. Reece was what is known as a catalyst. Arthur, Brian and Dominic were reliably daft, but it was only when Reece was added to the mixture that things really got out of hand. Without Mrs Peters there as a restraining influence, the dangerously over-the-top behaviour started immediately.

Reece had no sooner sat down when he was into Arthur's bag. Having grabbed his can of coke he ran into the far corner of the classroom with it. Arthur promptly gave chase. Reece began shoving tables and chairs into his path to slow his friend down. He skidded round the room, using the shoulders of seated children for leverage. He leapt on to their tables and over them, turning the form room into a kind of assault course.

Gordon sighed. He looked out of the window to see if he could see Mrs Peters coming. When he couldn't, he pushed his chair back, ready to intervene as usual. He found Nick's surprisingly strong grip on his arm, holding him where he was. Nick was already on his feet and turning towards the capering Reece.

"Sit down, NOW!" he told him, authority oozing from every pore, "before you hurt someone."

Reece skidded to a halt with an incredulous grin. What was this? Nervous, little, downtrodden Nick telling him to sit down?! What was the world coming to? Here was a game worth playing.

"AARRGGH!" he yelled in mock terror. "Save me lads! Knickerlarse the Nerd is after me. DON'T LET HIM HIT ME!" He ran behind Brian and Dominic and made a great show of peeping out in fear. "Keep him off!"

Arthur retrieved his coke. Chelsee, Debra and Britney screamed with laughter. Nick gave him a withering look of utter contempt. "This classroom's the wrong place for you," he told him. "You need a sandpit and a bucket and spade."

There was an explosion of giggles from Grace and Miranda. Gordon couldn't help himself. He gave Nick a measured, slow hand-clap of applause. Nick turned back to them, grinning. He'd waited a long time for this moment. He went to resume his seat.

"That's put you in your place!" Brian said to Reece, who was dimly aware that the tables had somehow been turned. There was no way he could let Nerdy Nick get the last word. The rest of the class was watching expectantly. There had to be consequences.

He stood up and walked round his table towards Nick. Nick spun smoothly round to face him. Again, Gordon went to stand up in order to get in the way – old habits die hard – only to find Nick's hand once more firmly on his shoulder.

"Leave it to him," Zack advised, grinning. "I'm looking forward to this."

"Who do you think you are, all of a sudden?!" Reece demanded, truculently.

"Don't you know?" Nick said. He looked him straight in the eye in a way that was frankly disconcerting. "I'm one of the nerds people like you are going to end up working for - that is, if you ever make it to being employable."

There was a collective intake of breath. That was unmistakably fighting talk. Reece was out of his depth. He was also centre stage, with a reputation to uphold. He was facing a window as well, and could see Mrs Peters hurrying across the playground clutching their register.

"Peters to the rescue," he jeered, turning back to his seat. "Run back to your seat and hide behind the Gay Gordon, like you always do."

Nick stayed where he was. "I've had you, and people like you, up to here," he told Reece's retreating back. "So anytime, anywhere."

When Mrs Peters came through the door, she was surprised and pleased to find a completely silent, well-behaving class. Nick was standing in the middle of it by himself. There was an atmosphere. She looked questioningly at him. He just smiled at her and sat down.

She thanked her lucky stars nothing awful had happened in her absence, and got on with calling the register.

At break, their set was slightly delayed packing up in Science, so it was a minute or two before they made it to the playground. Reece, his mates and those who wanted to watch were waiting for Nick to appear. As soon as Reece saw him, he began striding self-importantly in their direction, flanked by the small crowd. The humiliation of a victim is always more enjoyable in front of an audience.

"Let me do this on my own," Nick said to his friends. "Just wait here." He set off, walking steadily and quickly straight towards Reece. They were clearly going to meet in the middle of the playground, in full view of everyone: the perfect place for a public demonstration.

When they were only ten feet apart, Reece stopped. He expected Nick to do the same. In affairs of this kind, there is normally a verbal exchange before the onset of violence. It's much like the way male cats stalk round each other with their backs up, growling while waiting to see whether one or the other will think better of it and back down.

Reece had worked out what he was going to say if he encountered the usual scenario: Nick standing behind Gordon while Gordon dealt with the flak. He'd had to forget it when he saw that - for the first time ever - Gordon and their two snotty swotties were staying put. Nick was striding out on his own.

That was a turn-up for the book, and by rights it should have put him on his guard. But there he was, surrounded by mates and an eager audience. And after all, this was only nerdy little Nick he was dealing with. He'd never been known to say boo to a goose before this morning.

He got his opening sneering remark ready. He even opened his mouth to say it, but he never got the chance. Contrary to all expectations, Nick didn't stop. He took the remaining three strides and slapped Reece on both cheeks. His hand had moved so quickly Reece hadn't seen it coming.

There was a collective gasp of disbelief. Reece took in a swift shocked breath, bared his teeth in a snarl and threw a wild punch at Nick's jaw. Effortlessly Nick grasped the incoming fist in his left hand while slamming his right into Reece's solar plexus. Reece dropped on to one knee, fighting to get his breath back, all the wind taken out of his sails.

Without a word, Nick turned and began to walk back towards his friends. He'd taken about ten paces when Arthur seemed to wake from some kind of dumbstruck reverie and set off in pursuit. The honour of his oafish mate was at stake.

Nick heard the running feet. He glanced over his left shoulder and judged the intervening distance to perfection. Pivoting on his left foot, he scythed his right foot round in a head-high sweeping movement worthy of a karate master. The sole of his shoe was suddenly a foot from Arthur's incoming face.

Arthur's brain didn't have time to register its presence. His forehead met the stationary foot while his legs carried the rest of his body forward. He thudded backwards on to the concrete and lay there dazed and disorientated.

Nick stood for a moment, calmly surveying the amazed onlookers. His expression clearly conveyed the question: "Anyone else fancy it?" A full ten seconds went by and nobody else moved. Nick turned again, and resumed his walk back to his friends.

That breaktime went down in the annals of playground mythology. The story grew in the telling of course, as stories always do. In the old days, it would have been turned into an epic poem, told in the mead hall when the feasting was done, and the drinking was into its stride.

Chapter 39

It's In Your Genes

After supper that night, Nick sat his mum down. "I've got something to tell you," he said.

"I know," Angela said simply. She smiled at him, folded her hands together and waited quietly.

"You may find it very hard to believe," he said, a little awkwardly.

"No, I won't," his mum said patiently. There was just a hint of sadness in her voice, as if there was something inevitable about this moment.

"The thing is," Nick went on. "I recently found out something, something about myself. It's something I had no idea was even possible."

"You're a wizard," Angela said calmly.

Nick stared at her, flabbergasted. "How did you know?"

His mum shrugged. "There was always a 50/50 chance. You're at the age now. I've been watching for the signs."

He had not anticipated that. He'd asked her about his dad before, when he noticed that other children had fathers as well as mothers. She'd told him his father had been a kind and wonderful man who had contracted a rare tropical disease while doing voluntary service overseas in a country in Africa. There was no known cure. He had died just before Nick was born.

It was a sad story, but his mum said she would always be grateful to his dad for giving her a wonderful son who looked just like him. After that, he understood that he was now the man in her life. He promised he would look after her forever, just like his dad would have done, if he'd had the chance.

"I really think it's time you told me about my dad," he said.

She looked at him, and saw how grown up he had become. His gaze was so steady, his voice so firm, and his whole manner so suddenly confident and strong. She nodded. "You're right," she said. "It is time I told you."

Her eyes were bright with the memory of the young man she had first met when helping out at a soup kitchen for the homeless, one Christmas. They had stood shoulder to shoulder for an hour, ladling soup and cutting bread. She had admired the easy way he had with the men who came off the cold streets to get some welcome shelter and a hot meal. He'd been so friendly afterwards.

Young men, in her experience, were normally full of themselves, but he had that rarest of qualities: he was a good listener. He was also gentle and funny. He had kind eyes and perfect teeth, which you couldn't help noticing because he smiled so often.

Their paths crossed again, soon after that, at a charity event, which perhaps wasn't surprising. But then he started turning up at meetings organised by various local societies she was interested in. He even enrolled in an evening class she'd told him she was attending. That's when she knew for certain that, for some reason she couldn't fathom, he was interested in her.

They shared the same tastes in music and the arts, the theatre and cinema. There was often a concert, an exhibition, a play or a film that it would be more fun to go to together than alone. Within six months, she knew that she wanted to spend the rest of her life with him.

One evening, he had sat her down and told her he loved her more than he'd ever thought possible. He'd never been more certain of anything in his whole life. But before he could ask her to marry him, there was something he had to tell her. It was something she would find hard to believe. He was afraid she might want to end their relationship there and then.

"He was a wizard," Nick said. Relief washed over him. It explained everything.

His mum's eyes were misty. "I loved him so much. For a dreadful minute I thought he was going to confess to something awful. I thought he might be married already, or that his family was involved in organised crime, like in *The Godfather*."

She smiled at the memory. "I thought he might have a rare genetic disorder, or that he could never have children. Your mind races over all the possibilities." She giggled. "It was almost a relief when he said he was a wizard. I thought it was a joke at first. I mean, there's no such thing, is there! - witches, wizards, Father Christmas, the tooth fairy. I just laughed. I started singing 'Those fingers in my hair, that sly, come-hither stare ...' Then I noticed he was serious."

Nick could understand that. He'd expected incredulity from his mum tonight. He'd wondered how she'd cope when he told her exactly the same thing.

"How did he convince you?" he asked.

"He held his right hand up and there was suddenly a wand in it. I applauded. I said something like 'Look out, Paul Daniels!' Then he flicked it like a conductor's baton and said 'Up!' I felt myself rising from the sofa. I took him seriously after that."

Nick smiled, imagining that happen to his mum for the first time. "You mean like this?" he said. His wand was suddenly in his right hand. He gave it a gentle flick.

"Yes, just like that, Darling," his mum said drily. "Put me down please." She sank smoothly back to the sofa and readjusted the cushion behind her back. "Where did that wand come from?" she wanted to know.

Gordon and Grace had agreed it was only fair that Nick and Miranda should bring their parents into the loop, whenever they decided it was the right time to do so. It was a worry, of course. The more people in the loop the greater the chance of its secrets leaking out. If a secret shared is a secret halved, what about a secret eleventhed? When does it stop being a secret? They would have to see.

"Gordon and Grace," he told her. "They 'acquired' four wands in Chester a couple of weeks ago. They're still being mysterious about how." He owed his friends so much. "Gordon put two and two together. He worked out that Miranda had to be a witch and I had to be a wizard, just like Grace and him. Well, maybe not just like."

"Do Edith and Victor know about all this?" Angela asked.

Nick nodded. "I think his mum started to find out when he was eleven. Gordon told them everything after Grace showed up at our new school."

His mum pursed her lips. "You said "maybe not just like Gordon and Grace." What does that mean?"

"I don't know," Nick confessed. "It was something Gordon said. We're all finding our way at the moment, but he seems to think he and Grace might be different again in some way."

Angela smiled. "Isn't being a wizard or a witch different enough?"

Nick pulled a face. "It's different enough for me, that's for sure."

His mum was suddenly serious. "Your father told me that some witches and wizards out there aren't nice to know. He said we didn't have to worry as long as we never said anything to anyone."

She looked worried. "He did his best to make sure we didn't have anything to do with his 'other' world. He wouldn't tell me anything about it. I think there's condemnation of any wizard or witch who marries outside the magic circle."

She grabbed his hand. "We've got to be on our guard from now on. There may be dangers."

Nick enfolded her hand in his. "I'll look after you," he promised her. "I won't let anything bad happen to you."

Angela smiled sadly. "That is almost word for word what your father said to me."

And suddenly Nick knew. "He didn't die of some rare tropical disease, did he?" he said.

Angela shook her head. "We'd been married just six months. I was pregnant with you. He was a faithful, wonderful husband, looking forward to being the best dad he could be. Nothing was more certain."

"What happened?" Nick whispered.

"He became preoccupied about something. He tried to say it was nothing, but I knew him too well. Something was seriously wrong."

Nick stared at her and waited. He knew that this time he was being told the whole truth.

"I told him that, whatever it was, we would handle it," she went on. "He gave me that look that meant I had no idea how far out of my depth I was. It had to do with his 'other world', he said. I wasn't to worry. Some of the 'wrong sort' were making waves. They couldn't be allowed to get away with … something. He was dealing with it. Everything would be fine again."

"And it wasn't," Nick guessed. He set his jaw. If there were people out there who'd hurt his father, they could look out.

"When he didn't come home," Angela said, with a little wobble in her voice, "…I phoned a colleague of his at work. Apparently, he hadn't come back after lunch. They'd thought he might have gone home ill."

Unconsciously she had begun to rock gently, backwards and forwards. "I contacted the police. They made all the usual noises. 'There was probably some perfectly logical explanation. He would almost certainly turn up within the next twenty-four hours.'" She sighed heavily. "When he didn't, they made all their usual enquiries. They found no trace of him. He had just disappeared."

"As if by magic," Nick growled through gritted teeth.

"A young woman who worked in the same building disappeared at the same time." Edith went on. "The police thought the most likely explanation was that they'd run off together. I told them there was no way, but they weren't interested any more. They'd found no suggestion of foul play."

"And you never heard from him again." Nick thought how terrible that must have been for his mum.

She shook her head. "Promise me you'll be very *very* careful." She hung her head, to hide the pain in her eyes. "If anything happened to you, I don't think I could bear it."

"What work did my father do?"

"He worked for a pharmaceutical company."

Chapter 40

A Family Reunion

Miranda found herself drawn to her wand. There was something instantly comforting and supportive about it. It was kind. It always understood. It wanted to help in any way it could.

She loved holding it, even though she could see the advantages of being able to activate it while keeping it hidden. When it was in her hand she found herself stroking it. She talked to it, sensing its attentiveness and responsiveness.

When it was hidden, she would activate it ('Power on!'), close her eyes and send questions and worries into the innermost recesses of her heart and mind. In a little while, back would come answers and suggestions. They were laced with calm, reassurance and resolve. It was almost as if the wand had a voice that only she could hear.

There was something very special about that. It was like being under the protection of a guardian angel. The next time she went riding, the instructor was amazed at the difference in the relationship Miranda had with Polly. The pony was calm, attentive and responsive. Miranda seemed suddenly to have the skill of a horse whisperer.

Not only that: she was lighter in the saddle, and able to anticipate and respond to every movement the horse made. It normally took years to achieve that level of rapport, and often not even then. The transformation was magical. It was like touch telepathy.

She rode her four times during the two weeks immediately following the arrival of her wand. Polly's posture became almost majestic. She began holding her head like an Arab thoroughbred. Her trot became as high and as measured as a miniature Lipizzaner. With

Miranda in the saddle, her canter was worthy of any dressage arena. It rivalled Belinda's on that gorgeous chestnut gelding Belinda's daddy had paid an absolute fortune for. Her instructor was blown away by the transformation. She could hardly credit it, but seeing was believing.

More than once, Miranda caught Belinda looking at her in a calculating way. She asked the wand why. Back came the answer: Belinda was wondering whether she would have some serious competition at the next local gymkhana. For years she had scooped the board at that gymkhana. Her proud father had provided her with several trophy cabinets.

Most importantly, Miranda came easily and compassionately to a better understanding of her dad's new wife. The wand showed her how. A lot of Isadora's briskness and over-efficiency sprang from how nervous she was of her new husband's strong, quirky, barely polite daughter. She was so conscious of being constantly compared to a dead mother, knowing she could never compete with such a powerful ghost.

A lot of Isadora's clinginess around her dad – the constant flattery, the overloud laughter at every single one of his silly jokes – stemmed from her insecurity. She was staking her claim on the affections of a man who already had two very important females in his life: a daughter whom he worshipped, and a wife of blessed and much loved memory.

She asked the wand what it thought she should do. When its gentle advice came back to her, she took it. She became friendlier and more helpful. She began clearing up after meals without being asked. She made sure her room was clean and tidy. She found there were lots of little things she could do for her new stepmum without fuss or comment. It didn't take a lot of effort on her part.

She started asking Isadora's opinion, and listened to what she had to say. She even spoke up for her once or twice, when her dad was in teasing mode, or being stubborn about something. She felt the overall calming effect this change in her behaviour was having on her stepmum. Isadora's gratitude and appreciation was touching.

Isadora began confiding in her. She began asking her opinion on clothes and food. She wanted to know which of two things Miranda thought her dad would prefer. They began doing things together.

Miranda made sure her dad noticed, and saw how happy it made him. Towards the end of week two following her acquisition of the wand, they had their first group hug. Miranda had still not decided, however, whether or not it was a good idea to tell either of them that she was a witch. She'd only just piloted the family ship into calmer waters and filled its sail with a fair wind. It didn't seem like an ideal time to risk rocking the boat.

But could there ever be an ideal time to tell an unsuspecting parent something like that?

She asked the wand's advice one night, as she was lying in bed, waiting for sleep to overtake her. "Should I tell him? Should I tell her? Should I sit them down together and tell them both? She sent the questions into the deepest recesses of her mind, knowing the wand would give them careful consideration. Her consciousness followed them down, and she fell into a deep sleep without receiving any answers.

More importantly, she hadn't deactivated her wand.

And then she was walking along a path through a wonderful wood. The last time she had found herself in a forest, the path had led her with her basket to Grandma's house. This time she was certain she was in no danger at all. Furthermore, she was conscious that being there was an immense privilege.

The path turned a corner, and she emerged from the trees into a glade. She could hear the raucous cawing of rooks and the ascending flutes of skylarks. She could see rabbits bobbing and hares leaping. She caught a glimpse of a fox slinking from bush to bush in a blush of red fur.

The air was alive with butterflies - Tortoiseshells, Peacocks, Red Admirals ... She could hear the steady hum of bees. And there! - standing alert at the edge of the wood on the other side of the glade - was a magnificent stag. Miranda counted seven points on each of its huge antlers.

To her right, a broad path led to steps carved in a jagged hill of rock. On top of the hill stood a castle of grey stone. It grew out of the granite like a living thing. Warm sunlight bounced off its topmost towers, bathing them in a warm, enchanted glow. To her left, the glade ran down to a lake. It sparkled, clean and crystal clear, and its waters were as still as mirrored glass.

There was a woman standing beside it. She had her back to her, and was gazing peacefully at the beauty she beheld. Miranda hoped with all her heart that she wouldn't disappear before she had a chance to speak to her, because the closer she got, the more certain she became.

She knew who it was.

When she was within ten feet, the figure turned, and Miranda saw that she had been right. Her mother gave her a radiant smile, and held her arms out wide in welcome.

Chapter 41

Cosa Nostra

They enfolded each other in a crushing embrace. Her mum was reassuringly solid. Miranda was now tall enough to wrap her arms right round her. She squeezed really tight, and for several precious seconds she entertained the possibility of holding on forever.

"Look at you!" her mum said, pulling away and laughing. "How you've grown! I like what you've done to your hair." She reached out and stroked it.

"You don't look any different," Miranda said. "You're exactly as I remember you, not a day older."

"Her mum smiled. "I will always be as you remember me." She linked in, and they began strolling along the side of the lake. "I hoped I would see you here one day; but it's never certain, particularly when one parent doesn't have the gift. I'm so proud of you: that you have found your way so soon."

"It's my wand," Miranda said. "It's wonderful. Grace and Gordon boosted it with their magic. Now it's helping me so much I don't know where I'd be without it."

Her mum patted her arm. "And where do you think it would be without you?" she asked. "You're a great witch. I can sense it. The force is much stronger in you than it ever was in me."

Miranda looked up at her. "You were a witch too? I've inherited this power – whatever it is – from you? You never said! I never knew."

Her mum shook her head. "I met your father and fell hopelessly in love with him. He isn't a wizard, he could never be a wizard; but there was something about him."

Miranda squeezed her mum's arm in happy concurrence. There definitely *was* something about her dad.

"Marrying outside the magic circle is not something a witch or wizard does lightly. There are secrets to be guarded, and fear and prejudice both within and without." Her mum's voice took on a harder tone. "Certain powerful families of witches and wizards claim descent from those who first laid down the L.O.A."

"L.O.A.?" Miranda repeated, puzzled.

"The 'Law of Apartheid'. To them, the L.O.A. is hard and fast. It must never be broken, and woe betide any witch or wizard who strays from its narrow path."

Miranda looked up at her mum and saw how suddenly stern her face had become. "Anyone judged to have broken any part of it can expect the ultimate penalty. 'Better the death of one, rather than the dishonour of many' is the creed those families go by."

"That's terrible," Miranda said. "What about the dangers of in-breeding within a depleted gene-pool? Even royal families nowadays understand the need to marry outside a charmed inner circle. Look at Wills and Kate."

Her mum's face remained grim. "For some, the clock runs backwards. They would take us back to some imagined "better" time, when their ancestors were in charge and everyone else knew their place, and did what they were told."

She shuddered. "The 'punishments' were terrible in those days, and there was no recourse to law or independent judgement. The 'Lords' and 'Ladies' had total control over anyone lower down the social scale."

"Did you belong to such a family?" Miranda asked.

Her mum laughed. "No," she said. "My parents were enlightened and progressive. They brought me up to think for myself." Clearly she had loved them very much. "When I told them of my feelings for your father, they warned me that what I was thinking of doing was highly dangerous. If I married him, I would put myself beyond the witching pale."

She shrugged her shoulders. "I would be shunned, and never be allowed to return to our world. If it suited those in power to claim that I had divulged - or just might divulge – any secrets, my life and the lives of every member of my family could be forfeit."

"How DARE they?!" Miranda cried. "It's an outrage! It's mediaeval, barbaric."

"Yes, it is. And it's how it will go on being, until someone comes along with the power to change it. It's the reason I never told your father. He knows nothing about it to this day."

They were still linked in. She gave her precious daughter's arm a squeeze. "Of course I never told you. You might never have shown any magical ability at all, then that would have been that." She sighed sadly. "I didn't have the power to change any of it, and I wasn't going to give your father up. So I left the community."

"Quite right," Miranda cried. Who did they think they were, telling other people how to run their lives? She owed her very existence to her mother's quirky strong-mindedness.

"Quite wrong, according to some people," her mother told her. "One family in particular was determined to make an example of me and my parents."

This part of her story was clearly very painful.

"My father was summoned before a tribunal under that family's control. He was humiliated as a weak, over-indulgent parent. They berated him for having no control over his feeble wife and his self-indulgent daughter."

Her mum's voice shook a little at the sheer injustice of it. "It was claimed that he had exposed the local wizarding community to avoidable risk. An example would be made of him, to deter others from doing what I had done. The cancer of 'defection' would be 'surgically removed.'"

"How?" Miranda wanted to know.

"They said my father had one chance to save his errant daughter's life. He could volunteer to enter the regime's service and perform certain 'unpleasant but necessary tasks.'"

They had made it sound as though they were doing him a favour. "He could help 'further the regime's noble ends'. However, if he flinched, my sentence would be death. The price of 'disobedience' was high.

"I'm not surprised you left a world like that," Miranda said. "Our history teacher told us someone once said 'power tends to corrupt, and absolute power corrupts absolutely.' Your world sounds like an awful place."

"It wasn't always like that," her mum said. "When I was growing up it was kinder, fairer, more democratic. That was before the coup."

"What happened?" Miranda wanted to know.

Her mum shrugged again. "What always happens in a coup? Those in power are toppled by those with more power. The topplers say they are acting on our behalf to root out corruption and inefficiency."

Her tone dripped with sarcasm. "They promise to stay in power only as long as it takes to reform everything, after which time there will be a return to democracy, stability and prosperity. They will let us know when that time is right."

"And that time never arrives," Miranda guessed shrewdly.

"No, it never does. Meanwhile they go on grabbing more and more power and influence. And somehow, enormous wealth always goes along with it. That buys even more power and influence, until they have it all. After that, any opposition is simply crushed."

"What did your father have to do?" Miranda asked.

"To protect my mother and me, he did whatever they told him to do."

"Such as?" Miranda whispered.

"He never told me, and believe me, you don't want to know," her mum said. "But I saw the effect it had on him, what a terrible toll it took. I begged him to stop. I told him just to say 'Enough! No more.'"

"And did he?" Miranda asked.

"He asked for an appointment with the man who had the power to release him. The appointment was granted, and he went on his knees. He begged to be excused further 'duties'. He had done whatever they'd asked for eight years, and would be haunted by it for the rest of his life."

Her mum's voice trembled as she focused on this image of her broken father. "He asked to be allowed to fade into obscurity, to live as before, posing no threat to anyone. He would never speak of anything they had made him do."

Miranda's heart went out to her grandfather, whom she had never met - presumably for her safety as well as his. He had harmed others in order to protect her, her mum, and his wife.

"What did the man say?"

"He said my father understood nothing. He said that his request was an act of disloyalty, and disloyalty must always be punished. He said he had always found pain to be a most effective way of conditioning servants."

"Oh my God," Miranda said, horror-struck.

"When eventually he got tired of listening to my father scream, he told him his "duties" would be doubled." Miranda did not want to think what those 'duties' might be, but her mother thought she needed to know.

"The regime uses pain to oppress opposition. Sometimes it's inflicted on the opposers themselves. Sometimes it's on their children, while they are forced to watch."

She put a protective arm around her daughter's shoulders. "He was told that his 'pathetic' plea had prompted the signing of my death warrant. Any future sign of reluctance on his part to do anything required of him – anything at all – and the regime would find his wife guilty of treason. The penalty for treason is agonising death by fire. Their loved ones are made to watch."

Miranda did her best to shut out the horror of it. It wasn't a very good best. "So that unpronounceable disease was them?"

"Yes," her mother said. "I wasn't the first, and I won't be the last while that regime and that family has a stranglehold on our world." She turned to face her daughter and gripped her shoulders. "From now on, you must be very, very careful, you *and* your friends."

Chapter 42

Heard But Not Seen

Grace was simply astonished by her wand. Having seen what Mr Wynfor was able to do with it, her first experiments were in musical reproduction and image-projection. She found it responded to her much as an orchestra responds to its conductor, and as a cast and crew respond to a director.

She let her requests and requirements flow through her fingers to the wand, and it dutifully conjured up exactly the sounds and images she wanted to hear and see. It had access to an inexhaustible library of sound and the surround sound capabilities of a first-class hi-fi system, plus it had a quality of hologrammatic projection not yet seen in the non-magic world.

She sat her two mums down one evening for a concert and took requests. Vivian asked for the opening of Elgar's *Cello Concerto in E minor* performed by Jacqueline Dupré. Grace closed her eyes, waved the wand, and it was is if they had been transported back more than 40 years to watch this exceptionally gifted young woman giving a live performance with a wonderful symphony orchestra.

Elaine chose the *Lacrimosa* from Verdi's *Requiem*, because – like the Elgar – it was music you wouldn't mind dying to. Effortlessly, the wand wafted them into a different concert hall and the amazing experience not only of a wonderful orchestra but also stunningly gifted solo singers and the majesty of a massed choir.

Grace then remembered Miranda's question in Gordon's back garden, and conjured up *Take That* live at the City of Manchester

Stadium. By general consent, however, she shut it down after a minute or two, as it wasn't doing anything for any of them.

The memory of the pain that nasty wizard Mr Mortlake had fired into her brain prompted her to explore what protection the wand might be able to offer her. She tried the command 'Shield!' and got Zoë to hurl pillows and cushions at her. Zoë said it was really impressive. It looked as though the object had hit her, whereas it had merely impacted against a Grace-shaped forcefield about an inch from her body. The shield completely encased her.

Zoë then tested the strength of it with a walking stick. She started tentatively, and then increased the vigour. Eventually, she was jabbing and whacking as hard as she could from all angles. It withstood every blow.

That could turn out to be very handy, but would it work against spells? Grace made a mental note to get Miranda, Nick and Gordon to fire off some spells at it. It's always sensible to have your defences tested by friends, before you try them out in the presence of enemies.

The nature of the shield was interesting. Clearly it wasn't impenetrable, or she wouldn't have been able to breathe. Would her spells pass through it from the inside? You wouldn't want a spell rebounding, but deactivating your shield beforehand would leave you vulnerable to attack.

She reassured herself that her wand wouldn't do anything to put her in harm's way. It would use the sense it was born with, and if it could let air in, surely it could let a spell out?

She set up some targets in their back garden and was soon excellent at knocking things about from a distance. She found she could send spells in all directions while Zoë was hurling missiles at her from all angles. Zoë was very strong, and a terrific shot. The missiles bounced off the shield with impressive force.

They were in the back garden, just over a week later, when Zoë came up with a brilliant suggestion. "Try asking the wand to project an image of your surroundings on the inside of your shield. See if it can make the image opaque."

"Why?" Grace asked.

"Because if the image is opaque enough to block you out, whoever is looking in your direction will only see an image of whatever they would see if you weren't there."

"Ooh," said Grace. "Let's try." She thought for a moment. "Cloak!" she said and spun herself through 360 degrees. Obediently, the wand projected an exact image of her surroundings on to the shield. Zoë clapped her hands in delight.

"You're invisible!" she said excitedly. "Welcome to the club."

How useful was *that*! She couldn't wait to pass that particular discovery on when they hit school again on Monday.

"Try running around," Zoë said. Grace darted past flower beds, round a tree and back to the French windows. Zoë shook her head in wonder.

"I've no idea where you are," she told Grace. "Can you see me?" A second later she gave a yell and leapt about a foot in the air. Grace giggled. It had been fun to blow in her ear for a change!

Miranda had told them about the ruthless oppression in the world of witchcraft and wizardry. Their combined skills were building into an effective arsenal.

It seemed likely that they would need one.

Chapter 43

A Chamber Of Secrets

Gordon was grateful to the others for concentrating on the attack and defence capabilities of their wands. It meant he could concentrate on what he thought he needed his wand for most: to explore and map regions of his mind that had not previously been available to him.

Ever since he'd met Grace on his first morning in secondary school, he'd been exercised by her ability to know what he was thinking. Yet when Myrddin appeared in the dell that fateful September two and a half years ago, he had said to her: "You are wondering why you cannot tell what I am thinking."

So clearly, it was possible to hide your thoughts from a mind-reader.

He'd been able to get inside Mortlake Senior's mind. He didn't know how yet; it had just happened. And a very unpleasant place it had turned out to be. He'd heard him say "I read your pathetic little mind" to Mr Wynfor. So mind-reading was a skill some wizards had.

Wynfor hadn't been able to hide his 'disloyal' thought from Mortlake. Yet Mortlake had been able to repel Grace's mind-probe by sending a jolt of pain through her brain. His defences had kept her out, but not Gordon. Why?

Gordon had several important items of information to keep safely under lock and key. There was his ability to travel to Avalon and to consult with Myrddin. There was the location of the dell. There was the existence of Zack and Zoë. Not least, there was the fact that he had the power to get into Mortlake Senior's head without that exceedingly unpleasant gentleman knowing he was there.

It was essential he master the thought-cloaking technique before he met Mortlake again. That meeting could come at any time, do there was no time to lose. Just being inside Mortlake's head had given him an inkling of how it was done. He had sensed the slippery thoughts sliding past him. They were on their way to some deeper part of Mortlake's mind, a part that he kept under lock and key.

Gordon hadn't tried to follow them. He'd been too intent on rescuing Wynfor from the torment Mortlake was about to inflict. But something told him a time would come when he would need to find his way through that dank darkness. And when he unlocked Mortlake's 'Chamber of Secrets', he had better be prepared for the horrors he would find lurking in there.

It was therefore essential he develop a technique for exploring the deepest cellars in his own brain. He told Zack that was what he was going to do, and asked him to mind the shop while he was gone.

Zack looked very doubtful. "It's bound to be a labyrinth," he warned. "There may be miles and miles of twists and turns. What if you get lost? What if you can't find your way back?"

Gordon was interested. "Do you think that's what happens to people when they're in a coma, or in a trance?" he asked. "They get lost in the labyrinth?"

Zack shrugged. "How are you going to make sure you get back?" he insisted. He could just imagine how Gordon's mum would take it. "I'm sorry, Mrs Bennett. Gordon went potholing in his own brain, and I've no idea when - or if - he'll find his way out."

"OK," Gordon said slowly. "I'll ask the wand to lay a trail – like Theseus with his ball of string, or Hansel with his bag of little white pebbles. And I'll ask it to provide me with enough light to see by."

The plan developed twists and turns of its own. "I'll memorise the route as I go. I'll tell myself a story with the same number of twists and turns in it as I take on the journey."

"You know what I'm going to say, don't you?" Zack said grimly.

Gordon grinned. "I do, and I will. But as you also often say, 'the path to knowledge is unfolded truth'. I have to walk that path."

When his journey began, it seemed to him that he was travelling along a pleasant, well-lit, one-way thoroughfare. He passed under a sign that identified it as *Recent Thoughts Drive*. It wasn't long before he reached a much broader avenue, lined with skyscrapers. The intersection was controlled by traffic lights. The sign said *Process Parade*.

The lights turned green and he turned right. Judging by the numbers on the streets, he was heading "uptown". In every building, the windows blazed with light. He was conscious of machinery whirring away, processing vast amounts of data, conducting urgent business.

In size, layout and structure, it reminded him of the Island of Manhattan. He'd seen it several times in films: New York New York, 'so good they named it twice'. The blocks were defined by equidistant streets. Each street contained rows of buildings of varying sizes, designs and purposes: shops, offices, houses, factories ...

Along the Parade - and along all the other avenues, boulevards, drives, roads and streets that led off it - vehicles thronged, ferrying goods and passengers between locations. Traffic lights controlled the flow. Licensed personnel were on hand ready to deal with any gridlock and make any impartial judgement necessary.

This was *Gordonopolis*: a well-ordered, apparently smooth-functioning urban hub. It was a metaphor of the mind: Operations HQ. The street names were illuminated: *Zack Street, Grace Lane, Nick Boulevard, Mum and Dad Close* and a signpost for *Myrddin Avenue*.

"In my father's house are many mansions..."

He knew he could turn down any of these streets: open any door, go inside any room, and there he would find itemised memories relating to the individual highlighted in the street name. This was his conscious mind. This was where his terabytes of R.A.M. were keeping his life very well organised and under his control.

In the quieter outer suburbs there was much less going on. The buildings had fewer and fewer lights. There was less and less traffic on the thoroughfares. It was appreciably darker. Before long, he had reached the city limits.

By now he was in almost total darkness. The streets had no names. There was almost no sign of life or movement. Out here, the buildings were smaller, silent, standing by. They were awaiting future development.

He spotted one lighted window in one small house off to the side, right on the outskirts. He smiled, knowing what was in that room. It was his first realisation that Nick had to be a wizard and Miranda a witch.

He had grasped the technique while in Mortlake Senior's head. He'd tried hiding his very next thought in the remotest building he could find at short notice. It had worked: Grace hadn't been able to find it. She probably wasn't used to going much further than Recent Thoughts Drive.

Gordon, however, wasn't sure that anywhere within his city limits would be safe from a determined spy with the necessary skills. His purpose now was to go far beyond it. He was heading for uncharted territory, to seek out new secret locations for his most private thoughts and memories, to boldly go where he had never gone before.

He felt the capsule cross the city line and pick up speed. Quite suddenly it dipped, and now it was diving through the R.A.M.-less regions of his inner darkness. The glow from the wand's tip only lit up the space immediately around him. He wasn't able to anticipate the many changes of direction. He began to feel queasy.

The trajectory became steeper. It was almost like going over a waterfall. It combined the twists and turns of an Xtreme rollercoaster with the swirl of water going down a massive plughole. Gordon felt his ears pop. He closed his eyes and held on to his stomach. His R.O.M.-run regions had seemed the ideal place to look, but how far would he have to go?

What part of him was doing the travelling? The threads of connection he was travelling along could only be a few atoms thick. How fast was he going? He was inside a biological computer containing goodness knows how many microchips. Each chip contained goodness knows how many pathways. Each pathway performed a specific function within the microcosm.

If he was inhabiting a pulse of energy for this incredible journey, he must be travelling at the speed of light. His notion of remembering the route by telling a story with the same number of twist and turns now seemed utterly ludicrous. He would have to rely on his wand, and on Mabon's ring. They would get him home. He didn't doubt it for a nanosecond.

"This has to be far enough!" he thought, when throwing up had become the most likely thing to happen next. The capsule obediently slowed …

He opened his eyes, and a broadening beam of intense light sprang from his ring like a powerful headlight. Ahead of him was a substantial hill of jagged rock. On its top was an enormous castle. It grew out of the granite like a living thing. The crenellations on its impressively high walls were perfectly spaced. It had ramparts and a wide moat, a drawbridge and guard towers. There was a heavily portcullised gateway in and out.

He used his bionic zoom to read the motto engraved in wrought iron across the arch: "Memor Tua Rei". "That'll do," he thought.

His capsule came to a halt in front of the gate, and he climbed out of it. The castle seemed to recognise him! The portcullis creaked up and the drawbridge creaked down. Clutching his wand tightly, he strode across it, under the arch and into what appeared to be a ghost town.

Inside, it bore a marked resemblance to Chester-Within-The-Walls. There were hundreds of quirky, strong-minded buildings, and inside those buildings were thousands of odd-shaped rooms. Each house almost certainly had a dusty attic and a cellar from an earlier time. Within many a deceptively thick wall he knew there would be cunningly wrought secret passageways that led to hidden rooms marked with an X on a map he had yet to find. When he did, he would keep it in a place no-one would think of looking.

He wondered whether, in time, Gordon-Within-The-Walls might accumulate its own assortment of ghosts. He made a mental note to move all memories of his sixteen great grandparents in as soon as possible. He would reserve the best available accommodation for them. His SGGm would expect no less.

Maybe those memories could be put in charge of guarding the place against intruders. Might any intruder ever get this far?

He walked a little way down Northgate Street, expecting the cathedral to emerge to his left and the town hall to his right. It was an eerie experience. Some force had been able to remove all the people while leaving the buildings intact.

He didn't think there was any point in going much further on this particular occasion. He needed to get back, to face the challenge of sifting through his memories. It would be a painstaking business carrying and shifting, hoisting and lifting. He needed to move everything he wanted to keep secret from the likes of Mr Mortlake far away from Gordonopolis. He would relocate those thoughts and memories here, deep within the confines of Gordon-Within-The-Walls.

Curiosity, however, took him as far as the Art Deco, Grade 11 listed Odeon Cinema building; and he was very glad it did.

As he reached the corner of Northgate Street and Hunter Street, he became aware of sound coming from somewhere inside the building.

"Oscar Deutsch Entertains Our Nation". Well not anymore, not in this particular cinema. It had closed some time ago. In Gordon-Within-The-Walls it should certainly not have been open, but he could definitely hear something.

Floating through the otherwise total silence was what sounded like the soundtrack of a film.

He asked the ring to dowse its light. In the consequent pitch blackness he could see a pale light shining in the cinema's entrance hall.

There was a memory in there.

He pushed open one of the big glass swing doors and walked in. The light grew brighter. He crossed the entrance lobby, passed the ticket-checking point and entered the corridor containing the entrances to each of the five screens.

The sound was coming from the end screen on the right. Wondering, he followed the dark passageway leading to that particular screen. Dumbstruck, he stood and watched the film that was playing in there. The focus was pin-sharp. The sound quality was impressive.

"Oh my God," Gordon thought. He stood alone in this cinema somewhere deep in the ROM-run regions of his mind. "So *this* is where they hid it."

Chapter 44

Questions, Questions

Grace and Gordon's initial brush with local witch-and-wizardry had been revealing, as well as disturbing. It had suggested they were more powerful than the witches and wizards they had met, at least those nearer their own age.

They had been able to supercharge their wands. They had made them far more powerful than they ever were when Todd, Petronilla and Astrid were waving them around. Grace had healed the snapped one, even though Wynfor had said it was impossible. She had never held a wand before, yet she had performed what the wand-master described as "a bloody miracle".

Nick and Miranda were showing huge potential. To achieve that much in such a short time was amazing. Nick had transformed himself. Miranda's mother said Miranda was a much more powerful witch than she had been.

Gordon and Grace were certain Miranda had met her mother in their glade in Avalon. They recognised it from Miranda's description. It made sense. She had been dead six years. But that Miranda had got there at all – albeit with the help of a supercharged wand – was extraordinary. It marked her out as no mean witch.

Even so, Myrddin must have had a hand in it, just as he had when Gordon first met Grace and Zoë there. That meant they should take Miranda's mother's warning very seriously indeed.

There were so many questions. Were Nick and Miranda more powerful precisely because their magically gifted parent had married outside the closed circle of the witch-and-wizarding world? Do fresh genes in a magic pool produce a stronger swimmer? Was that why the "gods" – so called - had involved themselves with two human females? Was that how Grace and Gordon came to possess the extraordinary powers they had?

Could those Greek-God lookalikes really shape-shift, as Miranda's Uncle Fergus had surmised, into the revered images of the many different religions on Earth? Had they found those images there already, or had they created them in the first place?

When did they first set up their bases? How long had they been involving themselves in human affairs? Was it long enough to have undertaken a selective breeding programme among primates?

If so, had they created the human race?

Where was their home planet? It must be - or must have been - aeons of spacetime away. Had they exhausted its resources, just like we are exhausting the resources of our own? Had they travelled for centuries in a massive mothership to reach a planet capable of sustaining them? If so, what happened to their mothership? And if they could shapeshift, were they now established on the planet in human form? Were they the word made flesh? Were the ancient gods actually aliens?

Is "God" an alien? When you think about it, what else can a God be but an alien?

Questions, questions ...

May turned into June. Each day brought revelations about the capacities of their new wands. They shared everything they learned, so it was no real surprise that their progress was astonishing. Each tended to be strongest in those functions they were the first to discover, but they were all eager to try everything. Practice makes perfect.

It took Grace a week to find her own memory of that dream. It was in a treehouse halfway up a massive oak in a patch of thick forest, where it couldn't be seen either from the ground or from the air. She heard it before she saw it. The forest itself covered a range of hills somewhere over the rainbow in her head. She had no idea how much of it there was. It was so utterly dark in there and out there, way beyond her conscious mind.

Scarcely trodden pathways wound through it. She could only keep track by leaving a trail. A fine thread of endless shiny silk oozed from the base of her wand. The light at the wand's tip glistened on the thread like the tiny eyes of spiders in the grass.

She found that particular treehouse because of the sound, and the pale light glinting through the leaves above her head. Then she realised there were thousands upon thousands of others, all hidden from the path because of their height above the ground and the density of the foliage.

She could hide all her private thoughts and memories in them, well out of sight and earshot from one another. The amount of light and sound each one generated would only attract attention if you happened to be standing right underneath the tree it was hidden in.

The thought that aliens had been that far inside her mind was uncomfortable, but she would have to live with it. After all, in some way more complicated than she could ever hope to understand, her father had been one of them, or maybe even all of them.

Gordon had described his version of the dream in vivid detail. Once Grace was able to fill in additional details from hers, they had a pretty complete picture. Miranda and Nick hadn't found their versions yet, though their déjà vu moments were getting more and more frequent.

It was almost as if their dreams were trying to find *them*. Maybe dreams and dreamers are always looking for each other, inside that amazing labyrinth casually referred to as the human mind. Maybe it was harder for Nick and Miranda to find their way through it because aliens had not been so directly involved in their conception.

Wynfor had told them Grace's wand would know if Mortlake was hurting or threatening him. She had been watching and waiting for some sign, but hadn't sensed anything yet. She hoped that meant he was all right for the moment.

Both she and Gordon were grateful for this trouble-free training period. From the little they had seen of Mortlake Senior, they didn't think it would be long before he made another move against them.

His family seemed to have a stranglehold on the Chester area. Had he just taken it upon himself to become a local feudal lord? Or was he part of some national network ruling the world of witchcraft and wizardry the length and breadth of the British Isles? Either way he had money and power. That meant he had soldiers and servants - lots of both, probably - and no scruples whatsoever.

So it was no real surprise when the call came, one Sunday evening towards the middle of June. The telephone rang in the Bennett household and Edith answered. Gordon heard the hesitation in her voice when she asked "Who is this?"

He was on his feet and heading to the phone when she put her hand over the mouthpiece. "Someone with a Welsh accent asking for you," she told him. "Says his name's Wynfor, and that it's a matter of the utmost urgency."

Victor leapt to his feet. "Do you want me to take it, Son?" he asked protectively. Gordon still had almost two months to go before his fourteenth birthday. If any adult out there had any business with him, urgent or otherwise, he could have the decency to go through his parents.

Gordon shook his head. "Don't worry Dad. I'll hear what he's got to say, then we can plan accordingly." He smiled at his mum as he took the phone from her, trying to lessen the worry he knew she was feeling. At the same time, he knew he couldn't.

"Hi," he said into the phone, and waited to hear what Wynfor had to say.

Chapter 45

A Council Of War

Two minutes later, Gordon put the phone down. He turned to find two parents sitting bolt upright on their living room sofa on full alert. His dad pointed at the comfy chair opposite them. "Sit," he said. "Family conference."

Gordon sat. Anticipating the need for tea, Zack whizzed into the kitchen and put the kettle on. "That was Wynfor," Gordon said. His parents nodded. They knew who Wynfor was.

"What did he want?" Victor wanted to know. "Word for word, please."

"He said he has to meet us all as soon as possible. There are urgent things he wants to tell us, things he needs to warn us about. He said not to go anywhere near the Alley again, at least not until we've had the meeting. The Mortlake family has spies all over it."

That could explain why everyone shopping in Coincident Alley had scurried around with eyes averted, not meeting anyone's gaze.

"He wants us to find a place in our world that we can meet without arousing any suspicions. He wants all four of us – me, Grace, Nick and Miranda – and all our parents to be there."

Edith nodded vehemently. She and Victor would definitely be at that meeting. If anybody anywhere – it didn't matter two hoots who - was thinking of harming her Gordon, they'd have to get past her. It wouldn't be easy, because she'd be hitting them very hard at the time with the nearest weapon, blunt or sharp, didn't matter.

Victor patted her knee reassuringly, and she smiled bravely. She knew that her confidence stemmed from her certainty that Victor would already have grabbed them and be holding them still enough for her to get in a telling swipe.

Gordon knew all that, and he loved them for it. It would be the other way round, of course. He would be doing his best to ensure that they didn't come to any harm. Grace, Nick and Miranda would be doing exactly the same.

Their collective best had become a much better best in the last few weeks. That said, no-one was complacent about it. Any family with the power to terrorise a whole community had to be a force to be reckoned with.

"How about St Mary's Church Hall in Handbridge?" Edith asked. Not for the first time, her AmDram connections might come in handy. Chester Operatic Society used that space for rehearsals, and she had access to the keys. She also knew it wasn't normally in use on a Wednesday evening. The hall had a handy adjoining kitchen.

The living room door swung open, and a tray wafted in with three steaming mugs of tea on it. "Thanks, Zack, you're an angel," Edith told him as she took her mug. She was careful to get the right one: Victor's and Gordon's would have sugar in.

Victor sipped his pensively. Gordon knew what he was thinking. He also knew he wouldn't voice those thoughts, for fear of alarming his mum. He gave his dad a little wink and the merest nod of his head, hoping to convey the fact that the same thought had occurred to him.

Wynfor could be acting under duress. They could be walking into a trap. He wanted a meeting with Myrddin before they did anything else. Surely the most powerful wizard this world had ever known had a vested interest in the health and safety of his apprentice. Gordon expected Myrddin to have some useful advice for them all.

In school the next morning, Gordon gave them the news.

"I haven't even told my dad I'm a witch yet," Miranda said. Her brow was ploughed by the enormity of it all. "I'm going to have to, aren't I?"

Grace gave her best friend's arm a supportive squeeze. "I think you are," she said, "him *and* your step-mum. Your mum said these people stop at nothing. They'll hurt anybody to get what they want. That means your dad and Isadora are in danger as well." There was no ducking this issue. "They can't protect themselves against magic. Look what happened to your mum; even she wasn't able to stop it."

Miranda's bottom lip began to quiver.

"Don't worry!" Nick urged. "There's six of us, don't forget. I'll kill anyone who tries to hurt you or your dad."

Miranda managed a smile, though her eyes were threatening to brim over. It was hard to recognise Nick as the same boy who'd taken such a shine to her on their first day at secondary school. Then he'd been weedy and nervous in a blazer two sizes too big for him. Now he was her knight in shining armour.

"Why don't I come round to your house, and we can tell them together?" Grace suggested. Miranda nodded gratefully and cheered up a bit. As there was no way out of this situation, that would definitely be the best way of doing it.

Nick was boiling. "So they're coming after *us* now, are they?" he said. "Not content with murdering Miranda's mother, torturing her grandfather whom she's never met because of them, making my father disappear - and goodness knows how many others - they think they'll come after *us*?"

He stared at Gordon. "You know what? I'm glad. Let them come. It saves me the trouble of going after *them*!"

"I will do such things," Zack murmured, "- what they are yet I know not - but they shall be the terrors of the earth!"

Zoë smiled sympathetically. Nick was right, however. There were six of them, and unlike King Lear, they hadn't just given their power away. Quite the opposite.

Grace looked thoughtful. "This may be what it takes to get my father to put in an appearance," she said hopefully. "He had a reason for pulling that Angel Gabriel/Holy Ghost stunt on my mum, and I'm fairly sure it wasn't to have me bumped off by some psycho and his barmy army in this neck of the woods."

"How about a week on Wednesday, 8pm in Handbridge?" Gordon suggested. "I mean for our meeting with Wynfor, and whoever else he brings with him?"

The others looked at each other and nodded. They could check that date with their parents and confirm tomorrow.

"And how about" Gordon went on, "...another visit to the dell this Sunday? All of us this time, with our parents?"

He smiled at Grace. "Like you, I don't think Myrddin made me his heir so some tinpot dictator could take me out. I'd like to get his advice. It would help Nick and Miranda's parents know that they're not facing this situation on their own."

Grace nodded thoughtfully. "You know how protective my mum is of the dell," she said, "but I think she'll see the sense of getting Myrddin's take on all this, if we can."

They would have to see. But when the bell went for morning registration they were feeling better about it all. They were together, and they had a plan.

Chapter 46

Proceed With Caution

Grace accepted the Lansbury's invitation to stay for tea. She and Miranda insisted on clearing away and washing up, so Isadora could get to her baking circle in good time. The circle met regularly on a Tuesday evening, and on this occasion would be doing magic things with sourdough.

Miranda's father then found himself faced by two earnest young ladies with some very important and deadly secret things to tell him. One or two demonstrations later, he was rapidly getting his head round the fact that his daughter and her best friend were a couple of witches.

All it took was a vanishing act, a bit of telekinesis and a three-dimensional performance of *Bohemian Rhapsody* by a life-size, depressingly-young-looking group called *Queen*.

Robert took the news of his daughter's special talent surprisingly well. What was a lot more disturbing was Miranda's account of her recent vivid dream involving her mum.

He'd had many a dream of his own, of course - outpourings of love, longing and grief. At first they'd been overwhelming, but gradually they had healed to a bearable fondness for the happiness they'd shared.

To find out that she had been a witch was amazing. That she'd been murdered for marrying outside the witch-and-wizarding community was truly shocking. The probability that the people who killed her would now come after Miranda as a rogue witch outside their closed circle was terrifying.

How could he protect her? He couldn't take a story like that to the police, could he?

"Actually we already have," Grace had told him. "Gordon's dad is a Chief Inspector."

"Grace reads minds," Miranda told her gobsmacked dad. "You're going to have to get used to that."

"Leave Isadora to me," he told them. His new wife would take it hard, but she had to be told. They all needed to be on their guard from now on.

It was ironic really. With a name like Isadora, she was the one who sounded like a witch.

Mobile numbers were exchanged so that each family could alert the others if they had any reason to. Thankfully there was no need. The rest of the week passed quickly.

Sunday dawned without further incident, and they set off at different times in different directions, in case their houses were being watched. They took their time and checked their rear-view mirrors for following vehicles. They made their way via different routes to that B-road in the countryside beyond Mold.

Rendezvous was at 10.30 a.m.. The car-parking area was deserted, as it normally was. Family by family, they arrived safely. Robert and Victor each approved of the other's firm handshake. Isadora's evident anxiety and fluster was mollified by Vivian's serenity, Elaine's cheerfulness and Edith's strength of purpose.

Angela waved Nick away when her son showed signs of sticking closely to her. "Go and be with your friends," she told him. "You'll soon know if we need you."

"I will," he promised her. The child-like excitement he'd felt on his last visit to this spot had been replaced with more adult resolve and grim determination.

The four children went on ahead to recce the dell. The adults followed their offspring along the narrow path through the wood, talking in low voices about the perilous situation facing them all.

What they didn't know was that Zack and Zoë were sticking to them like glue. Gordon and Grace were leaving nothing to chance.

Once in the dell, Gordon wasted no time. He chose his spot in the centre and stretched out his arms on either side. "Summoning circle," he explained.

They came together, Nick on one side, Grace on the other, Miranda facing Gordon. They clasped hands and waited. "Let's close our eyes and beam our message. 'Please come at once,'" Gordon said.

"If you're not too busy," Nick added.

Gordon felt the cool touch of the torque as it wrapped itself round his neck. The light from his ring blazed into the centre of the circle. A glow spread from his hands through Grace and Nick to Miranda. All four children were encased in it. They prayed for intervention ...

... and within their circle the air thickened. In seconds it had solidified into the figure of a very old man. The wrinkles around his eyes were even deeper. He leaned more heavily on his staff, and his hair and beard were now as long as the robe. All three touched the ground.

"You can open your eyes," Myrddin told them gently. Nick and Miranda dropped their hands and took a step back, gazing in wonder. He bore such a striking resemblance to Professor Dumbledore. Or was it Gandalf the White?

"My predecessor's favourite rôle was Moses," Myrddin told them with a twinkle in his eye. "I've had many in my time. Prospero had style. Merlin too, of course. Lots of interesting adventures, but I was younger then."

He gave a little sigh. "And finally, I turned into Father Christmas." He gazed fondly round the dell. "But all good things come to an end.

And out of the end a new beginning, like a phoenix rising from the ashes." He put a friendly arm round Gordon's shoulders. "Speaking of which, how is my young apprentice?"

"I think you know," Gordon said.

Myrddin threw back his head and laughed in the booming hearty manner associated with Santa Claus across the globe. It was heard by their parents on the path. They quickened their pace. Apparently, things had already kicked off in the dell.

Myrddin held his hand out to Miranda. She took it and gave a little gasp as the healing power flowed through him into her. "I am sorry for your loss," he said gently. "There will be a reckoning."

He let go and offered his hand to Nick. "Master Nick," he boomed cheerfully, "My good pirate. That's a firm grip you have there. There's more treasure on its way to you." He looked up and beckoned to the parents to approach.

"The time is up for tyrants on this earth."

Chapter 47

A Leap For Victory

Hand in hand, Victor and Edith led the way into the hollow where Myrddin stood, still radiating. He was like a great star about to go supernova. Vivian, Elaine and Angela were right behind them. Robert and Isadora brought up the rear, largely because Isadora was hanging back. Her sense of security was fragile at the best of times, and she wasn't coping well with this recent tectonic shift in her world-view.

Myrddin held his arms out in welcome. "We meet again, as promised," he said to Grace's and Gordon's parents. He turned to Angela and Robert. "Thank you for the gift of your children."

He moved his compassionate gaze to Isadora. She was whimpering quietly, like a puppy in a sack. "Come here, Child," he said quietly.

Miranda went over to Isadora and took her hand. Her stepmum allowed herself to be led to Myrddin, though she couldn't bring herself to look at him. He placed his hand on her head and closed his eyes. A second or two passed ...

A smile began to spread across Isadora's face. Slowly her shoulders straightened and her head came up until she was staring into the kindest eyes she'd ever seen. She was completely calm.

"There's nothing to be frightened of," she said in wonder. Myrddin took his hand away and she turned to the other adults with absolute certainty. "Don't be afraid," she assured them. "There's no need to be afraid." She went back to Robert and grabbed his hand. "It's fine, really. Don't worry. Everything's fine."

Robert nodded. He smiled gratefully at Myrddin. That was one of his major worries dealt with. Now he could concentrate fully on the remaining one: his precious daughter's safety.

"Why isn't my father here to look after us?" Grace asked. "I want to understand why." She went over to her mum and Elaine and grabbed their hands. She turned to face Myrddin. "*We* want to understand why."

"Your father moves in mysterious ways," Myrddin said quietly. "You will see him soon. He'll fly through a magic casement on the far side of the moon." He smiled reassuringly. "Meanwhile, I am here to do his bidding. Let me assure you that will be enough."

He strode over to one of the two magnificent oak trees. They promised acorns aplenty in the autumn. "Right, Nick," he said playfully. "Let's see another jump like that one in Gordon's garden!"

Nick backed off and measured up. He looked like he was about to kick a penalty for the England rugby team. He clasped his hands, gave his bum a little wiggle, took two or three strides and launched himself into the air. Shooting up like a rugby ball in a neat arc, he came down like a cat on the topmost branches of the oak. He was a good 35 feet in the air.

His mum gasped. She grabbed Elaine's arm in fright and opened her mouth to tell him to be careful. Then she realised how silly that would be, in the circumstances.

Robert's eyes had widened in awe. Isadora linked in with him and smiled happily. "You see? I told you! Everything's fine. It really is."

Victor folded his arms and nodded. He hadn't needed any further proof, but if he had needed it, there it would have been, on a plate. Nick drifted down as light as a feather. He strove to keep his expression nonchalant, but there was a fierce triumph in his eyes. He held out his right hand, open-palmed. In it lay four shiny, perfect acorns.

He gave them to the great wizard. Myrddin smiled reassuringly at the parents. "Gordon and Grace, by virtue of their lineage, already possess a power that comes to them through the fairy line," he told them. "It flows from a spacetime beyond even the Tuatha Dé Danaan. It is normally beyond the reach of mortal magicians, who spring from a different stock."

He turned to Nick and Miranda. "Authority has been vested in me by those who rose in the beginning at the source. I now confer upon you the supreme honour of access to that power."

They looked at each other in wonder. What an awesome gift.

"You stand by Grace and Gordon in this fight. Our hope is that together you will show the human race a simple way towards a better world. Approach and kneel."

They did so, prompted by encouraging nods from their two best friends. Myrddin raised his ancient, twisted staff, and lifted his eyes towards the watching sky.

"We thank thee, God and Goddess of The Oak, for showing us the way. We ask you now to grant these children access to that power that flows through me. Our hope is with them. Help them in their fight against injustice, cruelty, greed, and the selfishness that blinds. Help them meet the needs that bleed."

Light from Gordon's ring began to pour with the power of a sunbeam through fragmenting cloud. It lit the spot between the oaks where Nick had uncovered his pirate's treasure chest. That had been just three life-changing months ago.

Myrddin brought his staff down firmly on that glowing, fertile earth. For a moment there was a palpable stillness, then the ground began to tremble. There was a rumbling sound beneath their feet. Water began to bubble round the tip of the rod. The ground a foot around it sank to make a bowl that filled rapidly. The water had enough pressure to form a small fountain in the middle.

And suddenly the air was filled with the most wonderful music - many voices, each one singing a different note. The chords merged and melted into each other. A haunting tune surmounted it, played on a set of pan pipes.

Gordon and Grace smiled at the memory of their fairy majesties' renewal in sacred Arden's groves. The adults looked on in wonder.

From pockets within the folds of his flowing robes, Myrddin produced sprigs of sacred mistletoe. He dipped them in the bubbling, sunlit spring, and sprinkled cool drops on Nick's head and on Miranda's. He gave them each a moistened sprig to hold.

Making the sacred sign of the endless knot above Nick's bowed head, his voice acquired tremendous power. The sound rebounded from the trunks of trees and rustled in their branches.

"I name thee Nick Sióg, Knight of Nuada of the Silver Hand, first human to be so honoured." He placed his left hand on Nick's head and raised the staff in his right hand high above his own head.

With incredible force a bolt of lightning ripped through the clear blue sky. All its power was channelled through the rod. Briefly the flash illuminated the priest/magician and his young charge. Almost simultaneously a tearing crackle announced a thunderclap so loud that all the adults flinched.

Nick never moved.

Taking his hand from Nick's head, Myrddin turned his attention to Miranda. Repeating the sign of the endless knot, he declared in the same ringing tones: "I name thee Miranda Sìth, Handmaiden of Scáthach, the first human to be so honoured."

Placing his left hand on her head, he raised his staff again. Again, the sky was split by the light of the bolt and ripped by its sound. Both figures were transfused. Miranda remained as motionless as Nick had been.

Myrddin lowered both arms to his sides and stepped back. "Rise," he said gently. Nick and Miranda rose so effortlessly they might have weighed nothing at all. Myrddin retrieved the mistletoe and returned it to a deep pocket. He handed them each an acorn.

"You must dip them in the waters of the sacred spring," he said. "There's room in this outpost of Avalon for two more oaks." He turned to the sunlit hollow. "Grace's rises in the east, Gordon's in the west. His ring will choose your ground. And Vivian once more has come prepared."

Vivian had popped the trowel into her bag as a precaution. Grace collected it and followed Gordon and Miranda into the northern segment of the dell. Mabon's ring located the optimum spot. She scooped out a trowelful of rich earth and leaf mould. "Get ready," she warned Miranda. "That acorn packs a punch."

Miranda pushed the moistened nut into the ground. She pressed the loose earth and mould back over it and stood back. With dramatic suddenness her head shot back and her body went rigid. "O-H-H-H-H-H" she moaned. It was a drawn-out exhalation of breath.

"Here we go again," Grace muttered. Miranda's dad started forward, his concern for his daughter written all over his face. Grace was quick to reassure him. "It's OK," she said. "It's just .. fulfilment."

Miranda took off backwards, her feet rising faster than her head, until she was horizontal. She rapidly gained speed round the circumference of the dell. Head first, flat on her back, eyes tightly closed, riding the sightless couriers of the air.

"It's fine, really it is," Isadora told everybody brightly. She watched her apparently unsupported stepdaughter circumnavigating the dell at high speed, six feet or so off the ground. "Don't worry; everything's fine."

Miranda slowed, and came to a halt just where she had taken off. She drifted delicately to the ground. Only then did she open her eyes. "The earth moved," she announced, to no-one in particular. "Can I do that again?" Grace and Zoë shook their heads emphatically.

"Your turn, Mate," Gordon told Nick. "I'll come with you." Grace handed him the trowel and they marched off to the southern side of the dell. Gordon trowelled out the ring-chosen spot. Nick dropped his wet acorn in and patted the earth down over it. He stood up.

"Oh, my goodness!" he exclaimed. Gordon, Grace and Miranda could see the crackling sparks of energy surrounding him.

"What's happening?!" Angela asked, alarmed at her son's exclamation. He was standing with his eyes tight shut, fists clenched. Grace tried to reassure her. "Don't worry. He'll be taking off any moment now."

The sparks were dying down. Nick opened his eyes. He was supercharged, so full of whatever force it was that he could hardly hold it in. "WOW!!" he said and shot up into the sky like a rocket. In seconds he was two hundred feet in the air. Gordon was right beside him.

"OSCILLATE!" Gordon yelled urgently. "Shimmer! - dart from side to side!" He knew from experience that shimmering was a good way of working off excess energy. It also minimised the chances of anyone reporting a U.F.O..

Both boys shot from side to side too fast for human eyes to follow. Once Nick had got a grip, they dived back down to ground level and he strove to slow himself further. The air he was displacing shook the bushes all round him. Gradually the choppy wind died down and he became visible again.

"Whoohh!!" he said in a high-pitched voice. "Sorry about that!" He looked around and his eyes lit up. "Zack!" he called out. He rushed over to him. "How great to see you! How are you, Mate?"

The adults were treated to the sight of Nick clapping some thin air on the back and shaking it by the hand. Edith's heart lurched as she watched Nick greet the son she might never see again. Nick transferred his attention to the space next to Zack. "Hi," he said shyly. "You must be Zoë."

Grace's head whipped round to Miranda, hope written all over her face. "Of course," Miranda assured her. She waved at Zoë and Zack. "Hi, Guys."

Gordon was delighted. "How about that!" he exclaimed. "We really are *The Super Six* at last!"

THE EIGHT-TEAM
CHRONICLES
Book 4
ROBIN CHAMBERS

Chapter 1

One Lifetime Has Never Been Enough

Gordon was filled with gratitude and hope. He went over to Myrddin. "Thank you," he said.

"You're most welcome," Myrddin said gently. He put a protective arm round his young apprentice's shoulder and handed him the two remaining acorns.

"One for Grace and one for you. Plant them at home. Hereafter, you may choose to plant acorns in any place you choose. You'll have plenty, and the need is everywhere."

He patted Gordon's shoulder. "Mortlake will be your biggest test to date. It is a project worthy of the name."

Gordon looked worried. "I wanted to ask you about that. I've been inside his head. He's done terrible things. He measures pleasure in units of pain. He's a torturer, a murderer and a tyrant."

Nevertheless, Myrddin's young heir was stricken by doubt.

"But who am I to sit in judgement? Can he be forgiven? Can he be redeemed? Can the evil in his heart be turned to good?"

He turned his young eyes up to Myrddin's face. "There are so many questions. And I'm not fourteen 'til August." Where else could he search for answers, if not here? Myrddin nodded, and Gordon had the feeling he'd just passed a test.

"Questions like those have always been easier to ask than to answer. Where would philosophers be without them? Remember too that doubt is almost always preferable to sweeping certainty."

For how many millennia had those questions been doing the rounds?

"If we had a decade or so to spare," Myrddin went on. "We might spend it identifying, defining and weighing the pros and cons of each and every direction mankind could take in any circumstance." There was more than a trace of weariness in his smile. "Each direction will have many problems associated with it, of course. Each problem will need to be identified, defined and weighed in turn, so that we may identify, define and weigh all possible solutions to it."

He pretended to give the matter serious consideration. "But having done that, we should then, one might suppose, be able to recommend a particular course of action to mankind."

He gazed down at Gordon. "And how would mankind respond, do you think, to our recommendation? Remember that it's based on thousands of years of experience and a decade of careful analysis and reflection."

Gordon gazed back expectantly.

"In all probability," Myrddin told him, "mankind would ask us which Christmas cracker we'd got it out of." He chuckled. "In the past, one might have said 'LISTEN YOU! Do it because God just told me to tell you to get it done. He even took time to carve it in stone while he and I were alone together on that mountaintop. He also said that if you don't do it, all hell will break loose, and he told me to see to that personally."

That last observation merited a heavy sigh. "The path to knowledge, as Zack would have to agree, is beset with thorns. It appears to be in the nature of things that each of us must walk it in our own moccasins."

He hummed a couple of bars – 'Dumb da-dumb (dumb dumb)' – "He's right about that tune as well."

He gave Gordon's shoulder a final, affectionate squeeze. "Until then, console yourself with this thought: one lifetime has never been enough. Remember my last words to you when I saw you last."

Gordon smiled wryly. "Be happy to do the best you can. We ask no more than that."

"Indeed," Myrddin said, "and in deed. You will not be surprised to know that I am needed elsewhere, but know also that my eyes never leave you. Now send me on my way."

A minute later, Myrddin was back whence he had come, and they were left with the challenge of putting their world to rights.

But progress had been made. Gordon was clearer about his remit and Grace was reassured about her father's commitment. Nick and Miranda were significantly more able to defend themselves and their families against the oppression of tyrants, petty, local or otherwise.

Before they left the dell, they refilled all their water-bottles from that bubbling sunlit spring. What remained to be seen, of course, was how events would unfold.

About The Author

Once upon a time, I was born in a place called Bootle (Liverpool 20). There was a war on. Later, I wanted to follow in the footsteps of J.R.R. Tolkien and C.S. Lewis, but instead was plunged into the challenging world of inner city education, where I taught English. In the 1970s I wrote some stories for children to see if I could, and Penguin published them. I thought then that I would try and write something really good when I retired from teaching.

After fourteen years of headship at Clissold Park and Stoke Newington School in Hackney, I took early retirement and came back up north to live in Chester, a compact, historical city in west Cheshire on the border with North Wales. There, I met my brilliant wife, Amy.

We looked after my increasingly ill parents full-time until they didn't need us to do it anymore, by which time I learned there was a shortage of teachers of English in the UK's secondary schools and I went back to teaching English, this time at Tytherington High School in Macclesfield.

In 2008, Amy and I set off for a life by the western shores of the Caribbean; but it was only after I survived a murder attempt by three local thugs in November 2010 that I realised how easy it is to die without accomplishing a cherished ambition.

So, we came back to the UK and I began to write the epic story I will leave behind. Its first version – *Myrddin's Heir* – was published in seven books, each of which included copious notes on the text designed to be helpful to any teacher of English wanting to use these books (as I would love to have done) in a high-school classroom.

I am now publishing a revised, 'non-didactic' version of the tale under the generic title of *The Eight Team Chronicles*. Both versions will remain available on Amazon Kindle and in Draft2Digital. However, *The Eight Team Chronicles* carries the story beyond the point it reached in the *Myrddin's Heir* series. How far beyond remains to be seen.

The Weight We Choose

Donald Watkins

The Weight We Choose

Table of Contents

Introduction
The Moment You Realize It's On You

There comes a point in life when things stop feeling light.

Not suddenly. Not all at once. But gradually—almost quietly—you begin to notice that the same actions carry more weight than they used to. Decisions linger longer. Mistakes echo further. What once felt manageable now feels consequential.

At first, it's easy to explain away.

You tell yourself you're just tired. That things will settle down. That once you get through this stretch, life will feel the way it used to.

But it doesn't.

Because something fundamental has changed.

You've moved from a life where momentum carried you... to a life where responsibility does.

Earlier in life, progress felt natural. Effort produced results. You could move quickly, recover easily, and adjust without much cost. The environment around you absorbed mistakes before they became defining. You were learning, growing, improving—and the stakes, while real, were still contained.

You didn't realize how much was working in your favor.

You didn't realize how much was being held for you.

That changes.

Responsibility doesn't arrive all at once. It builds. Quietly. Through expectations, through roles, through people who begin to rely on you in ways they didn't before.

And one day, without a clear transition, you realize:

If something goes wrong, it doesn't just affect you anymore.

It moves through you.

That realization is where many people begin to feel overwhelmed.

Not because they aren't capable—but because no one really teaches you how to carry weight well.

You're taught how to work hard.

You're taught how to compete.

You're taught how to win.

But you're not taught how to sustain.

How to stabilize.

How to be the person others depend on when things are no longer simple.

This book is not about success in the way it's usually defined.

It's about what happens after success becomes responsibility.

It's about the shift from moving quickly to moving deliberately. From chasing progress to maintaining stability. From living for yourself to carrying something larger than you.

It's about the quiet, often unrecognized transition into becoming the person things rest on.

Because at some point, whether you planned for it or not, that's exactly what happens.

The weight shows up.

And the question is no longer whether you can avoid it.

The question is:

How will you carry it?

Chapter 1
The Era of Accidental Wins

There was a time when wins seemed to arrive without asking much of you.

You worked hard—sure—but the consequences were forgiving. Mistakes were educational, not costly. Decisions could be undone. Risks carried stories, not scars. If something went wrong, it rarely followed you for long. You adjusted, recalibrated, and moved forward without much weight attached.

In that season of life, effort and reward felt closely linked. Put energy in, get something out. Show up consistently, improve a little, and progress followed. If something worked, you assumed it could be repeated. If it didn't, you chalked it up as part of the process.

It all felt reasonable. Predictable, even.

What you didn't realize at the time was how much the environment was working in your favor.

You had time—long stretches of it. Time to recover from mistakes. Time to experiment. Time to fail quietly. You had energy that replenished itself quickly. Sleep restored you. Rest actually worked. You could push hard knowing there would be space to recover.

You also had flexibility. Schedules could change. Plans could shift. Consequences stayed localized. And most importantly, you were the only one affected by your choices.

That last part is the one most people miss when they look back on early success.

When success comes early, it quietly teaches a dangerous lesson: that momentum is permanent.

You start to believe that things move forward because of who you are, not where you are. You confuse favorable conditions with personal mastery. You internalize outcomes without fully understanding inputs.

This isn't arrogance. It's human.

When effort reliably produces progress, it's natural to assume that relationship will hold. You begin to trust the rhythm. Work, win, repeat. Over time, it becomes part of your identity.

But momentum is seasonal.

And seasons change whether you're ready or not.

What early wins don't teach you is what happens when the margin for error narrows. When mistakes stop being educational and start being disruptive. When decisions echo longer than expected. When the cost of being wrong isn't embarrassment, but instability.

They don't prepare you for a world where other people absorb the consequences of your choices.

At some point, you begin to notice that the same approach doesn't work as cleanly anymore. You put in effort, but results lag. You move fast, but recovery takes longer. You make a decision, and it can't be undone without cost.

That's usually when frustration creeps in.

You tell yourself you're working just as hard as before—maybe harder. You wonder why things feel heavier. Why progress isn't as smooth. Why the same intensity doesn't produce the same outcomes.

The mistake isn't that life got unfair.

The mistake is assuming that ease was proof of strength.

Ease is often a condition, not a capability.

Early wins don't lie—but they don't tell the whole truth either. They show what's possible when conditions are favorable. They don't reveal what happens when conditions disappear.

And that's the transition no one names clearly.

The problem isn't that life gets harder.

The problem is that it gets heavier—and no one teaches you how to carry weight well.

CHAPTER 2
Effort Is Not the Same as Preparation

For a long time, I didn't understand why things were going well for me when they weren't for others.

We were all training.

We were all tired.

We were all putting in hours.

From the outside, the inputs looked similar. Sometimes they even looked identical. And yet the outcomes weren't.

If I was being honest with myself, there were moments when it felt like I was doing less. Or at least, not more. That created a quiet discomfort I didn't know how to name at the time. A sense that maybe I hadn't earned the ground I was standing on.

It's hard to admit that when you're young.

You want effort to be the currency. You want time spent to equal progress gained. It feels fair. It feels clean. And when you see others working just as hard—sometimes harder—it creates confusion when the results don't line up.

What I didn't understand yet was the difference between effort and preparation.

Effort is visible.

Preparation is selective.

Effort fills time. Preparation filters it.

Preparation asks questions that effort avoids. Questions like: *What actually matters? What am I weak at that I'm hiding behind volume?*

What am I spending energy on because it feels productive, not because it is?

As a Division I athlete, I benefited from something I didn't fully appreciate at the time: great coaching.

Not loud coaching.

Not motivational speeches.

Not someone telling me to want it more.

Real coaching is quieter than that.

It narrows focus instead of expanding it. It removes distractions instead of adding drills. It protects energy. It forces you to work on the things you'd rather avoid—and saves you from spending time on the things that don't move the needle.

I wasn't doing everything.

I was doing the right things.

That distinction matters more than people want to admit.

Many people confuse exhaustion with effectiveness. They equate long hours with preparation. They assume that because they're tired, they must be progressing.

But two people can work equally hard and prepare very differently.

One can be grinding.

The other can be refining.

One can be busy.

The other can be deliberate.

The difference doesn't show up immediately. That's why it's misunderstood. But when opportunity finally arrives—when timing and circumstance intersect—preparation reveals itself quickly.

Opportunity doesn't reward effort.

It rewards readiness.

Later in life, this lesson comes back with sharper edges.

No one cares how hard you tried.

No one measures how tired you are.

The outcome is the outcome.

Responsibility changes the scoreboard.

You stop getting credit for motion. You start being judged by results. And results don't care how much energy you spent getting there.

That's a hard transition for people who were raised to believe that effort alone would carry them.

It won't.

Preparation is quieter.

More uncomfortable.

More honest.

And eventually, it's unavoidable.

CHAPTER 3
A Calm Sea Does Not Make a Skilled Sailor

For a long time, my sea was calm.

Not easy—but navigable. Structured. Supported. There were systems in place that absorbed mistakes before they turned into consequences. Coaches corrected inefficiencies early. Guardrails existed, even when I didn't realize they were there.

Because of that, success felt natural. Almost expected.

When things go well early, it's easy to believe that's simply how life works. You learn the rhythms, trust the feedback loop, and assume that forward motion is the default state. Progress feels earned—and in many ways it is—but it's also protected.

That's the danger of calm seas.

Calm seas don't announce themselves. They feel normal. You don't recognize them as conditions; you interpret them as capability. You assume the waters are calm because you're skilled, not because the environment is forgiving.

And that assumption stays with you longer than it should.

A calm sea doesn't require you to learn how to recover. It doesn't teach you how to navigate when visibility drops. It doesn't force you to slow down, reassess, or choose restraint over speed.

It lets you move quickly without consequence.

Later in life, the water changes.

Not suddenly, not dramatically—but decisively.

There is no practice rep for a decision that affects your family. No timeout when exhaustion stacks up.

No coach pulling you aside to say, *"That doesn't matter—focus here instead."*

The buffers disappear.

What once felt manageable now feels heavy. Decisions linger. Mistakes echo. Recovery takes longer, if it comes at all.

This is usually the moment people say life got harder.

But that's not quite right.

Life didn't get harder because you became weaker.
It got harder because the conditions changed.

The sea got rougher because the stakes increased.

Early success wasn't a lie.
It just wasn't the test.

The test begins when you're responsible for navigating without protection. When judgment matters more than instinct. When restraint matters more than speed.

Calm seas teach confidence.
Rough seas teach competence.

And competence—real competence—is what later life requires.

You don't earn it by wishing the waters were calmer.
You earn it by learning how to sail when they're not.

CHAPTER 4
Great Coaching Is Invisible—Until It's Gone

One of the reasons early success is so often misunderstood is that the forces supporting it tend to work quietly.

Good coaching doesn't draw attention to itself. It doesn't feel controlling or restrictive. In fact, when it's done well, it barely feels like coaching at all.

It feels like clarity.

It narrows your focus instead of expanding it. It removes options instead of adding them. It protects your energy by telling you what not to worry about just as often as it tells you what to improve.

At the time, it's easy to assume this clarity comes from within. You believe you're simply disciplined, motivated, or focused. You don't see how much has been filtered out for you.

That's the illusion.

Great coaching functions like guardrails. It allows speed precisely because it prevents catastrophe. It corrects inefficiencies early, when they're small. It steers you away from wasted effort before you've invested too much in it.

And because it works preventatively, you don't notice it doing its job.

Later in life, that structure disappears.

There is no one filtering decisions for you anymore. No one sequencing priorities. No one telling you that something flashy doesn't actually matter. No one saving you from overworking the wrong problem.

You are suddenly exposed to everything at once.

Every option looks plausible. Every demand feels urgent. Every decision competes for attention. And without realizing it, you start spending energy on things that feel productive but aren't essential.

This is where many people burn out.

Not because they lack discipline — but because they lack direction.

When the coaching is gone, inefficiency creeps in quietly. You work harder, not smarter. You fill your days, but progress feels scattered. You move constantly but advance slowly.

And that's when a sobering realization starts to take shape:

A lot of your early success wasn't about how hard you pushed.
It was about how well you were guided.

That realization can sting if you interpret it the wrong way. It can feel like your accomplishments weren't earned.

But that's not the truth.

The truth is more nuanced — and more useful.

You did the work.
But you didn't design the system.

Later in life, you are asked to do both.

Adulthood isn't harder because you're weaker.
It's harder because you are now responsible for building the structure that once protected you.

You don't just perform anymore.
You design.

And design mistakes are more costly than execution mistakes ever were.

That's why responsibility feels heavier. Not because the work increased — but because the consequences did.

C HAPTER 5
When You Become the System

At some point, you stop being part of the system and start *being* the system.

There isn't a ceremony for it. No announcement. No clear moment where someone hands you responsibility and says, *"This is yours now."* It happens quietly, often without permission, usually before you feel ready.

One day you realize that if something goes wrong, there is no one else to catch it.

If something breaks, it breaks through you.

That realization changes how you think long before it changes how you act. You start noticing gaps you didn't see before. You think further ahead. You replay decisions at night, not because you're anxious, but because you understand that the margin for error has narrowed.

Consistency starts to matter more than intensity.

Earlier in life, intensity was rewarded. You could sprint, recover, sprint again. You could push hard in short bursts and rely on downtime to reset. But systems don't work that way. Systems require steadiness.

Reliability becomes the metric.

You begin to understand that showing up once isn't enough. Showing up repeatedly — predictably — is what actually creates safety for the people who rely on you.

This is where freedom subtly shifts.

Not into restriction, but into responsibility.

You have fewer options now, not because life is smaller, but because it's more specific. You don't get to chase every impulse. You don't get to experiment recklessly. You don't get to disappear when things get uncomfortable.

You are needed.

That can feel heavy if you fight it.

But if you lean into it, something else emerges: purpose that isn't tied to excitement.

Repetition stops feeling boring and starts feeling stabilizing. The routines you once resisted become the very thing that allows others to rest.

When you become the system, you stop optimizing for yourself alone. You optimize for endurance. For continuity. For outcomes that hold even when you're tired.

This isn't glamorous work.

No one applauds a system that functions. People only notice systems when they fail.

But if you're doing it right, failure becomes rare — and invisible.

That invisibility is not insignificance.

It's success.

CHAPTER 6
Be Less Impressed and More Involved

"Be less impressed and more involved." — Matthew McConaughey

Early in life, it's easy to be impressed.

You're impressed by talent, by speed, by people who seem to win effortlessly. You watch highlights. You compare paths. You imagine alternate versions of your life where things look cleaner, easier, more exciting.

Impression is passive.

It costs nothing to admire outcomes from a distance. It doesn't require commitment. It doesn't require responsibility. You can be impressed without being changed.

Involvement is different.

Involvement requires showing up daily. It requires boredom, patience, and follow-through. It demands that you stay when leaving would be easier.

When others begin to rely on you, impression becomes a liability.

Admiration doesn't fix problems. Presence does.

You don't need to be inspired.

You need to be consistent.

This shift is subtle but profound. You stop consuming stories about life and start maintaining one. You stop chasing feelings and start managing realities.

The work becomes quieter.

Involvement rarely looks impressive. It looks like repetition. It looks like doing the same things well, even when no one notices.

That's where maturity settles in.

You realize that life doesn't need to be admired — it needs to be *kept running*.

And keeping things running requires discipline that doesn't announce itself.

CHAPTER 7
When Rest Stops Feeling Like Rest

There was a time when rest actually restored you.

You could feel the edges of fatigue. You knew when you were tired, and you knew when you weren't. A night of sleep, a weekend away, or even a few quiet hours could reset you. Rest had a clear cause and a clear effect.

You stepped away, and you came back lighter.

Later in life, that relationship breaks.

You still sit down. You still sleep. You still take time away. But something doesn't fully shut off. There's a part of you that remains alert, scanning, listening. Even in quiet moments, there's a background noise you can't quite silence.

Did I forget something?

Is everything handled?

What's coming next that I should already be thinking about?

At first, you assume this is stress. Maybe burnout. Maybe anxiety. You look for ways to eliminate it, because you remember a version of yourself that could truly disengage.

But this isn't anxiety in the way people usually mean it.

It's responsibility refusing to clock out.

When no one depends on you, rest is clean. You can disappear for a while and return without consequence. When people do depend on you, disappearance has a cost. Even if nothing goes wrong, *something could*, and your mind knows it.

That awareness doesn't mean you're failing to rest properly. It means your role has changed.

You're no longer resting from life.
You're resting within it.

That shift is subtle, but it explains a lot.

Many people fight this by chasing old versions of rest. They plan bigger vacations. They add distractions. They look for silence loud enough to drown out responsibility.

It never quite works.

Because responsibility isn't a noise problem.
It's a structure problem.

Rest used to come from absence — from stepping away entirely. Now it comes from order. From knowing systems are in place. From having thought through problems before they arrive.

When things are handled, your mind softens.
When things are loose, rest stays shallow.

This is why the same amount of sleep can feel different depending on how your life is organized. It's not the hours. It's the confidence that nothing critical is waiting for you on the other side.

Eventually, you stop trying to reclaim an old kind of rest. You accept that it belonged to a different season.

And once you accept that, something unexpected happens.

Rest returns — quieter, less dramatic, but deeper.

Not because life got lighter.

CHAPTER 8 — *Comfort Becomes a Moral Obligation*
When you're young, comfort is optional.

You can live loosely because instability doesn't linger. A disrupted night costs you a morning, not a week. A bad decision becomes a lesson, not a liability. Chaos feels like part of the experience, not something that needs to be managed.

Discomfort even becomes a badge of honor.

You wear exhaustion like proof that you're doing something meaningful. You pride yourself on adaptability, on being able to sleep anywhere, pivot quickly, recover fast. You learn how much friction you can tolerate, and tolerance starts to feel like strength.

Later in life, that framing breaks down.

Discomfort stops being contained.

A restless night doesn't just affect your mood — it bleeds into the next day, the next interaction, the next decision. A poorly planned choice doesn't just inconvenience you — it creates downstream consequences that someone else has to absorb.

That's when comfort quietly changes categories.

It stops being indulgence.

It becomes responsibility.

Not luxury — comfort.

Predictability.

Consistency.

A sense that things will hold.

This is where many people feel internal resistance. Especially those who once defined themselves by grit. Choosing comfort can feel like choosing weakness, like backing away from challenge, like losing edge.

But that assumption misunderstands what comfort actually does.

Comfort, done well, doesn't remove challenge.

It removes unnecessary strain.

It clears space so energy can be spent where it matters instead of being wasted on avoidable chaos. It protects the people around you from having to constantly adapt to instability they didn't choose.

You stop asking, *"What can I handle?"*

You start asking, *"What shouldn't they have to?"*

That question changes how you organize your life.

You begin to value routines you once resisted. You eliminate volatility not because you fear it, but because you understand its cost. You choose boring reliability over exciting unpredictability, even when unpredictability looks more alive from the outside.

This kind of discipline doesn't feel heroic.

It feels repetitive. Thoughtful. Sometimes dull.

But it creates something rare: an environment where people can rest without bracing.

At this stage of life, comfort isn't about avoiding difficulty.

It's about making sure difficulty doesn't become constant.

And when you accept that, comfort becomes one of the most generous things you can provide.

CHAPTER 9
The Wisdom of Not Pretending

"The wisest man is the one who does not act like he knows what he does not know."

Early success rewards decisiveness.

You move quickly. You trust instinct. You commit publicly and adjust privately. Confidence reads as competence, and hesitation can look like weakness. When the stakes are low, this approach works well enough.

Later in life, decisiveness without clarity becomes dangerous.

When others depend on you, pretending certainty carries a cost. A wrong decision doesn't just inconvenience you — it destabilizes systems, erodes trust, and forces recovery work that didn't need to exist.

That's when wisdom starts to look different.

Wisdom slows down.

It pauses when certainty would feel more comfortable. It resists the urge to fill silence with answers that haven't fully formed. It allows ambiguity to exist long enough for clarity to emerge.

This can feel unnatural at first, especially if you were rewarded for speed earlier in life.

You're used to being the one with the answer. The one who moves first. The one who projects confidence even when you're still figuring things out.

Responsibility changes that equation.

Now, people don't need you to look confident — they need you to be accurate.

They need you to say, *"I don't know yet,"* when that's the truth. They need you to ask better questions instead of offering faster conclusions. They need you to hold uncertainty without turning it into anxiety.

This is harder than pretending.

Pretending is efficient.

Wisdom is patient.

You begin to realize that trust isn't built by always being right. It's built by being honest about what's unclear and thoughtful about how you resolve it.

Admitting uncertainty doesn't weaken your position. It strengthens it — because it signals that outcomes matter more than ego.

At this stage of life, wisdom isn't about knowing more.

It's about knowing when not to speak yet.

And that restraint becomes one of the quiet strengths that allows others to feel safe placing their weight in your hands.

INTERLUDE
What No One Warned You About

No one warned you that responsibility wouldn't feel heroic.

They warned you about stress. About sacrifice. About how tired you'd be. They told you about long nights and hard choices. They framed responsibility as something heavy, but meaningful — something you would rise to.

What they didn't warn you about was how *ordinary* it would feel.

They didn't warn you about repetition.

About doing the right thing every day with no visible payoff. About success looking like nothing going wrong. About your best work being invisible precisely because it prevented problems instead of solving them.

There's a quiet loneliness in realizing that stability only exists because you're holding things together.

If you stop paying attention, cracks appear. If you stop anticipating, things unravel. And because none of that happens when you're doing it well, it can feel like nothing you're doing matters.

This is where resentment can sneak in if you're not careful.

You look around and see people who seem freer. Less constrained. Less burdened. You wonder if you chose something unnecessarily heavy.

But this isn't punishment.

It's trust.

You were trusted with responsibility not because you asked for it, but because you were capable of carrying it.

And carrying it well rarely feels dramatic.

It feels quiet. Repetitive. Unremarkable.
That doesn't make it small.
It makes it essential.

CHAPTER 10 — *The Invisible Load*

There is work that doesn't announce itself.

It doesn't show up on calendars. It isn't measured in hours. It doesn't produce visible outcomes because its success is defined by what never happens.

This is the invisible load.

It's the mental checklist running quietly in the background. The awareness that stays switched on even when nothing is urgent. The sense that you're always slightly ahead of the moment you're in.

You're thinking three steps forward so no one else has to think one.

You notice patterns before they become problems. You catch tone shifts, energy dips, small inefficiencies. You make micro-adjustments that prevent larger disruptions later.

And because nothing breaks, it looks like nothing was done.

This is one of the most exhausting forms of work — not because it's intense, but because it's continuous. There is no finish line. No clear point where you can say, *"That's handled for good."*

The load resets every day.

This is where many people feel unseen.

They're not acknowledged because acknowledgment usually follows visible effort or visible repair. Preventative work rarely gets recognized because it succeeds quietly.

But quiet success is still success.

You're not tired because you're weak.
You're tired because you're vigilant.

Vigilance is a form of care. It's attention applied consistently over time. It's choosing to stay alert so others don't have to.

Leadership often looks like absence.

Absence of chaos.

Absence of emergencies.

Absence of fear.

Those absences exist because someone noticed something early and acted before it mattered.

Over time, you stop expecting this work to be seen. You measure success differently. You start paying attention to how stable things feel instead of how busy you are.

That's when you realize the invisible load hasn't drained you of meaning.

It has trained you in steadiness.

CHAPTER 11
The Loneliness of Being the Backstop

At some point, you realize that if something goes wrong, it stops with you.

There is no escalation path beyond your judgment. No one else to defer to. No authority to appeal to when the decision is uncomfortable or unclear.

That realization doesn't arrive all at once. It builds slowly, through moments where you look around for confirmation and realize there is none coming.

You are it.

This is where responsibility can feel isolating.

You don't talk about it much — not because you're trying to appear strong, but because the people who rely on you don't need to carry the weight of your uncertainty. They need to feel that things are handled.

So you absorb it.

You hold decisions privately. You process doubt internally. You make calls that no one sees and deal with consequences quietly.

This is the loneliness of being the backstop.

Not dramatic loneliness. Not emotional isolation. But the quiet understanding that some burdens are yours alone because sharing them would make things heavier for everyone else.

This isn't imbalance.

It's leadership.

Leadership isn't about being seen at the front. It's about being willing to stand at the end — the place where responsibility collects.

And over time, you come to understand that this loneliness isn't something to escape.

It's something to manage with care.

Because if you carry it well, others don't have to feel it at all.

CHAPTER 12
Providing Is More Than Money

Providing is often reduced to numbers.

Income. Savings. Security. The ability to say yes when something costs money and no when it doesn't make sense. These things matter, and pretending otherwise is naïve. Financial stability creates options. It removes pressure. It buys time.

But money is only one part of provision — and not the most enduring one.

What people remember long-term is not how much was available, but how it felt to live inside what was provided.

Provision also means emotional steadiness. Predictable presence. A sense that someone is paying attention even when nothing is urgent. It means being able to walk into a room and feel that things are handled.

This kind of provision is harder to quantify, which is why it's often overlooked.

You can outsource income.
You can't outsource stability.

There were times earlier in life when providing meant striving. Earning more. Achieving more. Creating upward motion. Progress itself felt like provision.

Later in life, provision starts to look more like maintenance.

Making sure systems don't erode. Ensuring that stress doesn't compound. Catching problems early so they don't become defining moments.

This is when many people feel tension.

You're doing more work that doesn't feel productive. You're spending energy preventing things instead of building new ones. From the outside, it can look like you've slowed down.

But what you've actually done is shift from expansion to preservation.

Preservation doesn't feel ambitious.
It feels responsible.

Providing at this stage of life means asking different questions:

- Is this sustainable?
- Does this create calm or chaos?
- Will this decision make tomorrow easier or harder for the people I care about?

Sometimes the most generous thing you can provide is not growth, but stability.

Not acceleration, but balance.

And when you understand that, you stop measuring your value solely by what you add and start measuring it by what you protect.

C HAPTER 13 — *Loving What You Have While Mourning What You Lost*

When our daughter was born, the first feeling was exactly what everyone promised.

Joy.

Purpose.

A sense that life had snapped into alignment.

There was an undeniable gravity to it. A feeling that something irreversible and important had just happened — not in a frightening way, but in a clarifying one.

What no one prepared me for was the second feeling.

I missed our old life.

Not in a dramatic way. Not as regret. And certainly not as a desire to undo anything. It was quieter than that. More disorienting.

The life before kids had been good.

We moved freely. We traveled without friction. We made decisions based on curiosity, not calculation. We could leave without planning, stay out without consequence, change course without explaining ourselves.

There was lightness in that season — not because it lacked meaning, but because it lacked weight.

Holding gratitude and grief at the same time felt confusing at first.

I wondered if something was wrong with me. If missing that life meant I wasn't appreciating what I had enough. If loving one season fully required disowning the one that came before it.

It doesn't.

This grief isn't regret.

It's recognition.

Life didn't just add responsibility.

It replaced versions of us.

And replacement hurts, even when what replaces it is meaningful.

Growth always costs something real. Not abstract potential — real identity. Ways of moving through the world that no longer fit the life you're building.

Over time, the grief softens. Not because it disappears, but because it gets contextualized. You begin to see the exchange clearly.

Freedom for responsibility.

Movement for depth.

Speed for meaning.

And slowly, the life you're living starts to feel less like a compromise and more like a progression.

Not because it's easier — but because it's truer.

C HAPTER 14 — *When Life Slows Down — and You Don't*
Before kids, life moved at our pace.

We decided on a Friday to leave on a Saturday. We stayed out late without calculating the cost. Travel meant packing bags, not planning logistics. Time felt flexible — something you could spend freely and replenish quickly.

Movement was the default.

After kids, life moves at a different speed — and it isn't yours.

Schedules tighten. Nights fragment. Days blur together. Simple decisions now require sequencing. Leaving the house takes planning. Rest takes intention. Momentum slows, not because you lost capacity, but because the environment changed.

If you were someone who lived in motion, this slowdown can feel disorienting.

The frustration isn't impatience.

It's identity lag.

Internally, you still feel like the same person. Your mind moves quickly. Your instincts still reach for possibility. But externally, the world has narrowed. And the gap between who you feel like and how you're allowed to move creates tension you can't quite name.

This is where people begin to feel trapped.

They tell themselves life has shrunk. That they've lost something essential. That the version of themselves they worked hard to become no longer has room to exist.

But what's actually happening is subtler — and more important.

Life hasn't slowed down to limit you.

It's slowed down to deepen you.

Depth requires stillness. It requires repetition. It requires staying long enough for things to take root. The traits that once helped you move quickly now need to be recalibrated for a season that values endurance over speed.

That recalibration is uncomfortable.

You're no longer optimizing for experience.

You're optimizing for continuity.

Continuity doesn't produce highlights. It produces presence.

Presence isn't dramatic. It doesn't announce itself. It's felt over time, in the way people trust you to be there tomorrow the same way you were there today.

Eventually, you stop fighting the pace.

You learn how to live inside it.

And when you do, you realize that life didn't slow down to take something from you.

It slowed down to teach you how to stay.

C**HAPTER 15 — *When Protection Becomes Personal***

The hardest nights weren't the sleepless ones.

They were the nights I could see the toll it was taking on my wife.

Not because she complained. She didn't. Not because she asked for relief. She rarely did. But exhaustion shows up even when words don't. In posture. In patience. In the quiet way someone moves through a room.

My frustration wasn't with the baby.

It wasn't even with the lack of sleep.

It was with the fact that something — anything — was challenging the sense of perfection I wanted for her.

That feeling surprised me.

Earlier in life, protection meant action. Fixing problems quickly. Removing obstacles decisively. Control felt like competence.

This was different.

I couldn't fix the nights. I couldn't eliminate the fatigue. I couldn't restore things to the way they were.

What I could do was stay present.

Protection, I learned, isn't control.

It's presence under pressure.

It's noticing when someone is carrying more than they're saying. It's stepping in quietly, without announcement, so the load redistributes without becoming a conversation. It's absorbing frustration so it doesn't spill outward.

This kind of protection doesn't feel powerful.

It feels restrained.

You want to do more. You want to solve the problem entirely. But instead, you learn to hold space for difficulty without trying to dominate it.

That restraint is its own form of strength.

You stop asking, *"How do I fix this?"*

You start asking, *"How do I help us endure this?"*

And that question reframes responsibility.

Responsibility isn't about removing hardship.

It's about making sure no one faces it alone.

A PASSAGE FOR MY DAUGHTER

You won't remember the nights that tested us.

You won't remember how slowly time moved, or how tired we were, or how unsure I felt some days about whether I was doing any of it right.

What I hope you remember — though memory doesn't really work this way — is how steady things felt.

Before you, I lived a good life. One filled with movement, freedom, and momentum. I don't regret that life. It shaped me into someone capable of carrying what came next.

When you arrived, life narrowed. And in that narrowing, it became clearer.

You didn't take anything from me.
You required something from me.

You slowed life down not to limit it, but to give it weight.

If one day you feel this same tension — loving what you have while missing what you once were — know this: it isn't a flaw. It's a sign that you cared deeply in both seasons.

You were never a disruption to my life.
You were the reason it finally organized itself around what mattered.

CHAPTER 16 — *Redefining Winning*

Earlier in life, winning was visible.

You could point to it. Measure it. Share it. Progress showed up as milestones crossed and momentum gained. There was satisfaction in knowing where you stood.

Winning felt like accumulation.

Later in life, that definition loses its usefulness.

Not because winning disappears — but because its signals change.

Winning becomes quiet.

It looks like systems that hold under pressure. Like routines that don't break when things get busy. Like relationships that feel safe instead of impressive. It looks like problems that never escalate because they were addressed early and carefully.

This kind of winning doesn't announce itself. It rarely gets recognized because its success is measured by what doesn't happen.

At first, this can feel unsatisfying.

Especially if your identity was once tied to growth and visible progress. You wonder if you've stalled. If you've settled. If you've traded ambition for comfort.

But what's actually happened is a shift in scorekeeping.

You no longer measure days by what you gained.

You measure them by what held.

Did things stay steady?

Did people feel supported?

Did you show up when it mattered, even when it wasn't convenient?

Those questions don't produce trophies.

They produce continuity.

And continuity, over time, becomes its own form of success.

You stop needing proof.

A life that functions well — quietly, consistently — becomes its own victory.

CHAPTER 17
Carrying the Weight Without Resentment

Responsibility only becomes heavy when you fight it.

The weight itself doesn't change. What changes is your relationship to it. When you resist the load, every step feels harder. When you accept it, movement becomes possible again.

Resentment often enters through comparison.

You notice people who seem freer. Less constrained. You see them moving quickly, making spontaneous decisions, living lightly. You wonder if you chose something unnecessarily heavy.

But comparison ignores context.

You are no longer in the same season.
You are no longer playing the same game.

Resentment fades when you stop measuring your life against lives you no longer want.

Acceptance doesn't mean pretending it's easy.
It means deciding it's worth it.

You begin to understand that the weight you carry is evidence of trust. Someone depends on you. Something matters enough to require your steadiness.

That doesn't make the days lighter.
It makes them meaningful.

When you stop resisting responsibility, something subtle shifts. The load doesn't disappear, but it settles. It finds its place. It becomes part of your posture instead of something you're constantly bracing against.

You stop asking, *"Why is this so heavy?"*
You start asking, *"How do I carry this well?"*
And that question changes everything.

CHAPTER 18
Gratitude for the Weight

"A calm sea does not make a skilled sailor."

For a long time, that phrase felt like a warning. A reminder that difficulty was inevitable, that struggle was coming whether you wanted it or not.

Later, it starts to feel like gratitude.

The weight you carry now is proof that you were trusted with something meaningful. It means you were invited into a role that requires judgment, patience, and endurance.

The weight refined you.

It taught restraint where speed once worked.

It taught care where freedom once mattered most.

It taught presence where ambition once dominated.

Gratitude doesn't erase fatigue.

It reframes it.

You begin to see that the sea didn't get rough to punish you. It got rough to prepare you. To teach you how to navigate without spectacle. To show you that strength isn't always loud.

Sometimes strength is simply staying steady when things could easily fall apart.

And that kind of strength is built slowly, under load.

CHAPTER 19
Choosing This Life Again

There are days I miss the old life.

Not because this one is worse.

Because the old one was lighter.

There were fewer calculations then. Fewer consequences. Fewer nights where being tired meant more than just being tired.

But when I ask the only question that matters — *would I choose this life again, knowing what it costs?* — the answer comes quickly.

Yes.

Not because it's easier.

Not because it feels heroic.

But because it's truer.

This life asks more of me than the last one ever did. It requires patience where speed once worked. Judgment where instinct once sufficed. Presence where ambition once dominated.

I no longer measure success by what I gain, but by what holds. By whether the people I love feel safe. By whether I show up consistently, even when no one is watching.

I don't need life to be impressive anymore.

I need it to be stable.

And in that stability, I've found something I never quite had before.

Peace.

Not the absence of struggle — but the confidence that I'm carrying the right weight.

AUTHOR'S NOTE

If you are reading this in the middle of your own transition — missing what was while learning to carry what is — know this:

You are not failing.

You are becoming.

And becoming always costs something.

www.ingramcontent.com/pod-product-compliance
Lightning Source LLC
Chambersburg PA
CBHW071312130726
47997CB00007B/2515